# The Grim Steeper

# Also available by Gretchen Rue

## Witches' Brew Mysteries

*Death by a Thousand Sips*
*Steeped in Death*

## Lucky Pie Mysteries

*A Pie to Die For*

# The Grim Steeper

## A WITCHES' BREW MYSTERY

## Gretchen Rue

CROOKED LANE

NEW YORK

Published in the United States by Crooked Lane Books, an imprint of The Quick Brown Fox & Company LLC.

Crooked Lane Books and its logo are trademarks of The Quick Brown Fox & Company LLC.

Library of Congress Catalog-in-Publication data available upon request.

ISBN (hardcover): 978-1-63910-865-7
ISBN (ebook): 978-1-63910-866-4

Cover design by Mary Ann Lasher

Printed in the United States.

www.crookedlanebooks.com

Crooked Lane Books
34 West 27th St., 10th Floor
New York, NY 10001

First Edition: September 2024

10 9 8 7 6 5 4 3 2 1

To cat lovers, tea drinkers,
bird watchers, and independent
bookstore browsers everywhere.

# Chapter One

Few things in life are certain. I'm told those things are death and taxes, but I think the two certainties in life are this: death and rain in the Pacific Northwest.

Sure, the overzealous environmentalists of the world would tell me the latter won't be such a sure thing a hundred years from now, but I was born and raised in Washington state. Standing in front of my tea and book shop, The Earl's Study, huddled beneath an umbrella, I felt confident of my assessment.

"Phoebe, tell me again why we can't look at this window from the *inside*? This hair was *not* cheap." My full-time employee and full-time friend Imogen Prater had pulled her long box braids forward, making sure her hair stayed safely under her own umbrella. She normally opted for a micro braid style with her signature color flare, but for the summer she had switched things up with thicker box braids that had hot-pink strands mixed into several of the plaits.

Rain poured down around us, practically obscuring the store's huge front window, and I had to admit my hopes for a dramatic reveal of our summer window display were a bit of a letdown.

On the opposite side of me, Daphne Hendricks huddled beneath her own umbrella, shivering slightly in spite of the muggy humidity that made the air as thick as a winter sweater but nowhere near as cozy. Her blonde hair was damp, and little ringlets curled at the base of her ponytail. For some reason she had decided to wear a filmy, lilac-colored sundress today, and while it looked adorable, there was a good reason she was shivering.

"I think it looks really nice, Phoebe," Daphne said sweetly.

"Thanks, Daph."

Inside, perched on the window's interior ledge, my chubby orange tabby cat Bob blinked slowly at the three of us as if wondering bemusedly what the silly humans were doing when it was so nice and dry inside.

The window *did* look great, in spite of the rain. It was a Raven Creek tradition to overdo things a bit when it came to seasonal decor, and while many of the other local shops were festooned with Americana to celebrate the upcoming Independence Day street festival, I'd opted to take a slightly different approach.

We had crafted beautiful mobiles with oversized papier-mâché birds meant to depict the local species we saw most often in our neck of the woods. Robins floated alongside downy woodpeckers, and brightly colored American goldfinches bobbed next to the dainty Rufous hummingbird.

I'd spent hours poring over bird books—which we presently had in abundance—picking and choosing the best options, and Daphne had helped make them all, putting her in-progress arts degree to good use. She'd built them on weighted strings so their wings could flap independently, and whenever the door opened and closed, the whole mixed-up flock appeared to fly.

There were stacks of books on narrow tables inside the window, all written by Sebastian Marlow, a renowned birder, with a huge poster advertising his upcoming book tour stop and birding excursion with us.

My stomach cramped nervously, something it had been doing a lot this past month, ever since we'd locked in a signing with him. Sebastian had an enormous social media following, where he was best known as the Backyard Bird Man. He posted videos of himself going all over the world—though primarily in the United States— trying to find rare birds and teaching a new generation about the joys of bird watching.

A tinkling bell sounded, drawing my attention to the shop beside ours. A plump blonde woman in her early forties emerged from the Sugarplum Fairy and hustled over to us, blinking against the falling rain. She hadn't brought an umbrella, so she tucked herself between Daphne and me.

"You girls look absolutely crazy standing out here," Amy Beaudry scolded in a downright motherly tone. Amy wasn't that much older than me, but she had a nurturing quality about her that made her immediately trustworthy and lovable. I was so lucky to have her shop right next to mine.

"I keep telling her we could see it just fine from inside," Imogen said again, smoothing her braids as if to confirm they were still flawless. They were.

"Well, you take these and then get your butts back indoors. Storm watch was just upgraded to a warning."

Up until now we'd just had days and days of rain but no thunder or lightning. It sounded like that was about to change. Maybe it would be what the bad weather needed to get over its foul mood and move on.

Hopefully before our book signing tomorrow.

Amy handed me a cardboard tray with three identical pink cups in it, and the scent alone was all I needed to know it was her famous Nutella lattes. Perfection in a cup. She was working on adapting an iced version for summer, but she hadn't *quite* perfected it—according to her. According to me, and the dozen different samples she'd insisted on me trying, it was already incredible.

I planted a quick peck on her cheek. She smelled like sugar. "Thank you, you're an angel."

"Oh shush," she said, blushing furiously. "That's just what friends do." She then darted out from under my umbrella, her baby-pink Crocs making little squeaky sounds as she hustled back to the dry comfort of her own shop.

"Okay, okay, you've both humored me long enough. Dual employees of the month. Best staff ever. Let's go inside."

Daphne and Imogen both let out delighted cheers in unison and did not need to be invited twice.

Inside the store we were greeted immediately by the warm scent of fresh sourdough coming from the compact kitchen in the back. The store wasn't designed to be a restaurant, but it was more than capable of churning out a few signature baked goods every day. We took advantage of Amy's wares to otherwise fill our bakery case.

The Earl's Study was my aunt Eudora's life's work. She'd spent decades traveling the globe, learning as much as she could about tea varieties and how best to mix and blend her own unique creations. As a passionate and motivated book lover, it had only made sense to her to combine books and tea together in one perfect package.

And so The Earl's Study was born. One part bookshop, one part tea shop, and one hundred percent charming. I hadn't been certain I had the mettle to keep up her store after she passed, but she'd had enough faith to leave it to me, and I had spent nine months getting my feet under me. I was *almost* convinced I was doing it right.

Since I'd taken over, we had digitized the store's inventory, started an online marketplace—which was doing gangbusters business, especially with our old first editions—and I was now in the process of adding in a cat adoption annex.

When I'd started bringing Bob to the shop with me every day, I'd been worried the locals would reject the idea of having a cat around. Instead, he'd become a bigger hit than I could have imagined. With Daphne's efforts on our social media pages, I soon realized that Bob had a bigger following of fans than our shop did and that we'd start to get comments if he wasn't featured often enough.

Daphne had even started a little vlog series told from Bob's point of view, and he narrated—her voice-over with a modifier that made it sound cartoonish—the woeful shortcomings of our treatment of him. The videos had become a viral sensation, and now tourists would often come into the store just to see him. I'd had to add a small sign under the OPEN light to indicate *Bob is in* or *Bob is out*, as sometimes I'd already taken him home for the evening or weekend.

This also meant I'd seen the willingness of our customers to embrace cats in the space. So, after many months of fighting tooth and nail with the town council—and more specifically one spitfire board member, Dierdre Miller—I had gotten approval to open Bob's Place, a small section inside the bookstore where we'd be able to host adoptable kitties from the Barneswood Humane Society.

Barneswood was the closest thing to a "big" town we had near Raven Creek, with more specialty shops, a dedicated vet, and its own shelter. But that shelter had to deal with animals from an enormous chunk of the state and was often filled to capacity.

Taking between two and four cats wasn't going to make a huge difference, but it would certainly help, and I was motivated to feature the cats who had been waiting the longest, hoping that a change of scenery—and quieter digs—would help them find the right families.

The grand opening to Bob's Place was scheduled for the following Wednesday, a couple of days after Fourth of July, once all the excitement over Sebastian's book signing and the outdoor excursion was over. I glanced over at the kennels, freshly constructed by my friend Leo Lansing. He had refused to let me pay him for his work—typical Leo—so I'd insisted on adding a little plaque to the kennels that read *Donated by Lansing's Grocery*. He'd made a solid effort at declining even that honor, but there was no way I was letting him build me gorgeous custom cat kennels and not do *something* to thank him.

Leo was the kind of guy who hated to have any kind of attention directed at him, so I think the entire situation embarrassed him terribly, but I'd be a bad person and a worse friend not to show how much his work mattered to me.

The timer I kept clipped to my apron started to beep, letting me know that the sourdough currently in the oven was ready to come out. Both Daphne and Imogen had already resumed working, grateful to no longer be outside.

Things had been going so well with our online shop recently that I'd actually been able to increase Daphne's hours, allowing her to work full-time. She needed the money to help pay for school, and I was grateful to have her around more frequently. Her social media skills and artistic eye were proving to be a genuine asset, and having an extra body in the store gave me time to work on fulfilling all our online orders.

I pulled the sourdough out of the oven and was hit with a blast of fragrant, warm air. Today's savory offering was a new one for me and had been a special request from one of our regular customers. It was a rosemary and olive loaf. Normally I would have immediately declined making anything with olives—they just weren't my thing—but I had recently tried a Castelvetrano olive for the first time and had to admit the buttery, light flavor almost made me like olives. So I had yielded and was trying something a little outside my personal comfort zone. Our sweet offering for the day was a blueberry lemon sourdough loaf with fresh blueberries I had picked myself.

I heard the bell over the front door jingle merrily and didn't think much of it until a moment later when Imogen came into the tiny kitchen.

"I think I'm going to need your help, or someone is going to wind up dead."

# Chapter Two

I stared at Imogen wide-eyed, not sure if I'd heard her correctly. "What?"

"Please rescue me, Phoebe. I can't handle these people." She held her hands together in a gesture of pleading and gave me her most heartfelt expression. How could I refuse, especially when it was a rare day indeed that Imogen couldn't handle an irate customer?

I wiped my hands on my apron and followed her out into the main part of the store. A group of four people had come in. One was milling around in front of the tea shop counter, sniffing our testers and nodding approvingly. One was inspecting the stack of books in the front window with a scrutinizing look, not with an eye to purchase but more like a teacher checking over my work, and the final two were waiting at the cash desk that sat between the two shops.

I might not have been the most social media–savvy person on the planet, but I recognized Sebastian Marlow at the desk immediately. His face was, after all, plastered all over my bookstore's walls, and I had recently unpacked over fifty copies of his books.

"Sebastian, what a pleasure to meet you. I'm Phoebe Winchester. I spoke with your publicist to arrange all of this." I gestured toward the display, which the young man in black horn-rimmed glasses I'd noticed earlier was now rearranging. "Um, sir, what are you doing?"

He ignored me and continued to change the entire presentation of the table. Daphne, who was standing on the window ledge beside him painting letters on the glass, cast me a helpless look. I just shrugged. I could change things back later; let the little weirdo rearrange books if he wanted to.

"Oh, yes. Deacon. My business manager. I fired Deacon."

My head swiveled back to Sebastian. He was an incredibly handsome man, with the kind of rakish good looks one might expect from a man who made his money in the wilderness. He had a bit of a Bear-Grylls-meets-Heath-Ledger-in-his-prime vibe that I'm sure helped explain why such a large portion of his fan base was female. Right now, he was looking bored and very much like he didn't want to be in my shop.

"Did you say you fired Deacon?" I scrunched up my brow, because surely I'd misheard him. Deacon Hume, Sebastian's publicist and business manager, had been the one to arrange this entire signing and the accompanying outing. I'd just been emailing him about final details and the weekend itinerary not even twenty-four hours earlier. There had to be some mistake.

The petite girl beside Sebastian piped up. "I'm Melody Fairbanks. I was Deacon's assistant. I'll be helping Sebastian this weekend in his place." She offered me her hand, which I shook politely, still not sure I really understood what was happening.

Something must have caused quite the rift between Sebastian and Deacon, because I had been under the impression that they were childhood friends and that it had been primarily Deacon's efforts and marketing savvy that had helped turn Sebastian from a guy who knew a lot about birds into the world's most recognizable bird watcher.

They'd even launched an app recently that helped novice birders identify nearby species with a quick photo or an audio recording of the bird's song. The Backyard Birder app was a mega-success; even I had it installed and had started using it almost every evening while sitting out on my front porch.

Whatever had caused the split between the two men wasn't my business, but I *was* a little surprised not to be seeing the person I had spent so much time coordinating everything with.

None of this was Melody's fault, though, so I fixed my best smile on my face and greeted her politely. "I'm sure Deacon would have shared with you all the arrangements and plans he and I worked out for this weekend."

"Yes, thanks, it was all very thorough. We're on our way to the bed-and-breakfast right after this to check in, but we wanted to stop and see where the reading was going to be tomorrow."

She glanced around the store, her lips pursing slightly, and then her nose wrinkling visibly when she spotted Bob sitting in one of the armchairs next to the big fireplace on the far wall. The fireplace was unlit for the summer, but it was still Bob's favorite place to while away the hours.

"Is that a *cat*?"

"That's Bob."

"Well, what is he *doing here*?"

I glanced over at my cat, then back over my shoulder at Imogen, who immediately pretended to be busy stocking new releases. I didn't know how she'd figured this group out so quickly, but I understood now why she'd passed the baton of helping them over to me.

In a way, it was probably for the best. I loved Imogen and she was spectacular at her job—and definitely overqualified to be working here—but she had a short temper and not a lot of patience. This would probably have pushed her over her limit.

In fact, from behind me I heard her mutter under her breath, "Well, he ain't shopping for the latest Dan Brown book, Melody."

Thankfully, my guests did not have as keen a radar for sarcastic snipes as I did and didn't appear to have heard her.

"He's a shop cat. He's here whenever I am."

"I sincerely hope you aren't planning to have him here for the signing tomorrow." Again, Melody looked as if Bob's presence were a personal insult to her. I'd met people who didn't like cats, but I'd never had anyone have such a viscerally negative reaction to my chunky baby before.

"As a matter of fact, no. With all the people who will be coming and going tomorrow, I didn't want to have to worry about him potentially getting out, so he will be staying at home." What I *wanted* to say was that Bob had every right to attend, since it was his store too, but I felt like that might not be the hill I wanted to die on here.

"Well, good."

Sebastian hadn't said much of anything. He gave my cat a quick once-over and I saw the faint trace of a smile on his lips, but I couldn't quite read the reason behind it.

"Now, before we check in, I just wanted to confirm, the B and B is really the *best* we can do?" Melody said this in a sweet voice, the way someone might ask for a favor right before asking to speak to a manager.

"If you're asking about finding a hotel instead, I'm afraid you're out of luck. Closest hotel that's not a B and B or motel chain is going to be an hour or so northwest in Leavenworth. And they'll most likely be fully booked, with it being Independence Day on Monday."

Melody chewed the inside of her cheek and gave me a long stare, as if my answer might suddenly change if she just waited me out.

"I promise you: the Primrose is the nicest bed-and-breakfast in a fifty-mile radius. They've won awards. There was even a Hallmark Christmas movie filmed there once. It's incredibly charming."

"I'm sure it'll be great," Sebastian said gamely. "It'll be great," he told Melody directly.

The young man in glasses had finished rearranging the table at the front, and when he joined Melody and Sebastian, he handed me a stack of Sibley field guides and slim *Birds of Washington* books. "You can find another spot for those, I'm sure. Do you have any more copies of *The Backyard Bird Man for Beginners*? Sebastian, do you want to sign stock now?"

I took the hefty collection of birding manuals and stared at the guy with glasses, who barely looked old enough to drink, let alone in charge of anything.

"No, I think they like it when I sign in front of them. We'll sign what's left tomorrow." He gave me a wink, suggesting we were in on this together. I imagine that might have worked on other women, and it might have worked on me if he were a dark-haired private investigator, but I was unimpressed.

"We'll stop by in the morning just to arrange the seating and plans for the signing afterwards. Are those shelves movable?" Melody waved a hand toward my heavily laden shelves of new and used books. "We're obviously going to need more seating."

"Don't worry," I said. "This isn't our first rodeo."

In the window, Daphne hid a snicker behind her hand and accidentally slicked purple paint into her hair in the process.

This *was* in fact my first rodeo, but I desperately needed Melody not to know that. And it wasn't the first signing we'd had here—plenty of local authors had done stops—but it was certainly the first one of this magnitude.

The tickets for Sunday's hike and bird-watching outing had sold out in minutes. I was starting to think I should have put a cap on the reading, but it was a bit late for that now.

"Well, make sure you're prepared," Melody snapped. "Because this weekend Sebastian is going to make history. He's going to put this little backwater town of yours on the map."

# Chapter Three

The lunch rush obliterated any opportunity we had to overthink what Melody had said about Sebastian. The group had certainly made quite an impression on us when they were front and center, but by the time I was packing up to head home for the evening, I'd all but forgotten the strange interaction.

I loaded Bob into his backpack carrier and hauled him, along with a tote bag of books, out to my car. I hated to drive to work when I could avoid it, simply because I lived so close to the shop, but it had been raining for several days straight, and Bob had much more genteel sensibilities than I did.

After placing his carrier on the back seat and buckling it into place, I made a quick pit stop at Lansing's Grocery. Bob—safely in his backpack—came in with me because I didn't want to leave him in the car alone, even for a few minutes. It was less a concern over his personal safety than it was a well-founded worry about what kind of antics he could get himself into when I wasn't paying attention.

There was a large poster in the grocery store window advertising the book signing and the scheduled hike afterward. It made my stomach knot up anew as I wondered if I'd planned well enough and hoped that the forecast for Sunday was right and we would have clear skies for the big birding hike.

I'd bought new hiking boots for the event and even gone through Eudora's things until I found a cute pair of binoculars I could bring along with me. I wasn't what one might call *outdoorsy* at the best of times, but I'd found I was actually very excited to be participating and looking forward to seeing more of the rustic landscape around Raven Creek. I'd explored woefully little outside the main streets in the months I'd lived here.

Inside Lansing's, I grabbed a cart, because I wanted to be sure I had everything I needed for tomorrow, even if that meant being *over-prepared*. Before I was even to the produce section, I saw a familiar white-blonde head bent over the fresh herbs.

"Don't you grow most of those yourself?" I teased, bumping my shoulder into that of my good friend Honey Westcott.

She jumped, briefly startled, then laughed as she put the bunch of parsley she'd been holding back down.

"One, most of what I have room to grow on that tiny patio of mine gets used up pretty quick, and two, that's a really dang good deal for mint. And as I know I've warned you, mint can be a risky thing to grow on your own, unless you want it to take over your entire property."

She had given me this very wise advice several months earlier when I was picking up plants to start my first garden. Since I ran a tea shop, I'd been thrilled at the notion of growing my own mint rather than having to source it, and Honey had been the one to offer me guidance and tell me to keep the enthusiastic plants in pots.

Those pots were now overflowing with mint, and I could barely make enough iced tea to keep up.

"Tell you what," I said. "Why don't you just come by my place and help yourself to as much free mint as you can handle. That's an even better deal."

"A smart witch never turns down free herbs," she said with a laugh. "Unless they're offered with ill intent."

"I would *never*," I replied, feigning offense by clasping my hand to my chest but keeping my tone light so she would know I was only teasing. "Witches need to watch out for each other."

We both kept the phrase *witch* quiet, as if protecting a secret.

There had been a long-standing rumor in town that my aunt Eudora had been a witch. People believed it primarily because she lived alone in a big Victorian mansion with her cat and sold special tea blends that happened to help a little *too* well with things like finding love and getting a perfect eight hours of sleep.

But like a lot of small-town rumors, it was one of those things that people *said* without actually believing.

Except Eudora *had* been a witch.

And once I'd moved into her house, I'd learned I was too.

As it so happened, discovering my own innate magical abilities in my late thirties was an awful lot like trying to learn to skateboard in your late thirties. Not that I'd attempted that. But it was hard, painful, and I often felt absolutely ridiculous and out of place doing it.

From my understanding—and what I'd learned from Honey, the only other witch in town—most witches discover their powers around puberty. I was a bit of a late bloomer. Some people at midlife get divorced and buy themselves a fancy, too-expensive car. I had learned I was a witch. Basically the same thing.

But just this week I'd been starting to have some issues with my magic, and I wasn't sure it was due to me being a late bloomer. Maybe it was a good thing I'd bumped into Honey.

"Hey, have you ever had your, um, *gifts* act up out of nowhere?"

"Acting up how?"

A few days earlier I'd been washing the dishes and suddenly gotten sprayed with water. I'd thought it might just be old-house problems, but soon realized—after a costly plumber visit—it had to be due to magic and not malfunctioning sink hardware. But even today I'd had things go awry.

"Well, this morning all the windows in the house started opening as I walked by them. But then of course they would close the second I got near them." I let out a long sigh and a helpless shrug. "So far nothing is causing any damage to me or the house, unless you count some very wet kitchen tiles. And Bob would argue he's incurred personal damages because he did get his paws damp."

Bob let out a plaintive meow from his backpack to let Honey know I was downplaying how traumatic it had been for him.

"Aww, Bob," she cajoled sweetly. "Poor guy."

"I just can't figure it out. One week I'm practicing small stuff, just like you said, and now it's like I'm living with a poltergeist, except *I'm* the poltergeist."

We started to walk together, and I filled my cart with things to make specialty teas for the signing the next day. The event was being catered by St. Pierre's, the only restaurant in town I might dare to call *fancy*, and they were bringing specially selected hors d'oeuvres. But since we *were* a tea shop and our summer iced tea menu was exceptionally popular, they had accepted my offer to make three custom mixes for the signing.

As I put plastic tubs of blueberries, strawberries, and nectarines into my cart, Honey and I continued to chat.

"Do you think I accidentally did something to permanently screw up my powers? Like maybe all the situations where things got scary and my time-stopping powers were engaged, did it maybe deplete a magical battery I didn't know I had?"

My time-stopping ability was actually a rare gift for witches known as probability magic. In the most lay terms, I was able to very briefly stop what was happening around me and take the opportunity to change the outcome.

Probability magic was a tricky thing, because I didn't control *it* so much as the power just activated when I needed it most. So I couldn't practice using it. I had, however, started trying to learn how to do the smaller things most witches figured out when they were a lot younger.

Honey gave me a smile, her big gold hoop earrings shining under the overhead lights of the store. Her Afro had started to grow out a bit, and today she had it twisted into chic Bantu knots. She looked much too ethereal and stunning to be hanging out in a small-town grocery store.

"I don't think your magic is permanently screwed up. You're not the first person this has happened to, and you won't be the last. Now, usually magic gets all messy when teenage emotions get involved, but that's not the case here."

"Then what *is* the case?" This fun little experiment in wayward magical skills had been going on for over a week, and while it wasn't something that happened every day, I was starting to worry an accident might happen when I was around other people and it was going to be very difficult to explain myself without revealing an even stranger truth to them.

"How about I ask around in the community? The *witchy* community, not Raven Creek. I'll ask my mom, because I swear she's heard every story about every witch in the US with something that went wrong at one point or another. The best I can suggest is that maybe it's mental? Stress can do weird things to the body; it stands to reason it would do the same for magic."

"Oh great, so it's all in my head? Are there therapists just for witches?" I sighed.

"Wouldn't that be nice?"

We finished up our shopping and headed to the checkout, but before we could even get to the cash desk, I heard a sound that was both familiar and utterly alarming.

Leo's voice was unmistakable, but what I had never heard before was the way it sounded when raised and angry. Leo was *yelling* at someone.

Considering Leo Lansing was the very definition of gentle giant, basically looking like Paul Bunyan minus a blue ox, he tended to make himself smaller and less intimidating by being quiet and withdrawn most of the time. He must have had some pretty strong feelings about whoever he was talking to, because this was the first time in my life I'd heard him yell.

"And you can think twice before you ever set your good-for-nothing self back in this store. If I ever see you again, I'll throw you out of here with my bare hands." Leo's fists were clenched with rage, and what was visible of his cheeks under his dark, bushy beard was flaming red.

Feeling like this situation might be getting out of control, I left my cart with Honey and put myself between Leo and the man he was arguing with. The man, a stranger to me, was wearing a black suit and a shirt so white I assumed it had never been worn before. His shoes, however, looked scuffed and ready to fall apart. The man had thinning hair brushed into a comb-over and wore wire-framed glasses at least a decade out of style, but he had a young face, and I was willing to bet he was probably only in his early thirties.

"Whoa, hey. What's going on here?"

The sight of a woman in a T-shirt that read *No Shelf Control* and wearing a plastic turquoise backpack holding a cat in it must have been enough to shake both of them out of their angry focus on one another.

Leo's hands relaxed, and his body sagged immediately when he laid eyes on me. He glanced around and realized all the early-Friday-evening shoppers had stopped in their tracks to watch this drama unfold.

# The Grim Steeper

The strange man pushed his glasses up his nose and gave Leo and me a severe and overtly judgmental look. "You may want this to be over, Mr. Lansing, but you'll find that my client is very motivated to make this deal happen. You *will* see me again."

He pulled a handkerchief out of his pocket and wiped his hands, even though I was pretty sure he hadn't touched anything. With one final sneer at the entire group of townspeople gathered in the store, the man left, a cloud of noxious-smelling cologne trailing behind him. As he passed through the automatic doors, he nearly collided with Melody, Sebastian's manager. Melody gave a little start of surprise, and the two shared a mutually unfriendly look before the man vanished into the parking lot.

I turned so I could look at Leo. "What on earth was that all about? I've never seen you get that mad before. I've never seen you get mad before period. Are you okay? Do I need to go after that guy and kick him in the shins or something? Because I'll do it." I bounced and weaved like a fake boxer until Bob let out a protesting howl from my backpack, not enjoying being jostled around. "Oops. Sorry, buddy."

This brought a smile to Leo's previously rage-creased face.

"I'm sorry you had to see that, Phoebe. That's not who I am." He was still red-faced, but now from embarrassment rather than anger. "I don't know why I let him get under my skin like that, but something about that weasel makes me so mad I could spit."

"Who was he?" Honey had come up next to me, carrying both our baskets. "I didn't recognize him."

"He's a lawyer, apparently for some development firm I've never heard of, and if he hasn't gotten to you yet, just you wait. It sounds like he's making a menace of himself all over town trying to see what kind of price he can get for pieces of property. I guess this secret client he's working for has finally figured out that Raven Creek is a

19

tourist economy, and they want to open up a bunch of short-term rentals here. And they want to convert this to a chain grocer. One of those ones with the coffee shop inside." His frown deepened, like the mere thought of having a Starbucks in a grocery store was a sin.

In fairness, Raven Creek might have been one of the last towns in Washington that didn't host one of the famed Seattle coffee company's stores. We kind of liked it that way, though admittedly I did miss my usual order sometimes.

"He was trying to get you to sell the store?" Lansing's had been a family-owned business for multiple generations. It was one of the longest-running businesses in Raven Creek and as much a part of the community's history and charm as the covered bridges and vista views.

"I ain't selling the store." Leo bristled visibly, and I placed a hand on his arm, giving it a gentle rub to assure him everything was okay.

"You said he's trying to buy up other businesses in town?"

"Said anything that looks suitable to be converted into one of those rentals you get online, you know?"

That would mean the lawyer would need to talk to a local real estate agent, and we had only one of those in Raven Creek. So if I wanted to find more out about what the mystery lawyer was looking for, it meant I would need to talk to my least favorite person in town.

Dierdre Miller.

Unfortunately, I suspected that conversation was going to come to me one way or the other, because being a witch wasn't the only secret I was hiding from the people of this town.

I also happened to own half of Main Street.

# Chapter Four

I didn't have it in me to have a conversation with Dierdre today, not with the big book signing looming over my head tomorrow. To voluntarily have a chat with the most frustrating woman I'd ever met wasn't going to be high on my weekly to-do list, but it had to happen one way or the other. I could at least go to her in the guise of asking how her nephew's plans for his new store were coming along. He was planning to open a very fancy artisanal soap and candle shop in about two months' time. I'd been watching his Instagram with some interest because I selfishly wanted to know what all those adorable-looking soaps smelled like in person.

First, I just needed to make it through this weekend in one piece.

Honey followed me from the grocery store to my house in her own car and collected some mint before heading home for the evening herself. She promised she'd be at the book signing the next day and confirmed our plans for dinner the following week.

Once Bob and I were alone, I needed to clear my head. The day had been high-stress and confusing, and things weren't about to get any easier. The one thing I could count on to calm my nerves would be preparing tomorrow's iced teas.

I had three teas planned to serve our guests as well as our full hot tea menu at the ready. We also had a fridge stocked with our signature black tea with lemon, which was so popular we needed to make it by the bucketful.

I unpacked all the fruit I'd bought at the store and set it in a full sink to clean it off while I fed Bob his dinner. He was being unusually quiet this evening, as he would normally yowl at me and weave between my legs in an effort to either convince me or kill me—I was never wholly sure which.

After topping up his dry food and giving him fresh water, I filled his wet-food dish, and he immediately began purring and eating in unison, which made a particularly funny *brr-nom-smack-brrr-brrr* sound. Knowing he was content, I headed to the basement storage area, where all the surplus tea and tea-making supplies for the Earl's Study were kept.

I hadn't changed much about the way Aunt Eudora had arranged things in the basement. While her filing systems elsewhere could be a little chaotic—I still hadn't found many of her personal documents after nine months of house sorting—the tea supplies were exceptionally well organized. Everything was alphabetical, and there were neat, laminated cards in each of the metal tins telling me how to mix the blends. The individual ingredients, like the various tea bases and add-ins such as marigold petals, jasmine flowers, and vanilla sugar, were all kept in clearly labeled and alphabetized tins and jars on their own shelf.

Metal tins were always the best way to store tea ingredients, because they kept light from damaging them or diminishing their potency, but I think Aunt Eudora just believed that some things—like the flowers—were too pretty not to be in jars, and I agreed.

I wanted to use three different tea bases to make my special blends for the signing the next day. A white tea would have a lovely light flavor; a green tea would give a nice grassy, herbal vibe; and a black tea would provide a deeper, richer flavor. Since our signature tea also had a black tea base, I would need to make sure the two black teas were distinctive enough to stand apart.

Rather than starting from scratch and making unique teas blends for the iced teas, I decided to pick from some of our ready-made options. It would be the add-ins that made the iced variations more unique.

For my black tea, I couldn't resist our most popular summer tea, the Strawberry Earl Grey, which was a standard Earl Grey with extra bergamot and freeze-dried strawberries in it.

We didn't have a ton of varieties of green tea, but we had one I particularly enjoyed called Picnic Basket, which was meant to evoke the feeling of sitting out on a fresh-mown lawn on a summer day. It had lemongrass, orange peel, and vanilla sugar in with the earthy green-tea base.

The last option I selected was our white tea, and here I went with a jasmine and white tea mixture that contained freeze-dried raspberries, blueberries, and lavender buds. We called it Tea Party. This was actually a blend I'd recently custom-made all on my own, and its success at the shop was giving me a slightly inflated ego.

It was nice to know that magic wasn't the only gift Eudora had passed along to me.

I filled three mason jars with tea so I could bring it upstairs and also bring some extra along to the shop tomorrow in case we needed it. I suspected that when people tried these, they would want to bring the loose tea home with them as well. We'd had so many people wanting to recreate our iced teas that we'd needed to print out recipe cards that people could take with their purchase.

Back up in the kitchen, Bob had settled into his cushy bed on the fireplace hearth, a location he favored even when the fire wasn't lit.

As I started to chop the fresh fruit I'd bought at Lansing's, I couldn't help but think about how angry Leo had been when he'd been confronted by the lawyer. It churned my stomach to think about Leo's rage, because that simply wasn't the Leo I knew.

For someone to get that kind of reaction out of him, they'd really needed to push his buttons. Something about the lawyer had made my skin crawl, but I knew that if his goal was to buy up prime real estate in Raven Creek, I would hear from him one way or another. Maybe I'd prepare myself and ask a few other business owners in town if they'd also had the displeasure of speaking to him before he ultimately found his way to me.

Not many people knew I was the secret owner of the bulk of Main Street. The financial aspects of that were handled by a company called Mountain View, and most of the cash flow was siphoned back into making Raven Creek better. That had been the deal Eudora struck when she'd been given the opportunity to purchase the deeds decades earlier.

It wasn't a hard choice to continue to support the town the way Eudora had. I didn't *need* millions of dollars. I had a beautiful house, enough money to support my employees and myself, and the ability to keep rental rates low for the other business owners I cared about.

This town had taken me in when I had nowhere to go, they'd made me feel welcomed from my very first day—with the exception of Dierdre—and over the months I had finally settled into my surroundings and routine here. I cared about these people, and keeping the town as pristine and welcoming as it had been for me and Eudora was very important to me.

It was a no-brainer to just leave things status quo, and that's how I wanted them to stay. For this lawyer to come in and think he could take that away from us, well, it made me as mad as it had made Leo.

I'd been absent-mindedly chopping fruit while working myself up into a frothy rage, so it took me a moment to realize what was happening around me. It wasn't until I noticed that Bob had climbed up onto the kitchen table and was pawing at something red floating over his head that I set down my knife to see what he had found.

Which was when I realized that all my freshly washed berries were suspended in midair all around the kitchen. They'd floated up off the counter and were all the way up to the ceiling, hanging overhead like a chandelier.

"Oh," was all I could think to say.

My fritzy magic was apparently triggered by anger, or at least by high emotions, something I didn't think I'd realized previously. I tried to think of the past instances where things had gone awry, but I couldn't recall if anything had been making me more stressed than usual. It *had* all started happening when I'd begun to plan the big signing and hike, so perhaps I'd just been in a constant state of elevated stress since then?

Bob batted at a strawberry half, and it just floated calmly away from him, like it was in zero gravity. I poked a fat blueberry hovering over my head, and it sailed upward, slow and casual, not a worry in the world.

Though what worries a blueberry might have, I couldn't guess.

I pulled out my phone and snapped a quick photo to send to Honey. Since it seemed that the floating fruit wasn't all going to come crashing to the floor now that I'd noticed it, I set about collecting it all again. Thankfully, it didn't start to head back upward once I grabbed it and replaced it in the bowls, but it *was* a bit of an effort to get a few nectarine slices that had managed to find their way almost to the ceiling.

Bob was reluctant to let me have his strawberry, so after a few unsuccessful attempts, I relented and just let him keep it. He'd get bored eventually—either that or I'd find hovering strawberry over my bed later tonight.

I didn't want to tempt fate further, but the iced tea still needed to be made. I couldn't do it in the morning, because it was best left to steep overnight. So rather than letting myself get sidetracked by stress and negativity again—heaven only knew what other trouble my magic could get me into tonight—I put my phone on the shelf above the kitchen sink and put on an episode of *Parks and Recreation* so that Ron, April, and Leslie could keep me distracted while I worked.

This technique worked wonders. I continued to chop up fruit until it was finely diced, then macerated it in using my big mortar and pestle. I took three jumbo glass pitchers—the kind you might use for a big town picnic—and set them on my kitchen table, which was the only place in the small kitchen that could hold them all.

To one, I added the smashed strawberries and some crushed basil leaves I'd taken from the plant in the window. To the second, I added the blueberries and some fresh-sliced oranges. To the third, I added a nectarine mixture into which I'd tossed locally harvested honey.

I filled several biodegradable tea bags for each pitcher. Strawberry Earl Grey went in the first, Picnic Basket in the second, and Tea Party in the third. I then added a hefty serving of boiling water to each, filling them one-third full and adding a cup of sugar apiece.

The mixtures would steep for the next several hours, and then I would remove the tea bags and fill the rest of the containers with water. Allowing the tea to steep for hours rather than just a few minutes would give it a strong concentration of flavor—not something you normally wanted in a cup, but for a pitcher it was ideal. The extra water would then cut down the potency, giving it the perfect balance overall.

Satisfied with a job well done and no follow-up magical disasters, I left the tea on the table and made myself a grilled cheese sandwich for a quick dinner using some leftover cheddar jalapeño sourdough I had on the counter. While we rarely had leftovers at the shop after lunch rush, I sometimes got lucky, and yesterday had been one of those days. The trick to my perfect grilled cheese was to add shredded cheese to the pan right when the sandwich was almost finished cooking so it would melt under the bread when you did the final flip. This added a delicious cheesy, crunchy layer to the outside of the sandwich, and it was absolute perfection.

A greasy cheese-bomb was just what the doctor ordered after a stressful, rainy day, and Bob and I finished our night curled up together on the couch. I needed a nice restful sleep to prepare me for the day ahead.

# Chapter Five

No amount of sleep could have prepared me for the day of the signing. The extra stress didn't help matters much, because when I woke up in the morning, a breaker would trip off every time I entered a room, sending me into darkness.

It made things very frustrating in the shower and almost made me late.

I wanted to blame the wiring of the old house, but I knew better at this point. Something was up with my powers.

When I got to the Earl's Study, it was bright and early, barely six thirty, and we didn't open until eight. I unloaded the massive pitchers of tea, added the extra water, and put them in the fridge so they'd be nice and cold by the time the signing started at two that afternoon. With the planned chat and Q and A before and nibbles to follow, we expected it would last about three hours.

I hadn't realized until I started unloading my car just how accustomed I was to having Bob with me all day when I worked. Several times I double-checked the door before entering or exiting to make sure he wasn't underfoot trying to escape, and he wasn't, because he was at home.

I was sure most cat owners were used to being away from their fur babies for hours at a time, and less than a year ago I hadn't ever wanted to own a cat, so it had never occurred to me I might miss one as much as I missed Bob right now. His furry orange presence might be physically small, but it filled up the space around him.

I headed next door, leaving my umbrella in the shop, hoping Amy would be quick to answer. It would be impossible to carry boxes of pastries *and* my coffee *and* an umbrella. I was just going to have to get a little wet.

The continuing rain was putting a damper on my day already, because the big birding hike the next morning was going to be impossible if it was pouring. But even if it was clear tomorrow, it might have to be canceled just because of how steadily it had poured over the last week. No one wanted to be ankle deep in mud while they were hiking.

Thunder rumbled, letting me know this particular storm had no interest in letting up anytime soon. In spite of the literal dark cloud over my head, I decided to try being optimistic. For one, I'd recently learned that stress and negative thinking could seriously blow up in my face, and two, I really wanted to go on that birding hike tomorrow. I was even closing the store for the day so Daphne could come, since this whole thing was only happening because of her.

Amy answered the door almost as soon as I knocked, looking like her usual ray-of-sunshine self. Nothing seemed to get her down for long, and I tried to let her positivity wear off on me.

"We all set for later?" I asked, following her inside and up to the counter. The Sugarplum Fairy was what would happen if a six-year-old girl with a princess obsession were allowed to build her own bakery. Everything inside was soft baby pink with light wood fixtures. A hot-pink neon sign over the coffee bar was a new addition and read *Sugar, Spice, and Everything Nice*. Anything that wasn't pink was white or gold, and the whole shop constantly smelled like cotton candy.

Little white Parisian tables invited you to sit and stay, not that the glass cases of pastries forming an L shape around the back and side of the store weren't invitation enough.

Amy was already making my usual morning latte, and my two boxes of pastries for my own store were packaged up and waiting for me. Today she had drawn little bonbon candies on top in marker with a note that said *Stay Sweet*.

"I have everything ready to go for the signing, not to worry. The macarons are already packaged up, but I don't think you've got enough room for them right now, so I'll bring them by after your lunch rush ends. The cake looks stunning, if I do say so myself. Do you want to see?"

I nodded eagerly, and she lifted the panel that divided the staff area from the main shop. In the back, she opened a large cooler and held her hands out with a flourish to show me the custom cake within.

It was a two-tier cake that she had decked out impressively, with little fondant and sugar-paste birds all over the exterior as well as Sebastian's distinctive Backyard Bird Man logo on the top in icing.

"Oh, Amy, you've really outdone yourself with this one. Those birds almost look real."

The attention to detail really was flawless. You could practically see feathers on the birds, they were so beautifully painted.

"This was fun for me. We don't get a lot of orders like this—it's usually birthday or wedding cakes—so this was outside the box. I had a great time."

She closed the fridge, and we went back out front. "You feeling ready? I know this is your first big event; you've been so nervous the last few days."

"It's that obvious?"

Amy laughed. "If you were more highly strung, you'd be a kite, hon. I know this guy is some sort of big deal online, but in the immortal words of my gran, *Man's a man*. Don't let him get you all twisted up like this. You ladies run a tight ship at that store, and I know you're going to have a flawless event today. So take a deep breath, drink your latte, and tell yourself everything is going to be okay. Okay?"

I smiled at her, hugging the latte cup to my heart. "Amy, what would I do without you?"

"You'd probably weigh about five pounds less, but you'd definitely be more miserable, so it's a fair trade-off in my books." She winked at me. "I'll call you in a couple hours just to borrow a pair of hands getting this cake next door."

Back in the shop, I went about my morning routine of baking our signature Earl Grey shortbread and getting the sourdough in the oven. Since we didn't typically have a lunch rush on Saturday, I baked fewer loaves, today opting for the fan favorites of chocolate cherry and rosemary with black pepper. They were so frequently asked for that I could make them without looking at a recipe.

For someone who'd spent much of her former life as an office drone, living off takeout and using her oven to store dishes, it amazed me sometimes how different things looked now. I had found immense peace in the process of kneading bread dough and playing with new recipes, a meditative calm I had never dreamed possible before.

It was all-hands-on-deck today, with Imogen arriving for her usual morning shift around ten, and Daphne would be in at noon just to help do some final work on getting the store set up and ready.

Amy was right, we knew what we were doing, even though the draw for this event was going to be much larger than anything we—or at least I—had ever done before.

Moments after Imogen arrived, the door tinkled again, admitting a familiar wizened face.

"Good morning, Mr. Loughery," I called, turning the kettle on to get his usual cup of Irish Breakfast started.

Norman Loughery was, without question, our most consistent customer. He came in almost every single day, rain or shine, and he would sit in one of the cozy armchairs by the fireplace and read whatever dollar-bin thriller had his attention at the moment. He'd just finished reading all the Sue Grafton books and was now on a John Grisham kick.

He tipped his newsboy cap at us and shuffled over to his usual spot. While he was in his mideighties at least, he still had a youthful spark about him, though his body definitely wasn't on the same page as his personality some days. I suspected the constant rain was probably giving him some aches and pains. Eudora used to complain about the weather in the Pacific Northwest being a real bear on old joints.

As Mr. Loughery dropped into his chair, a copy of *The Pelican Brief* tucked under his arm, he cast a long glance at the empty chair beside him. I watched as he scanned the entire store, peeking under chairs, craning his neck to see the front window.

I smiled to myself.

"Bob's at home today, Norman."

He expression visibly darkened with disappointment, and he took his hand out of his coat pocket where I knew he kept treats at all times, despite a little framed sign I'd placed on the fireplace that said *No Matter What the Cat Tells You, He Doesn't Need Treats.* I let it go for Mr. Loughery, because he and Bob had the most delightful little bond, and I knew it mattered to the older man to spoil my silly cat.

Mr. Loughery had been the one to suggest I name the new cat adoption program after Bob, since it was spending time with the orange tabby that had convinced him he might like a cat of his own. That was how Norman had unofficially become the program's first adopter when I found Frodo, an older tuxedo cat I thought would be a perfect fit for him.

"How's Frodo?" I asked.

Mr. Loughery clucked his tongue. "He has discovered if he sits on the back of the couch, he can pounce at the window and give the birds at the feeder outside a little fright. Naughty boy." But the smile on his face told me he loved every minute of it. I had seen about a thousand blurry photos of Frodo on Mr. Loughery's ancient flip phone in the few months they'd been together, so I knew they were loving their mutual companionship. "You make sure to tell Bob I said hello, though."

"I will."

Mr. Loughery knew all about the signing and that we might need to rearrange the furniture at some point. Daphne arrived just before noon, her light-blonde hair a curly massy of frizzy flyaways. She looked for all the world as if she had just stuck her finger in a light socket, but that was just kind of Daphne's vibe. She was a pretty girl who just happened to look a bit like a mad scientist.

Today she was sporting a shirt that said BIRD NERD on the front with little squares meant to resemble the periodic table, except instead of *Na* or *Cl*, the boxes read *Ro* for *Robin* or *Ha* for *Hawk*. It was cute.

"I didn't realize you were so into this whole birding thing," I commented, giving her shirt the nod.

She laughed. "You know, I wasn't either until I started coming across all these bird feeder videos online, and it was just so relaxing to watch birds come and go. So now I've started keeping these You-Tube channels on while I study. I think they're actually meant for cat owners—they just have birds flying around and ambient background noise. They're great. The most embarrassing thing—I've started watching tutorials on how to befriend crows. Did you know they recognize people, so if you've been mean or nice to a crow, it will remember and treat you accordingly? Apparently, if you feed them, they sometimes start bringing you gifts."

"I'm sure your mother will be thrilled when her entire yard is filled with crows leaving you dirty paper clips and old pennies," Imogen said, though it was clear she was only teasing good-naturedly.

"She *was* wondering why I bought a whole bag of puppy food," Daphne admitted. "I can't decide if she was more relieved or more concerned when I explained I didn't want a dog, I just wanted crow friends."

I shook my head. I liked sitting on my porch and watching birds at my feeder as much as the next elder millennial, but I'd have to draw the line at befriending corvids. I could be the crazy cat lady in town, but I couldn't be the crazy cat *and* crow lady. That might just push me too much into *very obviously a witch* territory. I needed to maintain at least a little plausible deniability.

Before I knew it, lunch was over and a queue was forming outside the door for the signing. Sebastian and his crew hadn't arrived yet, but there was still an hour to go before things started. I'd let in as many people as I could ahead of the reading and signing, but there were still at least a dozen people huddled under umbrellas waiting outside.

Daphne went out to suggest they bide their time at Sugarplum Fairy before things got started, and a few took the cue, but some refused to budge. I might have severely underestimated the appeal of a handsome bird expert.

Thankfully for us, and for the people outside, the rain was starting to lighten somewhat, and by the time it was quarter to two, it was only a light mist outside. I had suggested to Sebastian and his group that they come through the back entrance just to avoid too much commotion out front, so when I heard a knock at the back door, I hustled over to let them in.

Melody was positively drenched, primarily, it seemed, because she had insisted on holding an umbrella for Sebastian but hadn't put it over both of them. She shivered visibly.

The group with Sebastian was the same three people who had come the previous morning: Melody, the kid with glasses, and a man in a suit who I hadn't been introduced to at the time. As I showed them all into the store, Melody gave me a quick introduction to the people whose names I didn't know.

"Phoebe, this is Connor Reeves." She gestured at the kid with glasses in a vague way, without looking at him. "He's Sebastian's social media assistant."

Connor jerked up his chin in greeting. "Yo."

Next, Melody pointed to the man in the suit, but I noticed that when she shook out her umbrella, she did it in his general direction. Whether intentional or not, it told me a lot about how she felt toward both these men. "This is Travis McClaren; he's with Sebastian's publisher. They're just trying to gauge how this kind of event is attended to see how many more they want to do."

I offered to shake Connor's hand, but he missed it, or else he ignored it on purpose to head into the main part of the bookstore, his phone already out and either recording something or live streaming. I pivoted and extended my hand to Travis, who was at least gracious enough to give it a firm squeeze. "Nice to meet you, Phoebe. I knew your aunt, at least in passing. The store has done some nice business for our house in the past, and I'm really looking forward to seeing what you've put together here today."

Melody was already on her phone, water dripping from her hair onto the screen as she typed furiously. There was a deep divot in the skin between her eyebrows, and I suspected she spent a good chunk of her day scowling at her phone, or her laptop, or at whatever poor soul happened to be standing in front of her.

"Melody, would you like to use my office? It's nothing fancy, I'm afraid, but you could at least sit down."

I wanted to offer her a towel, but I didn't have one. I briefly considered texting Rich Lofting, who lived right upstairs, but then I imagined how it might look to text the guy I *might* be dating to ask him to bring me a towel. No matter how innocent the request, that would just look weird.

"Oh." Melody blinked at me, seemingly just realizing I was present. "No, no. That's not necessary. Are we just about ready to go here?" She pushed past me without waiting for me to answer, taking a look around the store.

It was hard to read her expression, but it wasn't disgusted, so I took that as a minor win. We'd converted the small seating area in the tea shop into a buffet where people could grab the finger food Melody had ordered as well as our custom iced teas and the desserts we had brought in for the event. When Melody looked at Amy's cake for one brief moment, I saw her smile, and for the first time in a week I felt myself exhale. Okay, so this wasn't going to be a total disaster.

The minute I let my guard down, the front door opened and a young man with damp, dark hair came through the door.

When Melody laid eyes on him, her cheeks flushed red.

"What do you think *you're* doing here?"

# Chapter Six

If there's one thing small towns can't get enough of, it's gossip. The moment Melody made her very loud exclamation at the newcomer, every single person seated in the bookstore spun around to look at what was happening in the foyer.

This included Connor, the assistant, whose phone was pointed directly at the drama, and my own staff, who stopped in the middle of putting out more chairs to gape at Melody and the man.

Perhaps I should have intervened, but I was so surprised by her outburst I didn't have time to react to it. She crossed the short distance between her and the man and jabbed a finger into his chest. "What makes you think you can come waltzing in here after what you did? We told you to stay out of this."

My first thought was that I was witnessing some kind of lovers' quarrel and this was Melody's boyfriend. But the way she said *we told you* had me second-guessing my initial response.

Sebastian, who had been hanging around in the back hallway, came into the main part of the store, probably summoned by the yelling. He stopped dead in his tracks when he saw the man in the doorway. I shared a quick, nervous glance with Imogen, who just shrugged helplessly.

"Dude, you can't be here right now," Sebastian said. His voice was much calmer than Melody's had been, but he was keeping his words as quiet as possible across the distance. There was no way the crowd hadn't heard him, but I got the sense Sebastian was trying to limit the drama as much as he could.

"Can we just talk?" the dark-haired man asked. He was ignoring Melody entirely, his expression solely fixed on Sebastian.

"He doesn't want to talk to you," snarled Melody.

I didn't want whatever this was unfolding at the biggest event of the year. I stepped between Melody and the new arrival. "Hi. I'm Phoebe, and this is my shop."

"Oh, Phoebe, of course. I'm Deacon." He shook my hand eagerly, as if there was no tension in the room whatsoever.

Ah, well, that explained some of the response I was seeing, but perhaps not the level of vitriol that Melody was wielding like a sharpened blade. Was Deacon trying to get his job back? I didn't know what had happened with the work dynamic, but the pleading way he kept darting glances at Sebastian told me there was a lot that had gone unspoken.

"Look, Deacon, we're just about to start the signing. Why don't you have a seat in my office, and once everyone is gone, I'll make sure you all have somewhere quiet to talk. I just don't think now is the time." I waved toward the large crowd, who were all staring at us without even pretending to hide their curiosity. I loved my town, but I did wish that sometimes, just sometimes, they pretended to act like normal humans.

Deacon looked like he might argue with me, and I didn't need to check with Melody to assume she was twelve shades of purple. Finally, after an excruciatingly long moment, Deacon nodded. "Okay."

I gave a wave to Imogen, who immediately knew what I needed. She guided Deacon through the center foyer, past the kitchen, and into my office. I turned and gave Melody one quick pleading glance, and though she looked furious enough to blow a blood vessel in her forehead, she just let out a huffy sigh and moved out of the way.

"Good afternoon, everyone! I'm glad our little show got your attention. I'm sure you all know that drama is the name of the game when it comes to going viral on social media, but our guest today managed to do it by simply looking outside his back window. On any given day you can see blue jays or crows in your very own backyard, having their own little fights like the one we just staged for you now, and Sebastian Marlow has made a career out of helping us understand what those avian squabbles really mean. So, without any further ado, the reason you're all here today, Sebastian Marlow!"

I had no doubt that my little fib wasn't fooling anyone, but I needed to say *something*, and it was the best I could manage under pressure. Whether they believed me or not, the crowd applauded wildly, whistling and cheering as Sebastian moved down the aisle to where one of the big armchairs at the front of the room was waiting.

Janice Delaney, the leader of our local nature club—who knew we had such a thing?—had been kind enough to volunteer as the coordinator for the Q and A and conversation session before the signing, which was probably for the best, since I couldn't tell a purple finch from a pine siskin to save my life.

Things went without a hitch through the chat, but just as Janice was about to turn things over to the audience for the Q and A, Sebastian raised a hand to silence her midsentence.

"Janet, I really wanted to thank you for such a thoughtful discussion."

Janice's mouth formed a thin line, but she didn't correct him about her name, even though I could tell she was dying to.

"But before we go any further, there is something I need to confess."

A collective gasp ran through the audience, and I cast a worried look at Melody to gauge her reaction to this statement. Her eyes gleamed, and all the former rage in her expression was replaced by something akin to giddiness. Whatever Sebastian was about to say, she was not only prepared for it but also excited. Perhaps this was the thing she'd been hinting about yesterday when she said Sebastian was going to put Raven Creek on the map.

"You see, I have my own reasons for wanting to come to your town that had nothing to do with signing books—not that I'm not excited to sign your books." He let his megawatt smile travel the room so everyone in the audience felt like it was solely for them. "Even tomorrow's hike is just an excuse for me to get out in your pristine wilderness. Friends, what I'm about to tell you could change amateur birding forever."

Everyone leaned forward, and I hated to admit it, but I caught myself holding my breath. He just had a captivating presence in front of an audience. No wonder he'd amassed such a big following online. His charm radiated with every smile and wink.

"I have been looking for a bird believed to be extinct for over fifty years, and my research had led me to your town. I believe that the Pacific tanager might be right in your very backyard."

Janice, who had been listening to this speech, interjected. "Do you mean the western tanager?"

Beside me, Melody scoffed loudly. Sebastian was more polite in his response. "A close relative, but no. The Pacific tanager was thought to be extinct since 1957. I've been tracing potential sightings of it for most of my career. I believe it is here, and if it's not the Pacific tanager, it could quite possibly be an entirely new tanager subspecies."

Sebastian said this as if announcing he was going out looking for Atlantis in our mountains.

Everyone listening cooed and clapped appropriately.

"Do you think we might find it tomorrow?" one of the women in the audience asked.

"If the weather favors us, I think we could get lucky. I'm hoping so, anyway."

I grabbed one of the Sibley field guides we'd needed to relocate from the signing table. We'd put up a new display of more generalized birding and natural history books on the main foyer table, so it was right next to me. I flipped through to the tanager section, because I had no clue what he was talking about. A stunning array of small birds greeted me; some were black and yellow, some blue and green. The western tanager was one I actually recognized. It was a bright-yellow bird with an orange-and-red face, and I'd seen them in the trees behind my house before. They weren't birdseed birds, but sometimes I'd spotted their cheery feathers at one of my suet feeders.

These birds were simply stunning. I could see the fascination with wanting to find a new one, or one previously believed to be extinct. It would be huge news in the birding community, not to mention an incredible feather in Sebastian's professional cap. Pun not intended.

Melody hadn't been kidding about it putting us on the map. Raven Creek was already a huge destination for birders, but with a new—or newly rediscovered—species in our very backyard, we'd see a ton more people coming through during the season, hoping to spot it and add it to their life list.

I set the bird book back on the table. Janice was taking more questions from the crowd and Sebastian was wooing his audience, but things were beginning to wind down. The signing table was prepped and ready, with Daphne standing by carrying a fistful of extra Sharpies just in case Sebastian needed one.

Seeing that everything was going beautifully, I ducked down the hallway to my office, hoping to get a chance to ask Deacon a few questions while Melody and Sebastian were distracted.

But when I opened my office door, Deacon was nowhere to be found.

# Chapter Seven

I had been worried that the drama of Deacon's arrival might put a damper on the remainder of the signing, but by the time Sebastian wrapped up his question-and-answer session with the crowd and Connor and Daphne had pulled up a big signing table with books, it seemed like the showdown had been largely forgotten.

Sebastian finished signing someone's custom-made *Mrs. Backyard Birdman* shirt, and folks drifted into the tea shop to snack on the catering wares and try out my custom iced teas.

It never got boring to hear people say nice things about my offerings when they didn't think I was around. As I cleared disposable cups and plates from the tables, I kept an ear out for any commentary on the beverages. If they didn't like the food, that wasn't my fault.

I spotted Melody and Connor huddled together near the end of one of the service tables, their heads bowed toward each other conspiratorially and their voices in a low whisper. For all their efforts of appearing like they were in a spy movie, they didn't seem to notice I was in the room with them.

As readers finished their plates and left for the evening, I was able to move closer to the pair under the auspices of tidying up. They didn't react and just kept talking.

". . . he thinks that he's getting back in on this, then he has another . . ." Melody's grumbling dropping off as the bell over the door jangled. ". . . should get someone to look at the records . . ."

Connor, his expression drawn, was obviously a little concerned over Melody's laser-focused fury. ". . . don't think he'll try again. Let's not be . . ."

"And *Sebastian*," Melody spat through gritted teeth. She mumbled something I couldn't make out. ". . . could kill him."

At this, Connor seemed to nod sympathetically.

My confusion over what they were saying—obviously not helped by my inability to hear most of it—distracted me from what I was doing. I picked up a tray of canapes that had mostly been demolished, but I didn't get a firm enough grip on one of the handles.

The tray lurched, and before I had a chance to try to save it, something bizarre happened.

The tray froze.

For a second, I thought my time-stopping abilities might have kicked in at a fairly unusual moment, considering I wasn't in any physical danger, but then I noticed Melody and Connor were turning to look at me.

And the tray was slowly starting to rotate, the remaining appetizers spinning in place like little tops. Oh god, this stupid glitchy magic of mine was really picking the optimal times to mess with me.

If I caught the tray, the dancing appetizers would certainly raise a few questions, so I did the only thing I could think of in that moment of panic.

I smacked the tray to the floor.

Little balls of mozzarella cheese and tiny tomato halves went everywhere, but at least I didn't think anyone had seen the weird fritzing magic in action.

44

Melody gave me a dismissive sneer, checking her shoes to see if the balsamic glace had gotten on her. "Be *careful*," she snarled.

"Sorry, tray handle was slippery. My bad."

Neither of them bothered to offer me any assistance, and they moved back into the bookshop, where Sebastian had a group of lingering fans laughing up a storm—Daphne included. I quickly got the mess taken care of, but the magical mishap meant I never got to finish hearing what Melody and Connor had been saying.

\*　\*　\*

I was exhausted and relieved by the time I locked up the shop at six. Normally I wouldn't have stayed the whole day, but it had taken us a long time to clean up after the signing, and we'd had customers backed up at the cash desk for almost an hour.

The one nice thing about people being forced to wait longer to pay was that they had no choice but to browse the store, and as a result the stacks of books we were ringing through just kept getting taller and taller.

We had sold out of all the extra birding books I'd ordered, and we had only a handful of copies of Sebastian's book left, which he generously signed so that anyone who'd been unable to come to the event still got one.

Daphne carried hers out before close, hugging it to her chest like a baby, her cheeks flushed with joy. The rain had let up by the time the event ended, and everyone was enthusiastically talking about the next morning's hike and whether or not Sebastian would find his Pacific tanager.

I had a box in one hand with what scant remains there were of Amy's beautiful cake after everyone had left. I was too tired to cook anything, so I planned to sit on my couch with the box in my lap and have that for dinner.

I was just about to get into my car when a window over the shop's rear door opened and a familiar mop of shaggy dark hair popped out.

"You're here late on a Saturday," Rich Lofting said, resting his arms on the window ledge and smiling down at me.

"Wow, you really are a good private investigator. Did they teach you observation skills like that when you were a cop, or are you just naturally quick?" I grinned at him. He made me feel like I was thirteen again, because we had grown up over our summers together lobbing good-natured abuse as the only form of flirtation we had a grasp on. Little had changed now that we were adults.

"Where's your better half?"

"He had to stay home today."

"Oh no, Bob got stuck on time out?"

I laughed, opening my passenger door to put the cake on the seat. "We had a big signing this afternoon. Did you sleep through all the commotion?" Rich's job required him to work truly bizarre hours, so sometimes he was asleep until midday.

"I was actually in Barneswood until about fifteen minutes ago. Sorry I missed your event."

"Unless you love birds and a moderate sprinkling of high drama, I don't think you missed much."

Rich made a little face. "I can't say I love either of those things."

"Isn't drama your literal job?"

"I'm a PI, not a playwright."

"Ugh, go away." My cheeks hurt I was smiling so hard.

"Hold on, I had a legitimate reason for bugging you, and while this feels a little more *Romeo and Juliet* than I'd like, I was wondering if you wanted to grab dinner with me next week? Like, real dinner, not just Sweet Peach's."

While the food at Sweet Peach's, our local diner, was unbelievably good, so far it had been the only place we'd really been out together, which would have been fine if we were still teenagers, but it made it difficult for me to put a name on what it was we were to each other.

Rich and I were both recently divorced, and it had made us gunshy about jumping into a romantic entanglement. The problem was that we both very obviously liked each other, and ever since I'd gotten back into town, we had been playing a very stupid game of *When will they start dating?* It was a trope I hated in my real life even more than on TV.

We kept talking about doing things, and we kept accidentally doing things, but now was the moment he was *finally* asking me out on the long-promised real date.

"I would like that a lot," I told him. "Now, by *real* dinner, you're going to need to give a lady guidance on what to wear, because I normally dress like a very hip spinster librarian." I gestured to my jeans, cardigan, and silly book-themed shirt.

"Let me mull that over and get back to you."

We said our goodbyes and I headed home, ready for my dinner of cake.

\* \* \*

In the morning, I was greeted by the most unusual thing when I opened my eyes. It wasn't the big orange lump on my pillow; that had become a pretty standard part of my morning. When I looked out the big picture window in my bedroom, bright, butter-yellow sunshine was beaming through.

I sat up in bed with all the enthusiasm of a small child on Christmas morning. I could barely believe what I was seeing. After day upon day of rain, the sight of a clear blue sky and sunlight blasting over everything was quite possibly the most beautiful thing I'd ever seen.

My alarm had been set early, the plan being to head out on the hike in a big group by seven o'clock. The early Sunday start was both to allow churchgoers to make it back in time for an afternoon service and because there was apparently some truth in the saying that an early bird catches the worm, because an early birder sees the best birds.

I had a quick shower and decided to forgo my usual morning run, figuring the hike would give me more than enough of a workout. It did feel strange to skip over my usual long skirts and jeans in favor of a good pair of shorts and my long-ignored hiking boots. I couldn't resist letting my shirt have some personality and donned one that had an old-fashioned library card on it and said Sometimes I Overdue It in typewriter font underneath.

Bob watched as I hustled around to get ready. I was usually at the shop before seven every morning, yet for some reason I was running late today. Perhaps the signing yesterday had tired me out more than I'd expected.

Since I'd never make it on time if I walked or biked, I decided to drive to the little parking lot near one of the town's iconic covered bridges. There was a great—and relatively easy—hiking trail that started next to one of them, which was where today's event was going to begin.

I made my way through town, taking a different route than I normally went, since I wasn't going to the shop. It was funny how you could live in a town for almost a year and still find new things you'd never seen before. I decided I really should make more time to see all the different streets and avenues in Raven Creek rather than keeping to the five or six places I was most accustomed to.

I was soon passing the Primrose B and B, where we'd rented rooms for Sebastian and his crew, and I was so focused on getting to the hike that I almost didn't notice the two police cars and the ambulance. When what I was looking at finally registered, I slammed on the brakes and parked my car at the curb.

I spotted Melody almost immediately, sitting on the front step of the B and B, her eyes puffy and red, cheeks streaked with tears.

"Melody, what's going on?"

The police were coming and going, but the ambulance was eerily quiet.

"I-it's Se-Sebastian," she stammered. "Someone *killed* him."

# Chapter Eight

It took me a moment to process Melody's words. Sebastian had been in my bookstore just the day before, laughing and joking and taking pictures with fans. It seemed impossible that he was dead now, but this being Raven Creek, I had learned early that the Reaper could pop up for people at unexpected times.

"What do you mean, someone killed him?" Maybe the shock of the event had rattled her. If he had died, it must have been by natural means. This sweet little B and B was hardly the kind of place you would imagine someone meeting with foul play.

Melody, hiccupping from how hard she'd been crying, mimed a stabbing motion with an invisible knife. "Right in the back. I found him in his bed this morning." This set her off crying again, and a female police officer came over to see what the new commotion was about.

"Can I help you?" she asked.

I shook my head vigorously. "Sorry, she's just one of my . . . guests?" Was that even the right word? I *had* helped coordinate booking these rooms, so I couldn't help but feel a little responsible for whatever had happened to Sebastian at the inn. I'd brought him to

Raven Creek, and now he was dead. Was there some warning sign I should have seen, something to indicate the star was in danger?

I immediately thought about Deacon and how high-tension things had been at the shop yesterday. Chewing the inside of my cheek, I decided to see if Raven Creek's resident detective was around before I started to cast blame on complete strangers. But the argument in the store definitely pointed to some bad blood between Sebastian and Deacon.

But was a rift between former besties enough to drive someone to commit murder? I'd heard of stranger motives.

The police officer, whom I didn't recognize, seemed to infer from my statement that I worked at the B and B and just gave a nod. I didn't bother to correct her, because an overwhelming urge to see what was going on in the cozy little house had beckoned me through the door.

More uniformed officers buzzed around inside, and everything was such a hive of activity that no one noticed I had slipped in. In a small room off the entrance that I assumed was a sitting area or maybe a library, a few people were sitting together, whispering and wearing shell-shocked expressions. I didn't recognize any of them, so I assumed they were other guests at the B and B.

As I walked down the hallway, careful to avoid drawing attention to myself, I entered a large dining area at the back of the main floor. There I found some faces I knew. Connor, the social media assistant, was sitting at the large dining table with his hands folded neatly in his lap, his cheeks completely drained of color and a concerned but confused look on his face. I'd known he must be young, but right now he looked more like a little boy than anything else.

Beside him was Travis, the rep from the publishing house.

At the end of the table, much to my surprise, was the lawyer I had seen Leo arguing with a few days earlier. Unlike the suit-wearing, sneering man I'd encountered in the grocery store, this version of him still had pillow creases on his face and a robe over his pajamas that looked threadbare at the cuffs and elbows.

The B and B, while cozy, was an old Victorian house like mine and had at least a dozen guest suites, so I wasn't surprised to see so many people were checked in at the height of summer tourist season.

I turned my attention back to Connor and Travis, specifically Travis, who seemed to have realized I was in the room and wore a quizzical expression. "Ms. Winchester?"

Connor and the lawyer both looked at me, though neither reacted very much. The lawyer kept glancing around like he was looking for someone. Or at least looking for someone to complain to. Connor just seemed like he wanted to have someone tell him what to do. I was close enough to him that I placed a hand on his shoulder and gave it a gentle squeeze of comfort. His knees were bouncing, his scuffed Converse sneakers looking out of place with the pajama pants he was still wearing.

"I was on my way to the hike," I explained. "I drove by and saw the commotion and then saw Melody. Is it true?" I didn't have a reason to doubt Melody, since she had claimed to be the one to find the body, but I was hoping she might have misunderstood. For some reason the idea that Sebastian had been murdered was just too much for me to want to believe.

Travis nodded grimly. "I'm sorry to say, but yes. It seems someone killed Sebastian last night."

"When did you see him last?" I asked, wondering if the killer might have been someone else staying at the inn or if Sebastian had gone out and bad fortune had followed him home.

"I went to bed around ten. I think he was in the library then, making notes for the hike. Oh heavens, I suppose we need to cancel that." Travis glanced down at the phone in front of him but made no move to pick it up, as if the effort were just suddenly too much. "And the book tour." It was hard to tell whether he was more broken up about canceling the book tour or about Sebastian's death.

"I'll take care of the hike, don't worry." I pulled out my phone and sent Daphne a message, trying to keep things vague to limit worries. Sebastian can't attend the hike, please let everyone know they can go on their own or just head home.

I was oddly grateful—and felt guilty for my gratitude—that the hike had been a free event and I wouldn't need to issue a huge batch of refunds in light of what had happened today. That might have been callous, but the brain does funny things when confronted with tragedy.

Nodding at Travis to let him know at least one crisis was averted, I asked him and Connor, "Do you know what time he usually goes to bed?"

Travis shook his head, but Connor spoke up, his voice barely over a whisper. "He was really excited about tomorrow. He told me he was going to stay up doing more research. He normally goes to sleep by midnight, but I had messages on my phone from him when I got up this morning. The last one was around two thirty—he sent me a list of content ideas he wanted to focus on for today." He let out a little shuddering sigh. "He was so excited."

I didn't think I'd get much more out of the two of them. My gaze drifted over to the lawyer at the end of the table. It was obvious he'd been listening to us, but he was playing with the cuff of his robe as if it were the most interesting thing in the world. I knew sooner or later I'd probably need to deal with him about other issues, but now was not the time to confront him.

The unmistakable sound of a throat clearing brought my attention to the doorway behind me, where Detective Patsy Martin was standing, one hand propped on her hip and a clear expression of annoyance on her face.

"Phoebe."

"Morning, Detective."

"Mm-hmm." She jerked her head toward the hallway, and I followed her out of the room. "Now, I know your cat didn't stumble across this body, Ms. Winchester, so do you mind telling me what you're doing here?"

I quickly explained how the morning's schedule was meant to play out, and while I could tell she didn't really buy it as an excuse for my meddling, she did take notes on the things I'd learned before she arrived.

"There's one more thing," I added, wondering if I might regret bringing it up, but it felt reckless not to share what I knew. "Sebastian's former business partner showed up to the reading yesterday afternoon. There was some pretty obvious tension with him, Sebastian, and Melody. He was supposed to hang around to talk to them after the signing, but when it was all over, he'd just split."

"You think there could have been some bad blood there?" Detective Martin asked.

"Absolutely. You could ask any of the attendees in the crowd last night, because the three of them didn't do much to hide their feelings."

"Do you have a list of attendees from your event?"

I nodded. "I can send you the folks who prebought copies and RSVP'd for the signing. There were probably a handful more who walked in, but it would be most of them."

She took a few more notes before closing her pad. For a moment she just scrubbed her hand over her short black Afro, and then she let out a long sigh. "I'm going to regret this, I just know it." She said it mostly to herself, and then she looked at me, obviously still weighing whether or not she wanted to say what she was about to say. "Phoebe, it would appear you have some inside awareness of the people involved in this case and some of their dynamics. It would be *very* helpful to us if we could leverage some of that connection and your existing relationship with the witnesses to help our case."

I stared at her.

She stared back.

"Detective Martin, are you . . . are you asking me to help you?" I had been dead certain that the moment she saw me at the crime scene, I was going to hear no end of it in terms of a lecture. I had a bad habit of being in the wrong place at the wrong time when bad things happened in Raven Creek. For a while I'd been worried Detective Martin might start believing I was responsible for some of the unfortunate events I'd been around for. But it appeared that she was now realizing it might be useful to have someone around during investigations who wasn't a police officer.

"I'm already questioning my sanity, Winchester. Don't make me change my mind. I know you, and I know you'll make your PI boyfriend start snooping around anyway, so I think my best bet is to have you on my side." She pointed a pen at me. "But I draw the line at deputizing your cat."

"Bob has a finely tuned sense of justice; you have no idea what you're missing."

Before she could change her mind, I bid her a good morning and promised to be in touch when and if I heard anything, then I left the B and B. Just behind me on the steps were the EMTs. I half expected them to be carrying a zipped-up body bag, but they were merely toting their gear and sharing somber looks.

A moment later I realized why when the county coroner's van pulled up.

I supposed they didn't need an ambulance to move someone who was already gone.

Melody was no longer on the steps. She had started pacing up and down the sidewalk, though her attention was drawn by the coroner's van, and she began to cry in earnest again. She started muttering to herself between sobs. "I never should have let him switch rooms. This is all my fault."

What did that mysterious statement mean? Had someone broken into Sebastian's room? Why would Melody blame herself for that?

Or was there some other reason she was feeling guilty?

Now wasn't the moment to ask Melody logistical questions, considering the state she was in. Instead, I had to head to the trailhead to see if Daphne needed a hand explaining everything to the amassed bird fans. She was a capable employee but didn't have an assertive bone in her body, so I wanted to make sure no one was giving her a hard time.

When I climbed into my car, I sent Rich a quick message. Hike canceled due to murder, call me when you can.

I had assumed he'd be sleeping, but instead I got an almost immediate response.

If you didn't want to go on a hike you didn't have to commit a crime to get out of it.

# Chapter Nine

As predicted, Daphne had her hands full at the trailhead. While some people had accepted her news of the cancellation, others would not be deterred until she could explain in detail why Sebastian wasn't coming. When I arrived, there were still seven people clustered around the parking lot, all of them in a semicircle around my poor, flustered employee.

"I'm sorry, I really don't know the answer to that," Daphne told a woman in cargo shorts. "If you want to head home for now, we'll have more details later."

The woman was not going to take this as an answer. "Well, I want to know why Sebastian isn't here. Wasn't this whole thing so he could go find some gosh-darned tangerine bird or something? Did he get worried one of us would find it first? Typical influencer."

I wouldn't have described someone who made a living talking about birds as a *typical influencer*, and I was mad on Sebastian's behalf that this woman was being so rude about him when he couldn't even defend himself from beyond the grave.

"Good morning, everyone." I came to stand next to Daphne, and she visibly relaxed, her tight shoulders sagging as she took an almost imperceptible step behind me, letting me take over the situation.

"I'm terribly sorry about the last-minute cancellation, but Sebastian was . . . not able to come this morning. I know this is disappointing for everyone, but it couldn't be helped. The hike is on a self-guided trail, so everyone is obviously welcome to go on ahead and enjoy it, or to head home, but I can promise you Sebastian didn't go on the hike without us, and he isn't coming."

This caused a new buzz with the remaining group, and I could tell Cargo Shorts wanted to argue with me a bit longer, but one of her friends interjected, saying, "Well, we're already here, Louise; we might as well go on the hike."

"I don't even care about birds," huffed Louise. "I just like looking at him."

The crew of women, all in their late fifties, headed toward the trailhead, chatting loudly enough that there wasn't much risk of them seeing any birds anyway.

Once they were gone, Daphne audibly sighed with relief. "Well, that was exhausting."

"I'm sorry you had to deal with them," I said, turning to face her. She wore an obviously questioning look, and I knew she was dying to find out what was going on. I hated to have to be the one to tell her that one of her most beloved online creators had been killed.

"Daphne, you might want to sit down for a second." I guided her over to a park bench, and while she went willingly, I could see that this was ramping up her agitation. "Sebastian isn't coming because someone killed him last night."

All the color drained from her face, and she sank against the bench, her breath exhaling in a whoosh. "What?"

I explained what had happened that morning on my way to the hike, leaving out the more grisly specifics of what had been done to him. When I finished, her face made me recall Connor's back at the

B and B, reminding me just how young Daphne really was. Tears beaded on her eyelashes.

"That's just horrible. Do they know who did it?"

I shook my head. "Not a clue."

Though that wasn't exactly true, was it? Because I had a pretty strong suspicion of who the most likely person was, and it pained me to think it, only because all my dealings with Deacon before the signing had just been so lovely. I might not actually know him, but he hadn't seemed like the kind of person who could resort to murder over a lost job.

That said, I *didn't* know him, I reminded myself, and you could fit an entire universe inside the space left by all the things you didn't know about people. I'd done my part by telling Detective Martin what I knew, and in turn she had trusted me to keep an ear to the ground in case I heard anything else.

It was nice, for once, to be on the periphery of a murder case and not be considered a potential suspect.

I sent Daphne home—she had walked, so I didn't need to worry about her driving—and made her promise to text me when she was back at her place safely. She was in such a daze I offered to drive her, but she said she wanted to clear her head.

I considered going home and was sure Bob wouldn't mind the company through the afternoon. It was a gorgeous day, and I could finally get some much-needed weeding done in the garden, but I was too distracted by the murder to do that at the moment.

Instead, I drove over to the store so I could read through some of my old correspondence with Deacon. I didn't think it would include any obvious allusions to Sebastian's death, but it might be worthwhile to give everything another look.

It was odd to be in the store with no one else around. We were open seven days a week, and even when it was slow, it felt as if someone were always there. Left on its own, the place smelled overwhelmingly of old books. I didn't notice it that often during the week, because it would be replaced by the scents of baking bread or cookies or tins of loose-leaf tea being opened regularly. Now it smelled like an old library, and I smiled to myself.

This little shop had a secret life of its own when we weren't here.

I made myself a cup of Snickerdoodle tea. Despite the weather outside being gloriously sunny and heading in the direction of *hot*, I had a habit of making myself hot tea whenever I got into the shop. With my tea in hand and the scents of cinnamon and sugar wafting into the air, I hunkered down in the office and fired up our relatively ancient desktop computer.

Back in my previous life, when I'd worked a soul-sucking corporate office job, my manager had been in the habit of sending out emails at all hours of the day or night, with no sense of boundaries in terms of the division between work life and personal life. After leaving that job behind, I'd sworn to myself I would never live in fear of the email notification sound on my phone, so I left work at the shop and didn't check emails related to the business unless I was physically in the store.

Not that emails about books and special orders created any real sense of drama in my life, but it was nice to not think about *work* once I got home.

I opened the thread of emails I'd been sharing with Deacon about the signing. His tone was light, friendly, often peppered with *lol*s here and there or sweet little jokes at his own expense. Everything I read gave me the indication he was just a nice guy helping his best friend run a business.

Then I got to the most recent email, which he'd sent me only a day before the crew was set to arrive in Raven Creek. It was a list of preferences for Sebastian, some dietary requirements for the food I was having made—he'd ordered most of the other food himself—and some important bits of advice for a smooth event.

I had been so caught up in the minutiae of the email the first time I'd read it that I hadn't really noticed the tone, but now, reading it with fresh eyes and having gone through all our other correspondence, I could see it was remarkably different from everything he'd previously sent.

When he explained how the day should best be handled, he sounded annoyed, like a parent giving instructions to a babysitter on how to deal with a toddler who had been misbehaving recently. There was no joking, no warmth in the words. Everything was very utilitarian, with no sense of love or camaraderie. In previous emails Deacon had acknowledged that Sebastian could be difficult, but he'd done it in the way one teasingly talks about a sibling.

In this email he was almost cruel in his description of Sebastian, though you had to read between the lines to see it. *He can be overly demanding sometimes*, Deacon wrote. *He will make his displeasure known.*

Two things especially stood out to me in reading the email anew. At one point, Deacon mentioned that Sebastian preferred a room with a good view. He specifically wanted a room at the B and B with a good view. Apparently, he liked to bird-watch while he worked. I remembered making that request myself when I reserved the rooms.

Yet Melody had mentioned something about *letting* Sebastian switch rooms, so it sounded like he'd made a swap at some point.

If he'd moved, had he willingly given up the room he requested? Perhaps it hadn't been the view he'd expected and he'd wanted something different. A bird watcher might be interested in things the standard tourist wasn't.

Who had he swapped with, then?

The second thing that stuck out to me was a line in the middle of the email where Deacon was explaining some of Sebastian's pickier demands.

*I swear one of us is going to end up in an early grave.*

# Chapter Ten

A little turn of phrase about winding up six feet under isn't a big deal under normal circumstances. There was no doubt that the context of the email I'd received from Deacon screamed frustration. But given what had happened today and Deacon's very weird appearance and disappearance the previous day at the signing, there was an extra element of foreboding to the words.

I pulled Detective Martin's card out of my purse and forwarded the email to the address on the front. This was precisely the sort of thing she wanted from me. I knew better than to think she was asking me to go out of my way to find clues, but this one was right in my lap and seemed like a useful piece of information, even if it wasn't exactly a confession.

I waited a few minutes to see if she would reply before powering down the computer. I sat in the office staring at the wall calendar and the big red Sharpie letters announcing today as *HIKE DAY* in the Sunday box.

Tomorrow was the Fourth of July, and murder or no murder, the town was going to be swamped with tourists. I figured if I was already at the store, I might as well get a head start on tomorrow's baking and prep some sourdough loaves and an extra batch or two of our signature shortbread.

In summer there wasn't usually a huge demand for baked goods—not the same way people were buying iced tea like it was going out of style—but given everything Imogen and Amy had told me about the previous Independence Day festivities, tomorrow would just be the first day of a very busy week and everything that wasn't bolted down would be flying off the shelves.

It didn't leave me much time to poke around the investigation, but maybe that was for the best. Still, there was a lingering sense of blame on my shoulders that I couldn't shake. Sebastian had been in Raven Creek because of me. Had trouble followed him here, or was this all just bad luck? Had I put him in the sights of a murderer without meaning to?

I felt responsible in a way that had nothing to do with guilt and everything to do with a deep-seated need to find justice for this man. I'd picked his hotel, I'd brought him here, and no matter who had killed him, I had to do everything I could to see that that person was found.

With those heavy thoughts on my mind, I tossed an apron over my hiking ensemble—perhaps not the most ideal outfit to bake in— and cracked open the jar of sourdough starter on my counter. I was immediately greeted by a familiar fruity-yeasty aroma that made me think of little backcountry kitchens in France or old medieval bakeries—if such a thing existed. Sourdough starter smelled at once alive and ancient, an incredibly powerful fragrance.

I didn't want to go too outrageous with my flavor choices for the next day, because I wanted the lunch specials to be accessible for most people to enjoy. While I'd received plenty of compliments about Friday's olive loaf, it hadn't been my favorite and had me wanting a return to less divisive mix-ins.

For my savory loaf I opted to make a modern classic: everything bagel. We made our own everything bagel mix, and despite how popular certain store brands were, we did go through a lot of it—I used it to make crackers and biscuits with the sourdough discard—and it was insanely easy to make at home for significantly less money.

The choice for my sweet loaf for the next day was a little more interesting and outside the box, but I thought it sounded like just the thing for a hot summer day, especially with the forecast calling for clear skies tomorrow. I was going to make a lemon and white chocolate sourdough. Topped with fresh ricotta, honey, and some blueberries, it was sure to be a sellout.

Because of the time it took for the dough to rise, I would only do the initial prep today and either come back in the evening or add my mix-ins in the morning, but I wanted to take advantage of the time I had now.

I mixed the sourdough starter with water, flour, and salt and combined it until a dough had formed. I repeated this process until I had fairly depleted my sourdough starter and had eight loaves waiting on the counter to rise. Later I would stretch and fold each dough like delicious Play-Doh to help the gluten form, and that would be when the mix-ins were added.

I didn't need to make more everything seasoning—I had a huge glass jar of it on the counter—but I did want to pre-zest my lemons. They might lose a little of that initial zing sitting out overnight, but if I did it now, I could add the sliced remaining lemons to the batches of tea in the fridge to boost their flavor.

Because of how much tea we had been making over the summer, I had ordered bulk quantities of lemons from Lansing's. I grabbed a half dozen from the shelf on the countertop and pulled out my rasp. A standard cheese grater wouldn't be suitable for the task, and while I preferred a grater that took off long strips of lemon skin when I was doing my own cooking, the bread needed something a bit more nuanced. The rasp would give a nice, fine grate to the lemon peel.

By the time I was done zesting the lemons, the kitchen had a beautiful lemon-sugar aroma hanging in the air, my hands were sticky with pith, and I had a big sandwich bag loaded with zest for tomorrow. I popped that in the freezer, then sliced up the remaining lemons, dropping them in the big jugs in the fridge.

It was almost noon by the time I was done with the prep, hours' worth of work I simply wouldn't have been able to squeeze in the next day, so in a terrible way I was grateful for the extra time I'd been given in the morning.

The universe must have heard me thinking inappropriate things, because once I'd washed my hands and dusted off the thin coat of flour that covered me head to toe, I stepped out into the bookstore just in time to see Dierdre Miller press her face up against the glass.

While I briefly considered diving back into the kitchen to hide from her, it was obvious I was too late. She waved enthusiastically when she spotted me and actually declared, "Yoo-hoo!"

When I paused just a moment too long, considering my options, I saw her brow furrow and she tapped harder, declaring, "Phoebe Winchester, I see you in there."

Well, now not only did *she* know I was here, so did the entirety of Main Street. So much for enjoying a little private time to catch up on work.

I walked over to the front door, opening it just a crack. "Good afternoon, Dierdre, I hope you're doing well. Did you see the sign on the door?" I tapped the *Closed for Special Offsite Event* sign we had put up to avoid situations just like this one.

"Oh, I don't want to *buy* anything," she drawled, really overemphasizing her disdain at the very idea of her being a customer.

In fairness to Dierdre, the last time she'd been in and tried something, I had accidentally bewitched her, so I didn't take offense to her reticence over coming inside.

"Then why *are* you here?" I tried my darndest to keep the acid out of my tone, but it was just so hard for me to be nice to her. Dierdre had never done anything to make me feel welcome in town; in fact, she had gone quite out of her way on my arrival to convince me to leave.

She had been polite to me in the past just long enough to help secure the rental of a shop down the block for her nephew, and after I'd agreed to that, she had stayed mostly out of my way.

"I was hoping you and I might have a quick sit-down chat, just us gals." A false twinkle in her eye and her best real-estate-agent smile made me realize why she might actually be very good at her job and how some people in town might be convinced to like her.

Dierdre was in her midfifties and five feet tall on a good day. She wore considerably too much makeup, and her hair was dyed a bright, unnatural red. But as in the case of poisonous South American dart frogs, the color made her easy to avoid from a distance. She wasn't an unattractive person physically, but the way she carried herself and behaved made me wonder why *she* wasn't the one who had the town rumor mill abuzz with witchy rumors.

Right now she was staring at me with a focus that set all the hairs on my arm at attention and a false cheer that made me think she might be luring me off to my own demise.

"What is it you wanted to chat about?"

She let the veneer of sweetness drop, showing me her vicious annoyance in one quick flash before the fakeness was back and she swatted at my arm playfully—though just a bit too hard. "Come on, now, Phoebe, you make it sound like I'm up to something. Can't a gal just want to catch up with the niece of her old best friend?"

This was a manipulative ploy, bringing Eudora into things. I knew perfectly well Dierdre and my aunt hadn't been besties. In fact, my aunt had given me posthumous warnings to be on my guard around the pint-sized whirlwind. Still, this approach made me curious. Dierdre must really want something if she was being this aggressively nice.

I had no more vacant shop space to rent her, so it had to be something else, and my Spidey-senses were telling me it probably had something to do with the shady lawyer who had been getting Leo all riled up on Friday night.

"We can go next door if you want." I wouldn't mind having some extra scrutiny on the situation with Amy no doubt listening in on our conversation.

Dierdre seemed to recognize what I was angling for, because she shook her head vigorously. "Let's go to the Buzzy Bean."

I was so completely addicted to the flavor and convenience of the Sugarplum, I often forgot our town actually had *three* coffee shops. That might seem excessive on the surface, but we were a very caffeine-obsessed town, and during the peak tourist months it kept things from getting too overwhelmed at any one location.

I had passed by the Buzzy Bean many times—it was just a few doors down from Honey's new-age shop—but I had to confess I'd only seen the third shop, Theo's, once or twice as I passed it on my way out of town. It was definitely located to catch driving tourists on their way back to Seattle.

Since the store was closed for the day, I didn't have that excuse to put Dierdre off with, and while I would have preferred to continue poking around my emails from Deacon to see if there might be other clues or perhaps knock on Rich's door to see what insights he might have, I knew it was better to get this chat out of the way now; otherwise I'd just be haunted by a petite redheaded ghost everywhere I went for the rest of the week.

"Okay, sure, let me grab my bag."

We walked the short two blocks to Buzzy Bean in relative silence, which was a treat. Town gossip worked fast, but evidently not fast enough for Dierdre to know about the murder just yet, because she hadn't mentioned anything about it. This was surprising, given how the ambulance in front of the B and B and the cancellation of the big hike were groundwork for some very basic math. I gave it until the end of the day before everyone was talking about Sebastian's murder.

It was a lovely change of pace to be outside on such a beautiful afternoon, despite my present company. The sky was blue, and there were faint puffy white clouds overhead but nothing that hinted at foul weather. The weeks of rain had done all the flowerpots outside a world of good, and the charming, European-inspired street decor was gorgeously offset by overflowing baskets of orange and pink flowers.

A few fat bumblebees and at least one very brazen hummingbird zipped past us, making sure to stop at each basket in turn to sample the wares.

The Buzzy Bean was an adorable little shop that was about as different from Sugarplum Fairy as a place could be and still sell coffee. Sugarplum Fairy was, after all, a bakery first and foremost, while Buzzy Bean was all about the coffee.

It leaned hard into a Pacific Northwest theme, with exposed wood everywhere inside and framed art of redwood trees and verdant mountain landscapes. There were also closeup paintings of glossy coffee beans, and beneath those were large glass cylinders filled with identical life-sized beans.

The whole shop had the immediately soothing fragrance of fresh-ground coffee, which was one of the world's greatest smells. Suddenly it didn't matter who I was here with; what mattered was the daily special: a honey lavender oat milk latte. It was called The Bee's Knees, and it reminded me I hadn't had an ounce of caffeine since leaving my house bright and early that morning.

Dierdre very graciously offered to pay, and once we collected our drinks, we took them to a booth that looked like it had been carved out of the base of an enormous tree. It was surprisingly comfortable and gave the illusion of being hugged by nature.

I might need to start coming here more often when I visited Honey.

"I want to broach something of a sensitive topic with you," Dierdre began, her false charm suddenly switched to game-face mode. I was so surprised that she'd gotten right down to business that I almost choked swallowing my first white-hot sip of coffee.

"How sensitive are we talking here, Dierdre?"

She pushed aside the small black coffee she had ordered and put both palms down on the polished wood table. "Let's cut to the chase, shall we, Phoebe? I know that you are a very wealthy woman."

I was glad I wasn't still drinking at the moment, because if I had, I would have choked a second time. I had accepted that Dierdre knew about my holdings in town. It was impossible for someone as snoopy as her, who also had access to real estate details, to not know that Mountain View Property Management was technically me. No one else in town had figured it out, and I was shocked she hadn't blabbed about it by now, but there seemed to be an understanding within the town council that keeping quiet about where all the generous donations they received were coming from was the best way to *keep* those donations coming.

If people in this town knew I was a millionaire, things would get awkward very quickly.

I was about to reply when I noticed Dierdre's coffee shift a half inch away from her without her touching it.

*Oh no.*

Perhaps it was just my imagination, or maybe she had jostled it in a way I hadn't noticed. I tamped down the wave of unease washing over me and tried to focus on what she was saying.

"I'm really not, though. I mean, if you're going to ask me for something that requires a lot of flexible money on hand, I'm going to have to politely decline." What was she up to?

The cup moved again.

*No no no, not now, not now. Get it together, Phoebe.*

I tried to take a few calming breaths and focus on Dierdre, but the funny thing about anxiety is, it doesn't care about bad timing.

When I'd split up with my ex-husband, Blaine, and realized that every part of my life was in complete shambles, I'd started to get frequent anxiety attacks. Just out of the blue I would start to worry about the most random things. What would the guy at our favorite takeout place think when I stopped calling every Friday to get wonton soup and fried rice? Would he think we didn't like it anymore? Did I still need to give Blaine's coworker's wife that cocktail recipe she had asked for?

These random thoughts would send me spiraling for hours, and no matter how often I tried to tell myself that everything was okay and none of these things actually mattered in the grand scheme of life, I just couldn't calm down.

Now it seemed that, confronted with an uncomfortable conversation with Dierdre, I was very capable of dredging up a dozen different doom-and-gloom scenarios, and unlike my previous fits of nerves, this time around I had to contend with magical side effects.

I tried to remember what I was supposed to be talking about, but it was hard when my attention was locked on her coffee cup.

"I'm not asking you to invest in anything," she chuckled. "I'm actually bringing you an opportunity to make a great deal more money than you already have."

This took my full focus from the cup to the woman in front of me. My eyes narrowed suspiciously. "What are you talking about?"

Recalling my discussion with Leo a couple of days earlier, I had a strong suspicion I knew exactly where this was headed. A knot of worry pitted in my stomach.

The coffee cup moved an inch closer to her. She seemed perfectly oblivious to it.

Over at the barista counter, a whole stack of paper cups fell over. The girl behind the counter let out a gasp of surprise, and the older man who had taken our money started to scold her about being more careful.

I had to get out of here.

"I know you're relatively new here and don't have many attachments. I thought this might give you a great opportunity to help find a way to make some money and maybe return to a life in the big city. Wouldn't that be nice?"

"I think that sounds terrible, honestly." I was too distracted right now to pretend at politeness. I needed her to get to the point so I could leave before anything more disastrous happened.

"Oh."

"Dierdre, what are you hinting at?" I urged. Her coffee cup was vibrating, like it was trying to decide which direction to move next. If I tried to grab it, would that make things worse?

"I have been given an opportunity to help a new developer who wants to create a tourism oasis here in Raven Creek. And they're being *very* generous with their offers, Phoebe. Evidently, they've tried several times to contact Mountain View but have been told every time the properties are not for sale."

I wasn't surprised that the team at Mountain View hadn't bothered to tell me this. They knew how important this setup had been to my aunt, and I'd told them to keep it business as usual, which likely included them automatically declining sale offers.

I only got involved if someone—like Dierdre's nephew—wanted to rent one of my spaces, in which case I approved or declined the agreement.

"I don't know why you think coming to me directly is going to change the answer."

"Because I thought if I could explain to you their goals, you might see that this is a really wonderful opportunity."

I recalled, vividly, the way Leo had turned bright red and balled his fists up as if he were on the cusp of committing real violence. For my gentle giant of a friend to react that way, I knew I wanted no part in what these people were selling.

"My answer is no."

"You haven't even heard what I have to say," she protested. The vibrating coffee cup stopped stock-still, and for one moment I thought I had accidentally stopped time. Since my ability to toy with probability usually responded to immediate danger, it would have been strange for it to kick in then, but Dierdre's lips were still moving; it was just the coffee that had stopped.

I knew what was about to happen.

I knew it without a doubt in my heart, the way sometimes you go to pick up a phone before it rings because the certainty that someone else will be on the other end of the line is just so strong.

There was nothing I could do to stop this.

The coffee shot off the table like a caffeinated bullet, spilling right into her lap with such force that she was splashed from chin to dress hem with black brew. Thankfully, it had been sitting open long enough it wasn't scalding hot anymore, but she clambered to her feet, letting out a yelp of surprise.

"Oh my goodness, that's so unlucky. You should always put a lid on those." I darted across the café and grabbed a handful of napkins, handing them to her awkwardly. I was fortunate, because her ire immediately turned toward the barista and she had no notion that I was the one to blame.

"You need to fix that table—wobbly, useless thing just made me spill my whole drink."

The barista, still flustered from the incident with the coffee cups, stammered, trying to come up with the right thing to say. "I-I'm s-so sorry. Do y-you want a new d-drink?" The girl looked like she was on the edge of an absolute crying jag, and I silently crammed forty dollars into the tip jar at the front, feeling abysmal that I couldn't help shield her from the blame.

"Accidents happen," I offered. "Right, Dierdre?"

She was busily mopping up the front of her red dress, which was now probably ruined. I felt bad about that too. I didn't often feel guilt about things said or done regarding Dierdre Miller, but today was the exception.

My magic was on the fritz, and I needed help *immediately* before someone else noticed.

# Chapter Eleven

Honey's shop was open, the front door held ajar with a big chunk of white quartz and the inviting scent of sandalwood and sage wafting out from inside. The siren call of her new-age Spotify playlist that went from chanting monks to thunderstorms to singing metal bowls was currently playing the last, and it was an instant balm to my nerves as I passed over the threshold.

Inside, the shop was cluttered in an inviting way, with herbs and crystal charms hanging from the ceiling and rainbows adorning ever surface as the sunlight passed through dozens of dangling prisms.

Here the smell of various herbs and incenses was even stronger and it became more difficult to tell patchouli from Oudh, but the mix-match was wonderful rather than headache inducing.

Bins of colorful crystals ranging in size from a penny to hulking, faceted boulders invited bystanders. There was a sign next to some of the smaller crystals that read *Shoplifters will be Cursed*.

My friend popped up from behind the glass counter that hugged the back of the store in a big U shape. She was wearing a brightly printed scarf over her hair, and in place of her usual gold hoop earrings she was sporting dangly ones with peacock feathers on them.

"Howdy, stranger. How was your big hike?" She waved a hand toward the sporty ensemble I was wearing.

I handed her a Bee's Knees latte, since the barista had felt so bad she'd made me a new drink as well. Honey sniffed it and smiled. "Now, did you assume I'd like it because it's sweet like me, or what?"

"I just know you've got good taste; otherwise we wouldn't be friends."

She sipped the drink and smiled. "You didn't answer my question about the hike."

I grimaced. "You noticed that, did you?"

"Sweetie, you'll find there's very little that goes on in this town that I *don't* notice. So what happened?"

"Well, it didn't happen, that's a start. We had to cancel it."

She waited, so I knew she knew there was more, I just wasn't sure how much. "Someone killed Sebastian Marlow last night."

Honey let her breath out in a long exhale. So she'd known there was something up but hadn't known about the murder. There must be a branch missing in the town phone tree today.

"Murdered? Are you sure?" She didn't wait for me to answer before she started rummaging around behind the counter, littering the glass with bits of crystal and partially burned sticks of palo santo.

"Yeah, I was at the B and B this morning, talked to Detective Martin."

Honey's head shot up over the counter, and she gave me an appraising, almost motherly look. "You're not in trouble again, are you?"

I clutched some imaginary pearls at my throat. "Whyever would you imagine such a thing?" She began to rummage again, and I said, a little more quietly, "Well, at least I'm not in trouble about *that*."

Honey found what she was looking for and placed a large, light-blue velvet bag on the counter. Whatever was in it was heavy, because it made a *thunk* sound when she put it down. She untied a silver rope that was wrapped around the bag, and the cloth unfolded to show that it was one large square of material, not a real bag at all.

In the middle were a set of jade stones, all bearing gold inscriptions on them. I wasn't an expert by any means, but they looked like runes to me.

She picked them up in her hands and gave them a shake, then strategically let several fall onto the velvet before setting the rest of them aside in a big crystal bowl.

She pointed to one, its sharp design a complete mystery to me.

"Your magic is still misbehaving?"

"Yeah, how did y—"

She clucked her tongue and kept looking at the runes she had dropped. She pulled one into the center of the cloth and seemed to contemplate it for a long time. Honey wrinkled her nose like she was confused, though I also couldn't make heads or tails of what the runes were telling her.

Lining the five stones she had dropped in a row, she arranged them, then rearranged them, before pushing them all aside with an aggrieved sigh. "This doesn't make sense."

"Murder rarely does."

That made her laugh unexpectedly. "Oh, Phoebs. Murder tends to be one of the most sensical things in the world, just as long as you know where to look. What doesn't make sense is this." She nudged one of the stones.

"I have no idea what that means."

"It's not something I can translate directly, but in general, this one stone indicates confusion. It means that possibly a mistake was made, or I'll often see it doing love readings when a person is with the wrong partner. I'm not totally sure what it means in this context, but something along the lines of their being confusion with the murder? The wrong person, maybe?"

I stared at her and then at the runes, trying to make sense of what she was saying. Sebastian had been killed, but were the runes trying to suggest he wasn't the intended target?

It occurred to me then that I was looking at a set of shiny rocks to give me insight into a murder, and while I did believe in magic, I wasn't sure I could take what the stones said at face value, especially if even Honey wasn't clear about the translation.

"Honey, what are you talking about?"

She gently laid her palms down on the runes. "I know I've told you before that one of my gifts is dream magic, right?"

I nodded, though I wasn't sure where she was going with this. All natural-born witches could do any number of things with magic, but we each had something, a gift or two more powerful than the others. Honey was skilled at helping people find things and at interpreting and channeling information through dreams.

"Well, it might be unrelated, but the stones right now are giving me the same vibe I've been getting from my dreams. For weeks now I've been having the same one, over and over again. There are all these birds sitting on a power line. Just hundreds and hundreds of them. And there's this house under the power lines. Every night in my dream the house burns down and the birds sit and watch. Last night, though, the dream changed. The house stayed standing, and all the birds, every single one of them, they all flew away."

I wanted that to be enough of an explanation, but it didn't make any sense to me. I couldn't read dreams, and when I had one that was trying to tell me something, it usually involved a giant spider wearing the face of the person I least wanted to see, and I didn't want to have that dream again anytime soon. Honey could keep her dream magic.

"The birds were never supposed to fly away. They were protection."

"But you said the house burned down."

"Sometimes a house is *meant* to burn down." She picked up one of the runes, carefully running her thumb over the smooth green surface. "I'm worried what's going to happen now that they've flown away."

This didn't really tell me much about the murder, though the birds aspect was interesting, given Sebastian's career. Could the dream birds have been protecting him? Was he the birds in the dream? None of it made a lick of sense to me, and I was more than a little frustrated by this mystery.

When Honey glanced up, her eyes widened. "Oh. Yeah. Your other problem."

I couldn't fathom why she was changing topic in the middle of a serious monologue, until I glanced over my shoulder.

Every candle in the shop was now floating upright in the room, hovering near the ceiling. Inexplicably, at least three of them were also lit, giving off a soft, flickering yellow light from where they hung in midair.

"Yeah. That's sort of what I came to talk to you about."

# Chapter Twelve

Honey sent me home after I'd promised I would drink my weight in peppermint tea and try not to get stressed about anything. We had discovered the root cause of what was sending my magic haywire, but we still had no clue how to stop it, so for the time being our only recourse was to keep my anxiety at a minimum.

My guest author had been murdered, and Dierdre Miller was trying to convince me to sell my properties to a big developer that wanted to turn our town into some sort of tourist hellscape.

No chance of me getting stressed at all.

I got home and ordered myself an early dinner from our local Thai restaurant, because when anxiety comes knocking, the best thing to do is drown it in crab Rangoon and pad see ew. It also meant I wouldn't need to go into the kitchen, where there were sharp pointy things and far too many items I could light on fire.

Strawberries had been cute, but the flying coffee and accidentally flaming candles were causes for concern.

It was too early to feed Bob—not that he would have argued—and I had to wait an hour before my own food would show up, so I grabbed my laptop and settled onto the couch in the living room. It was a squishy old-fashioned number that had deep, sinking cushions, so once you sat down, you were never getting back up again.

The old house didn't have air conditioning, something that didn't seem like a big deal most of the time, but as the July temperature outside inched closer to ninety, I was missing it a bit. I turned on the overhead fan and a little oscillating one I moved from room to room and thanked Aunt Eudora's genius brain for having so many remote-controlled items in her home.

With the air circulating and time to kill, I set about doing pretty much exactly what Detective Martin had asked me not to and went searching for trouble by looking up Sebastian Marlow. I knew plenty about his public persona thanks to the videos I'd seen online as well as an in-depth info dump from Daphne, who seemed to have memorized his entire career.

Sebastian might have been known for his love and knowledge of birds, but as I started to dig into his credentials, I found website upon website dedicated to what they called "The Backyard Con Man." Apparently Sebastian had no formal study in ornithology and had no actual credentials whatsoever in terms of being an expert.

I was surprised I hadn't seen any of these criticisms before booking him. I had only briefly looked into him online when Daphne had made the suggestion, and everything I'd read before agreeing to the event had implied that Sebastian was the next big thing in terms of getting a new generation excited about animals and the outdoors.

Indeed, it seemed like he had raised a considerable amount of money for various wildlife conservation efforts. There was a lot of backlash from birding professionals about him not having a degree and not making it more apparent that he was just an enthusiastic amateur, but aside from that I couldn't see any real skeletons in his closet.

I did some basic searches on Melody and Deacon, but there was barely anything about Melody online, and everything about Deacon was connected to Sebastian, barring a few bylines in his college newspaper.

If there was something in Sebastian's past that had made him a target for murder, I wasn't seeing it. That didn't mean it wasn't there, but it wasn't obvious.

Staring at the photo of Deacon and Sebastian from their youth, I was taken aback by the warmth and obvious affection the two shared for each other. They were standing with their arms around each other's shoulders, twin megawatt grins, their faces splattered with mud from a charity race they had just completed.

How had they gone from *that* to what I had seen in the store on Saturday?

I set my laptop down as a knock sounded at the door. The legitimate struggle of getting up from the couch took an extra minute, and Bob was whipped up into a frenzy, pacing back and forth in front of the door like he was worried I might have missed the sound of the knock.

"Mreowwwwww," he declared.

"Buddy, I'm coming, it's not an emergency."

He did *not* agree with me. "Brr, brrrr, mrow." He butted his head aggressively into my shin, then trotted up to the door, where he began actively pawing at the wood. Not scratching, thankfully, but some very enthusiastic pawing.

"I got it, chill." I opened the door, expecting to be greeted with a bag of Thai food on my doorstep, but instead of crab rangoon, there was Deacon Hume.

Bob hissed, his striped orange tail lowering and his entire back end becoming denser as his fur stood on end. His tail looked like a bottle brush as he backed away.

It was *very* unusual for Bob to have such a negative reaction toward people, and it immediately set all my personal alarms jangling. Outwardly, however, I maintained a poised, even expression.

"Deacon, this is a surprise. What are you doing here? How did you know where I lived?" This latter question felt especially important, because I never gave my home address for event details or shipments, just the store's.

"Oh, I just asked at the grocery store, and someone pointed me down the road."

If I could have knocked my head repeatedly against the doorframe in that moment, I would have. I *loved* living in a small town, but there were some drawbacks. Like eager-to-help cashiers directing potential murderers to my front door.

"What are you doing here?" I asked again. I didn't want to come across as rude, but it was more than a little strange for him to be here, and I was not loving the way Bob was still growling behind me. Animal intuition was a real thing, and I trusted my cat more than I did this relative stranger in front of me.

"I just heard about Sebastian." My bristly exterior shield lowered slightly when he said this, because there was no mistaking how completely crushed he was. His whole face had paled, his shoulders slumped, and even in those few words his voice cracked with emotion.

Either this guy needed to get into acting, or he was genuinely distressed about the death of his former friend.

I also wasn't going to let a big heart be the thing that got me killed, so I gestured toward the two big armchairs I had set out on the porch. "Why don't you sit down and I'll get us some tea. We can talk about it."

He glanced over my shoulder into the house, as if perhaps he'd been expecting me to invite him inside, but while I might be too nosy for my own good, I also know at least one or two things about general self-preservation. When I waved my hand at the chairs a second time, redirecting his attention there, he took the hint and settled in. I closed the door behind him and locked it, then true to my word set about pouring two glasses of iced tea.

While doing this, I sent a quick text to Detective Martin to let her know what was happening. I would normally have sent this to

Rich, but since he had no context about the murder or who Deacon was, he would probably be more curious than concerned when I told him some random man was at my house.

At least outside, with Detective Martin clued in and my Thai delivery en route, I was probably mostly safe.

When I headed back to the door, Bob followed after me, biting my sock.

"Buddy, what the heck?" My hands were full, so I pushed him away gently with my foot. He bit my big toe. "Ow."

"*Mow*," he declared.

"Look, I promise you I'll be okay. I'm just right outside. Nothing is going to happen." Still, he stood in front of the door and angrily swatted at me when I tried to open it. I considered letting him win this round, but then there would be a random man just sitting out on my porch for heaven knew how long. If I went out, I could get rid of him more effectively than hiding would.

I pushed Bob back once again and snuck through the door while juggling the two glasses of iced tea. Deacon was sitting right where I'd left him, but he had shrunk in on himself even more in my absence. His chunky black boots had come untied at some point, making him remind me of a little kid. He was slouched over, his face pressed into his cupped palms, and it looked for all the world like he was crying.

I set the tea down quietly so he would know I was there, and when I sat in my own chair, he finally looked up, his face red and his eyes glassy.

"I don't know what to do, and I don't know who to talk to."

"What's going on?"

"I think Sebastian is dead because of me."

# Chapter Thirteen

I recoiled from his words, pushing myself as far back in my chair as I could. I knew it. I *knew* Deacon had been the most obvious suspect. No wonder Bob had been so distressed by Deacon's appearance.

I was going to give my murderer-detecting cat a thousand treats when I got back inside.

"W-what do you mean?" Scanning the street, I tried to see if my food delivery was anywhere to be seen, but there wasn't even anyone out walking their dog. I was all alone here, faced with the gravity of his confession.

Deacon brushed his dark-red hair back from his face, and I noticed then just how rough his appearance was. It looked like he hadn't shaved at all today, russet stubble peppering his jaw, and there were deep-purple circles under his eyes. Was this grief or guilt, or some powerful combination of the two?

"I made a huge mistake." He leaned back in his chair, staring out at the street like he was just talking to himself.

I darted a quick glance over to my phone, wondering if I could pick it up and send a 911 text to Detective Martin without Deacon noticing. But too late; his head swiveled, and suddenly his gray-green eyes were locked on mine. "Have you ever been in love, Phoebe?"

This was such an unexpected question given the current circumstances that I had to stop myself from letting out a nervous little laugh. "I have, yes."

"And did you let that love slip away?"

I was starting to realize what he was talking about, and suddenly all those chummy university photos, the long-standing business relationship, everything I knew about Deacon and Sebastian up until this moment started to take on an entirely different shape.

"For me, it wasn't that I let it slip away, it's that it ran away all on its own."

He nodded, back to his own contemplative world, looking more through me than at me. I couldn't have been more confused if I tried. I had taken his words to mean that Sebastian's death had literally been his fault because he'd killed him, but now I wasn't sure anymore.

"Deacon, what do you mean Sebastian is dead because of you? Did . . . did you do something?"

If he registered the implication of my question, it didn't show. He let out a long, quivering breath and waved his hand toward the view of town from my deck. It *was* a great view, considering Lane End House was perched at one of the highest vantage points in town.

"This is really nice. You must like living here." He started to cry, so silently I didn't realize it was happening until I saw the silvery droplets tracing down his cheeks and dripping from the bottom of his chin.

"Deacon?"

"I told him he could either have me in his life forever or have me in his life as his manager, but I couldn't do both. He picked business. He picked business over everything we had, and he told me he loved me but he didn't *love* me. After fifteen years. How . . . how does love just stop like that?"

My heart skipped a beat, and for a selfish moment I thought about myself, and my marriage, and I wanted to give this poor guy a hug, even if I still thought he might have killed someone.

"I don't know what happens to love when it goes away, but sometimes it does, and we can't hold on to love any more than we could hold on to a running stream, you know?"

Roughly he swiped away the tears on his cheeks. "I couldn't stay. After he told me that I couldn't keep being there with him every day, I just . . . I couldn't breathe anymore. I thought it was going to be best for both of us, so I quit. And he replaced me just like that." He snapped his fingers, and the sound of it was like a gunshot in the stillness between us. I jumped. "He threw everything away, and he gave it to her. And she doesn't *deserve* it. She doesn't care about him, just his money."

I assumed he was talking about Melody. I wondered if he really meant *everything*, because I certainly had gotten more of an overprotective-mother-hen vibe from Melody, not a romantic attachment to Sebastian. She had been pretty torn up over his death from what I'd seen, though, so perhaps I had misread that dynamic as much as I had missed the clues about Deacon and Sebastian.

I also noticed that Deacon had said he'd quit, while Sebastian had said he'd been fired. It was an important distinction, to be sure.

"Deacon, did you go see Sebastian after you left the shop?"

"I just wanted to talk to him."

"Did you?"

He balled his hand into a fist, hitting the arm of his chair with a hard thud. "He's so *stubborn*. Why couldn't he just listen? Why did he have to make it all so difficult? Maybe if he had just listened, he'd still be alive."

A car door slammed, grabbing the attention of both of us. A teenage boy in a Metallica T-shirt came trotting up the front steps with a big paper bag bearing the logo *To Thai For* on the front.

I got up automatically, wondering if I shouldn't tell the boy to wait with me a moment so someone would be here, but I wasn't sure what good a skinny teen boy would be against a grown man. I thanked him, handing him an extra ten dollars for a tip, and stepped back onto the deck.

Deacon was gone.

\* \* \*

Detective Martin arrived about ten minutes later. She looked ready for business in her tailored navy-blue pants and crisp white button-down, and with her mirrored aviators on she looked so cool I had no idea why they didn't make a TV show about her.

She joined me on my deck, where I was tucking into my pad see ew as Bob lounged at my feet and kept a watchful eye out in case the interloper returned. Martin sat down next to me, and I nudged a box of spring rolls in her direction. I thought she might decline, but she took one out of the package and bit into it with a satisfying crunch.

"Thanks, I haven't eaten all day."

I had explained most of my story to her over the phone, but between bites, I walked through it one more time.

"Why do you think he came to see you?" she asked.

This question had been plaguing me since Deacon disappeared. It was so strange for him to have sought me out specifically, so much so that he'd go to a public store and get directions to my house.

"I wish I could tell you. We were friendly in emails, but we certainly weren't *friends*. Still, he really doesn't know anyone else here except for the people he used to work with. Maybe he thought I was the closest thing he had to a friend in town, because it didn't seem like he trusted most of them anymore." I shrugged. "Maybe he just wanted to talk to someone."

"Did you get the sense from what he was saying that he might have been responsible for killing Sebastian?"

I set down my Styrofoam noodle container and leaned back in the chair, contemplating her question. "I feel like my answer to that changed with every other thing he said. He feels guilty about something, and a lot of what he was saying made me nervous, especially when he said he'd gone to talk to Sebastian last night. But he also just seemed so *sad*."

"Well, if what you said about their past relationship is true, he certainly had plenty of motive. We see so many cases like this with a lover scorned, and especially if his job and relationship were both lost at the same time. That can push people to unexpected places. He might have snapped and just acted in a moment of passion. It happens more often than you would think."

Bob jumped up on my lap and started to purr loudly while kneading biscuits into my thigh. When he thought I was distracted enough, he leaned over onto the table and took a big piece of chicken from the takeout container. Bold as he was, he didn't run off with it. He just sat there, happily munching.

I thought about everything Deacon had said, and it made me start thinking about Honey and her runes and the possible implication that the wrong person had died.

Obviously, Honey hadn't said that for sure, but the runes and her dream about the birds was something I couldn't shake. If that was true—and I still wasn't sure what to make of that entire rune-reading situation—then Deacon's confession became more confusing, because the object of his love and frustration was Sebastian. So if the motive rang true, then the *right* person had died, no matter how tragic it was.

"I wish I'd asked him more questions, I'm sorry."

Martin shook her head, taking one more spring roll for the road. "You did more than enough, Phoebe, believe me. This is honestly why I asked for your help, because it seems like no matter what you do, trouble has a way of finding you. Might as well harness that power for good." She smiled at me, pushing her sunglasses up now that the sun was almost gone. "Just promise me if he comes back, you call me right away, okay? I'll have someone drive by later tonight just to make sure everything is fine."

"Thank you." I didn't think Deacon planned to hurt me, but it was nice to know someone was looking out.

"And Phoebe?" Martin said from halfway down the sidewalk.

"Yeah?"

"Just because trouble *finds* you, that's not an invitation to go looking."

# Chapter Fourteen

I slept fitfully that night, tossing and turning, accidentally bumping into Bob on several occasions, and whenever I could drift off, I would have a bizarre dream about birds and a burning house. I knew this was because of what Honey had told me during our visit, but it was still weird to be inside the dream she had described.

When I woke up, for a full minute I was sure I could still smell burnt feathers, but the scent disappeared as soon as I pushed my duvet back.

It was early, but the sun was just starting to inch over the horizon. I could already feel the muggy heat that was going to permeate the day. The sky was clear, though, which meant we were in for a perfect Independence Day if all went well.

At least in terms of the weather.

The store was going to be open today despite the holiday, but for reduced hours. We didn't want to miss the enthusiastic tourist crowd in town for the festivities, and it was going to be all hands on deck for the seven hours we were open.

I wanted to get a run in before it got too gross out, because there was no way on earth I would want to go running later this evening once I finished with a hectic day.

I also suspected that news of Sebastian's death would have made its way around town by this point, and doubtless I was going to be bombarded with a million questions about that and the missed hike the previous day. That was all enough to exhaust even the toughest soul, so a run this morning would do me good.

Tossing my hair into a ponytail, I donned my usual running gear and slipped my earbuds into my ears.

I needed something upbeat to get me through my run today and to hopefully distract me from the doom and gloom of the day before. One thing had surprised me in retrospect when I thought back to my encounter with Deacon. Even when I'd been alone with him with no way to know if he was there with ill intent, my accidental magic flare-ups hadn't gone off.

Evidently there was some nuance to my newly discovered magical hiccups: anxiety could trigger it, but fear and anxiety weren't the same thing. It was apparently more refined than that.

Which just made it weirder and weirder.

To keep the stress and floaties away during my run, I queued up some ABBA, with the steady beat of "Mamma Mia!" ready to keep me distracted. I took my usual short route, though I was out a bit earlier than usual today. That said, some of my beloved neighborhood dogs were already out in their yards, and who can be stressed when there are very good dogs in need of petting?

I made several stops along the way, wishing I'd had the foresight to bring a little pouch with treats. Maybe I'd need to add that to my plans in the future, because it would probably secure me a few new best friends. Though I wasn't sure how Bob would feel about doggy treats in the house. He might think I was plotting something.

My usual run took about forty minutes, passing through populated and charming neighborhoods and only occasionally dipping into more wooded areas. Most days I really enjoyed those diversions over wooden footbridges and along paths dense with overhead foliage, but this morning, with it barely being dawn, I felt nervous, stricken with an unusual sense of dread.

More than once on my run, I paused for a non-dog-related reason, getting the distinct feeling I was being followed. A tickling sense of foreboding wouldn't shake off no matter how hard I tried to tell myself I was just being paranoid.

Someone out there had killed someone, and if it *had* been Deacon, he was proving to be a little too gifted at appearing and disappearing as it suited him. I refocused my thoughts, chasing the jangling nerves off as best I could. Until I better knew how to keep my emotions and my magic separate from each other, I needed to work with some good old-fashioned mindfulness and meditation to keep the disasters to a minimum.

As I jogged through one wooded area, something bright caught my eye—a little flash of blue and yellow that smeared across my line of sight before disappearing into the branches. I drew to a quick stop, trying to find the place among the leaves where it had gone.

There, a little flicker of lemon-yellow feathers bounding from one tree to another. A sharp cry, somewhere between a trill and a song, came from the branches, and it was unlike any birdsong I could remember hearing in the area before. I couldn't identify birds by their call, but I knew enough that I recognized repeated songs, and this was new.

I inched closer to the edge of the trail. After taking a moment to check my surroundings and make sure there was no one lurking behind or ahead, I pulled my phone out to try to get a photo of the feathery critter. Even with everything that had been going on the last couple of days, I remembered what Sebastian had said during his signing, that there was the possibility of a previously thought extinct bird species living in the area. I knew pretty much nothing about tanagers, but I recalled the page in the guide where they'd been so brightly colored, and this little guy seemed to fit the bill.

The bird moved again, flicking to a lower branch, and as I lifted my phone, the rain-dampened soil beneath my feat shifted under the extra weight and gave way entirely. Soon, with barely enough time to let out a *whoop*, I was sliding down the side of the hill.

I was only about ten feet down when everything froze, a familiar bit of magic taking over from my sheer panic. The air around me was still, not a breeze, not a single birdsong. It was as if someone had pressed pause on the world and I was the only one still moving.

Motes of dust and debris hung in the air around me where they had been stirred up in my fall, and bouncing rocks were suspended below my feet.

Before I did anything else, I caught my breath, taking a calming gulp of air and assessing my surroundings. I had never really looked off the side of this trail before, but it was a relatively steep drop right down to the river below. It was strange to see the usually burbling water just stuck like it was frozen over. Even in the winter it didn't freeze over.

I climbed awkwardly to my feet, keeping my balance by clinging to a nearby tree trunk. The hill was steepest at the top, too sheer to climb back up, but below me was a less treacherous angle; this would keep me from getting too bumped and bruised by comparison.

I could walk down the hill from here and hike back to the nearest footbridge.

As I took my first wobbly step down the incline, using other trees for aid, the sound and movement of the world returned with a slight popping of air pressure in my ears. The river continued its lazy meandering, falling rocks skittered down the hill, and someone was yelling.

Wait.

Yes, after I paused a moment to be sure I wasn't imagining things—stopping time can really mess with your head—I was certain I heard two distinct voices bickering only a few yards away.

While it was still dim within the woods, I immediately dropped to the ground, crouching low to avoid notice and hoping to minimize any sound. Though if they were continuing to verbally spar even after the racket my fall had made, there was a very good chance they weren't listening to anything going on around them.

I scuttled closer to the sound of the voices, and soon I could hear snippets of what they were saying rather than just the muddled sound of angry tones.

". . . said there was no risk, and I'd say him *dying* was not something we had talked about." This was a female voice that sounded familiar, but I couldn't quite place it.

". . . don't seem to understand the risks. We had . . ." Here I lost what the man speaking to her was saying, the sound of the river and of waking birds in the trees making it hard to hear everything. He picked up again, saying, ". . . careful, or maybe it'll be your turn next."

Her response to this was unmistakable. "Are you threatening me?"

His tone lowered, and I could barely make out a single word he was saying, but the menace of his tone didn't need words to be understood. ". . . be stupid."

". . . not stupid, but maybe you should talk to Connor about . . ."

I got close enough to where they were standing that I could catch brief glimpses of them through the trees. The man had his back to me and was wearing a dark jacket and baseball cap, giving me no help in identifying him. I'd thought perhaps I might spot a flash of Deacon's telltale dark-red hair, but if it was tucked under that cap, I couldn't tell in the poor morning light.

The woman, however, was immediately recognizable, and my breath caught in my throat.

Melody.

# Chapter Fifteen

There was no mistaking her face, even if I'd only met the woman twice. I recognized her doll-like features, the delicate upturned nose and perfectly arched eyebrows, even from my hiding place in the branches and mud.

She looked awfully different now, arguing with this man, than she had just one morning earlier with her eyes red and her skin blotchy from crying. The woman I was looking at had a fierce, angry focus, and any of the sensitive grief she'd been overtaken by earlier was gone.

"... think you can manipulate me," the man was saying.

"... know exactly what ..."

"... not interested in empty ..."

Melody laughed at this, but there wasn't an ounce of humor in the sound. "... nothing empty about it," she snarled.

I had no idea what these two were talking about, though the death they'd mentioned earlier had to be referring to Sebastian.

I didn't dare make a move, no matter how much I wanted to try getting a better look at the man to see if he was anyone I recognized. Logic told me he must be, because who else would be here talking to

Melody except one of the people she had come here with, or Deacon, who she also knew?

I'd listened in on Melody and Connor's whispered discussion at the bookstore, and the man speaking didn't sound anything like the young social media manager. Plus she'd referred to Connor by name, meaning it couldn't be him.

Any of those people who were part of Sebastian's entourage had the means to kill him; they were all staying at the same B and B. I knew Deacon had motive, but did Melody? Did the man she was talking to? I wanted to get a foot or two closer to better hear what they were saying or catch a glimpse of the man, but then I heard him say, "Just get me what I want, and this whole thing goes away."

Melody snorted. "I'd like to know how you expect me to do that now."

"I don't care. Just get it done."

Of course I'd be able to hear them with crystal clarity *now*, when it was obvious the conversation was over. The sound of gravel under-foot accompanied them away from the side of the river and back to a small parking lot near where the running path had started. I waited a minute or two until I knew they were gone, then scooted my way down to the riverbank.

I was covered in small scrapes, a few places on my legs were bloody from where I'd been cut up by the rocks during my fall, but all things considered I wasn't in bad shape. It would hardly be the first time I'd hurt myself in some outdoor activity.

Following the river back to the parking lot, I jogged the rest of the way home at a slower pace. Walking would have been easier, but I wanted to get back to the comfort of my house and get myself cleaned up. There was someone I wanted to talk to about what I'd just overheard, and while I knew that person *should* be Detective Martin, it wasn't.

Once I got home, I pulled out my phone, only to see there was a nice fresh crack all the way across the screen. Cursing the fact that my magic had been able to protect me but not my electronics, I was grateful to see that my phone was still functioning.

I sent a quick text to Rich saying I was going to stop by this morning before the store opened and I promised to ply him with coffee as penance for making him wake up early. By the time I was showered and had bandaged up my hands and shins, there was a reply waiting for me that said, **There better be a breakfast pastry too. I don't wake up for just anyone.**

While this was technically a business call, or at least a professionally themed discussion, I couldn't help but think of Rich's dinner invitation and the actual date we had been putting off for months. I'd need to go to work after leaving his apartment, but that didn't mean I couldn't put in a tiny bit of extra effort to look nice.

I applied my usual minimal makeup but then added a smudge of brown eyeshadow, which made my blue eyes pop, and put on a little bit of a red lip stain called Melted Popsicle. I slipped into a pretty floral sundress I'd been looking for *any* excuse to wear; the bad weather lately had been killing the vibe.

I would bring a cardigan to wear in the store—otherwise the air conditioning would destroy me—but it felt nice to dress up. I hadn't done anything to make an effort to impress a man since leaving Blaine, and Rich and I were taking things so slow it could be classified as glacial, so perhaps a strategic use of spaghetti straps would help pick up the pace.

Bob was waiting by the door, looking for his carrier backpack, which I normally left there. Since he hadn't been to the shop in the past two days, I had tucked it away in a closet to avoid the tripping hazard.

He yowled at me, as if he knew I was considering leaving him home a third day in a row. The shop was going to be busy, and it wasn't even a full day. It made sense to just leave him here.

He had other opinions.

"Okay, okay, fine, you win." I pulled the carrier out of the closet, and he was instantly purring so loudly I could hear him down the hallway. When I got to him, he weaved between my ankles and batted at the straps over his head. The second I set the backpack down, he climbed inside and sat primly, as if to show me what a good boy he was going to be.

"You're not fooling anyone, kid." I planted a quick kiss on his furry head, then zipped him in.

I biked to the store, wanting to enjoy the nice weather. All the rain had forced me to drive more than I would like, and it was nice to feel the breeze on my shoulders.

I felt rejuvenated when I arrived at the shop. Sugarplum Fairy was already open, and I waved to Amy through the window as I locked the bike up to a rack out front. I had learned an enchantment that warded off thieves, but frankly I wasn't really trusting my magic at the moment and thought it better not to tempt fate.

I quickly moved through my morning errands, dropping Bob inside the store and getting my order from Amy. Since her shop was open, she was bustling with customers who wanted a tasty treat to start their day. I didn't have time to chat with her, only to order two lattes—one with extra espresso—and two of her hand pies. Today's specials were goat cheese, chive, and fig and a truly delicious-sounding sausage, cheddar, and banana pepper.

I also collected my usual order of pastries, so by the time I got out the front door, I was balancing two big to-go cups and three boxes of various treats for both me and the store.

Thank goodness there was a very handsome man standing outside the Earl's Study waiting for me.

"Hey, you," Rich said, taking the tray of coffees in one hand and
balancing the boxes easily in the other, freeing up both my hands so
I could unlock the door. "When I said you should bring me a treat, I
didn't think you'd go this overboard." His honey-brown eyes twin-
kled, laughing at his own joke.

I held the door open for him, pointing him in the direction of
the tea counter. "As much as I like you, you're going to have to share
those with paying customers."

"I mean, I pay rent to live over the shop; doesn't that count?"

I snorted. "Nice try."

While I emptied the pastry boxes onto the clean trays waiting in
the display cooler, I gave Rich a quick once-over. Was it just my imagination, or had he put a little effort into looking nice too? Rich *usually*
looked nice; it was a by-product of being very, very handsome. But
today he was wearing a nice pair of jeans and a plain black T-shirt,
and that T-shirt fit him so well it appeared to have been made for him.

How was it legal for someone to look *that* good in a plain T-shirt?

Once the cabinet was full and I knew Bob was settled in his
favorite chair, already snoozing, I handed Rich the smaller box of
hand pies. "Let's go have a chat about murder, shall we?"

"Don't threaten me with a good time, Ms. Winchester."

I had two hours before the store opened, so I wasn't worried
about being behind on the baking, but I really wanted a sounding
board to discuss what I'd overheard by the river this morning.

We headed upstairs to Rich's apartment—yet another piece of
Main Street real estate that I owned—and he made a beeline for the
kitchen, so I followed behind and perched myself on one of his
barstools.

It had been months since I'd been to Rich's apartment, and in that time it had stopped being such a spartan bachelor pad. He'd hung some gauzy curtains that gave him extra privacy but still let the morning light filter in. On the walls were an assortment of framed photos, including one of him in his old police uniform, shaking hands with an important-looking man in a suit while receiving some kind of medal.

Rich didn't talk about his past a lot, neither his failed marriage nor his time as a police officer, and I didn't want to pry into things that might be painful to discuss. My wandering gaze caught another framed photo, this one in aged color, but I immediately recognized it.

It had been taken on the front porch of Lane End House over twenty years earlier, and showed me, Rich—or Ricky, as I'd called him then—and Leo. We were probably about twelve years old in the photo, one of our last summers together. I was sitting on the porch step, my knees battered and bruised much like they were today, a missing tooth in my big smile and dirt smeared across my forehead and cheeks. Leo stood behind me, leaning against one of the pillars. His hands were stuffed in his pockets and he couldn't quite look directly at the camera, but there was a hint of a smile at the edges of his mouth. Rich looked disheveled, his dark hair messy and grass stains and dirt covering almost every inch of him. His expression was borderline dour, but that same twinkle in his eyes I'd seen earlier this morning was also in the photo. His arms were draped over the porch railing, and there were three fishing poles leaned up next to him.

The memory of my childhood with those two was laced with bittersweet regret. We had been thick as thieves when we were younger, but with hormones and the pressures of being cool—not to mention the rough home life that Rich had been trying to avoid—we drifted apart, the way childhood friends often do. Soon I thought I was too cool to spend summers in a small town with my aunt when there was so much to do with my friends in Chicago. I regretted that too, even though my summers had been fun. Now that Eudora was gone, I wished I had spent more time learning from her.

I wished I'd known *then* I was a witch and spent all those summer absorbing her knowledge instead of having to do it all as an adult now.

Rich leaned over the kitchen counter, following my gaze. "What a bunch of goobers."

"Some of them still are." I turned and looked at him. "Where on earth did you find that?"

"Oh, your aunt gave them to me and Leo a few years ago. Thought we might like to have them. Mine was tucked in a book for a while; I found it while I was cleaning some stuff up and figured it deserved to be hung up."

"It's great."

"Yeah, well, you're great." And while he might have meant the collective *you* of both me and Leo, I somehow suspected his compliment was much more direct. I blushed.

Suddenly feeling more scrutiny than I'd expected, I returned to my stool at the counter and opened the box of hand pies. Rich grabbed us two plates, and we split the pies in half so we each got to try the different flavors. The scents of crumbly sausage and tart goat cheese wafted into the air. Amy's pastry was flaky and buttery, everything you could want in a perfect breakfast delight. She swore to me these were easy to make, but I still felt intimidated by the process. Why learn when you can just buy them from an expert?

For a few minutes Rich and I sat in a companionable silence, something I liked that we were able to do. No one felt the awkward need to say anything just for the sake of avoiding too much quiet. As he bit into the goat cheese hand pie, he let out a noise of obvious delight, and I smiled to myself for a job well done in making our breakfast choices.

Once we had finished eating, Rich put the plates in his dishwasher and grabbed one of the extra stools so he could sit across from me.

"So, let me guess, you've been meddling around in an investigation that has nothing to do with you again? Are you a suspect?" He propped his chin on his folded hands and grinned at me.

"One, rude. Two, how dare you? And three, what do you take me for?"

"So that's a yes, then."

"In fairness, I am *not* a suspect, and I was *asked* to help."

He gave me a dubious look that said volumes. "Sure."

"I *was*. Detective Martin asked if I could keep an ear open and share anything that might be useful."

"And so you decided to come share your useful information with me and not the person who asked you for it?"

"I'm never bringing you pastry again."

"We both know that's not true. I've ensnared you with my devilish charms; you'll never be free of me now. But seriously, you must have had a reason for wanting to tell me this first and not Patsy. I know she can be intimidating, but that's definitely not what it is." Rich's teasing tone had become a bit more serious and he raised an eyebrow at me, as if challenging me to be honest with him.

"Since you asked, I think my reasoning is that I've *been* under police scrutiny for a crime before, and I don't want to start throwing people under the bus for something if they're already processing through their grief, you know? If Melody isn't up to something nefarious, then I don't think it's fair of me to tell the detectives she is."

"I have no idea who Melody is, so why don't you walk me through this from the start so I have all the information I need, and *then* I will tell you what I think."

I explained the book signing and all my interactions with Sebastian's team. I walked through everything I'd seen at the B and B and my unexpected visit from Deacon, and I ended with a play-by-play of the argument I'd heard by the river only a couple hours earlier.

When I was done, Rich sat quietly for a minute. He took a long sip from his coffee while he processed everything.

"That is a lot to consider," he declared finally.

"It's a bit weird, right?" I had left out the weirdest part of all, which had been Honey reading the runes and telling me that Sebastian wasn't the right victim. Rich might know I was a witch, but adding elements of the mystical to a murder investigation felt like a bit too much to load onto him.

I hadn't forgotten, though, and I was going to have to circle back with Honey soon to see if I could find more explanation. My little magical snafu with the candles had derailed any other kind of conversation yesterday.

"If I'm thinking like a cop," Rich said, "then Deacon is still the most obvious suspect. Everything you told me points to him being the logical one. Troubled breakup or unrequited love, a loss of his longtime job—that's enough to set anyone off to act foolishly. He was here, you said he talked to the victim the night of the murder. If there's sand and there's salt water, you've probably got yourself a beach."

"But then where does the whole thing with Melody fit in? We can't overlook that. I got the vibe from Deacon that his guilt might have just been because he wasn't able to protect Sebastian, not because he killed him. Now maybe I'm reading something into it that wasn't

# Gretchen Rue

there, but I also don't want to jump to conclusions." I shrugged help-lessly, then picked up a nearby napkin, wringing it in my fingers just to give my hands something to do.

"You didn't overhear enough of that conversation to make it sound like a confession. I agree it's certainly weird and very suspect, but if you brought that to a DA, they'd laugh you out of their office before prosecuting."

"That's you looking at it like a cop. What about a PI?"

Rich grinned at me. "If you want me to look at it like a PI, you and I are going to need to go on a field trip."

# Chapter Sixteen

With a promise that Rich would come to my place that evening to pick me up for our stakeout date, I headed back down to the Earl's Study to get my morning duties completed.

I was amazed that in the short time I'd been upstairs with Rich, the street was already bustling with activity. The tourists were obvious at first sight, their cameras out to capture the idyllic charm of our little European-inspired town, where you might find an English-inspired bookshop next to a Parisian-inspired bakery.

There were food trucks parked at the end of Main in front of Lansing Grocery, and the queue for various treats was already running up the block. I thought nine in the morning was a bit early for grilled cheese or nachos, but it was Independence Day, after all, and if there was any day you should be allowed to eat and drink whatever you want, it was July Fourth.

In a few hours Main Street would close completely to vehicle traffic, but right now cars were still able to come and go. There was a junky-looking sedan parked in front of Amy's shop that drew my attention almost immediately. It wasn't uncommon to see cars in rough shape in Raven Creek. Like most Pacific Northwest towns, we were no strangers to a nomadic population of new-age-philosophy and van-life folks who tended to smell like patchouli and know where all the best truck-stop showers were.

This looked different, though. It was an early-2000s Toyota with a bumper so rusty it was probably hanging on by magic more powerful than anything I could muster. But most importantly, it didn't look like it belonged to a modern wayfarer.

Something about it prickled my interest, and I stopped to take a closer look. The back seat had a suitcase in it that was partially opened, with clothes spilling out, and a hanger dangling in front of one of the rear windows had a suit jacket on it.

In the front seat were a sea of fast-food wrappers, and . . . was that a *law textbook*?

The phonebook-sized tome was half covered in Burger King bags, but it was pretty apparent what I was looking at.

A yellow legal pad was sitting on the front seat, and with one quick glance I could see familiar names in messy scrawl on it. *Lansing Grocery* was emphatically crossed off. Under the pad was a familiar-looking flyer for Sebastian's book-signing event.

"Can I *help* you?" came a voice that was pure malice. It was so unfriendly I actually gave an involuntary shudder before turning around.

The lawyer—I couldn't recall ever learning his name—was standing barely a foot away from me with a nasty expression twisting his otherwise bland features into something more memorable.

"Just checking," I said quickly. "The street is going to be cleared soon for the festivities; I wanted to make sure no one was planning to leave this long-term." It wasn't a *great* lie, but it was close enough to the truth that he seemed satisfied.

"I was just leaving. Do you own the block or something?" This was obviously said to be dismissive, but I had to choke back a laugh.

"Or something."

The lawyer continued to stare at me as he rounded the car and got in the driver's side. He was just so *unnerving*; I could see why he'd managed to rub Leo the wrong way immediately. There was just something instantly loathsome about the guy.

As soon as he drove off, I ducked into the Sugarplum Fairy, only to find Amy loudly banging baking trays in the back.

"Amy?"

She came out a moment later, her cheeks flushed red and what looked like a hint of tears clinging to her eyelashes.

"Whoa, are you okay?" I asked, making a beeline for the counter.

"Is he gone?" Her voice was strained.

"The lawyer? Yeah, he just drove off in possibly the ugliest car I've ever seen. What did he want?"

"Oh, he must have gotten it in his head that I might be an easy target for his little scheme of buying up property around town. When he found out that I rented, he was pretty quick to suggest that if his buyers had their way, my shop would be one of the first that got the boot. I know I shouldn't have let him bother me; I *know* my landlord isn't going to just sell to some corporation with deep pockets. If they were like that, they'd have done it years ago. But it just ruffled my feathers so much I couldn't help but give him a little bit of an earful."

She tossed a business card on the floor, and I picked it up so she wouldn't need to deal with collecting it later. The name on the very simple card said ANDREW BACHMAN and gave contact information but no company name.

I also knew perfectly well that her landlord wouldn't sell to Andrew, because I was her landlord. But *she* didn't know that.

The bell over the door chimed, and the massive form of Leo hulked into the shop. He smiled when he saw us, but if I wasn't looking I might not have noticed that the smile brightened considerably more when it landed on Amy than on me.

And almost as quickly it faltered when he saw her face.

"What happened?"

Amy offered him a smile that was *almost* convincing and waved a hand in the air, as if dismissing his concerns would be so easy. "It's nothing. Just that lawyer."

Leo had a thick beard, making it hard to tell when he blushed, but I had no problem whatsoever seeing how red his face got at the mention of the lawyer.

"Where is he?" Leo snarled.

For my soft-spoken friend to get so angry, the resentment of his previous encounter with Andrew must still be fresh on his mind.

"Don't you go doing anything rash, Leo Lansing. I'm a big girl, and I already gave him what for, okay?" She gave him a look, and I . . . was she . . . flirting? There was certainly something about their shared expressions that caught me off guard.

Amy was a little older than Leo but by no means *old*, and neither of them had anyone in their lives at the moment. For a while I'd thought Leo might be harboring a bit of a crush on me, and it was hard not to have a soft spot for the gentle giant. But Rich had stolen my heart, even if our courtship was moving at a snail's pace.

Leo and Amy . . .

Or maybe I was just misunderstanding.

"If he comes back here, call me," Leo insisted.

"He won't come back," Amy said. "Now that he knows I don't own the place, he can't bully me. Let me go get your order."

She returned a moment later with a big sheet cake box and lifted the lid. Inside, the cake was decorated in a Fourth of July theme with red strawberries and deep-violet blueberries and a finely piped *Thanks for Your Work* message.

"'S for my staff," Leo explained. "Didn't want the bakery to have to make their own thank-you cake." He flushed, embarrassed by his own thoughtfulness, and picked up the cake as if it weighed nothing.

I grabbed the door for him, though I was sure he could have managed. "I'll check in with you later, okay?" I said to Amy. "And if you need anything, I'm right next door."

"I know. Get out of here." She seemed to have already recouped, and I suspected it was in no small part due to Leo's appearance. I returned to the Earl's Study, but I was still put off by the unsettling encounter with the lawyer. I tried to refocus myself but found that every time I was out in the store, I let my gaze drift to Main Street, expecting to see the return of the shoddy-looking car.

My brother, Sam, was a lawyer, so I shot him a quick text while I worked.

Can you look up another lawyer for me?

I wasn't expecting an immediate reply—Sam frequently took days to respond to texts—but at least I'd put it out there. Maybe he could tell me if Andrew really was who he claimed to be. Something about him rankled me, and apparently everyone else in town.

Trying to boost my spirits, I set about getting everything ready for the day. Taking inspiration from the holiday, I put the usual loaves and cookies in to bake and set about prepping the day's themed iced teas. I had made the three usual bases the day before—white, black, and green—and I was planning to turn them into red-white-and-blue-inspired teas.

I took fresh berries from the freezer, where I'd placed them two nights earlier. They'd help chill the drinks more quickly when frozen. I pulled the already chilled teas out of the fridge and immediately started to prep new batches that would steep and chill while we served these.

If we continued to sell iced tea at the rate we were this summer, I was going to need to explore different options for storing and serving it next year. As it was, we were barely keeping up with demand, which was a great problem to have but still a problem.

With the big glass jugs on the counter, I started to sort out my ingredients for each tea. The white was going to be the most obvious base for my white tea, and while I was disappointed I couldn't actually make a clear tea to amp up the theme, I figured people would get it.

Into the white tea base, I added a homemade pineapple syrup and diced up young coconut. Almost immediately the kitchen was a piña colada–scented dream, with the two mingling scents transporting me to another country where I could dip my toes in the ocean and lounge around in the sun. I knew instantly this would be a hit.

The green tea base would be the perfect complement for our red tea, which also used a homemade syrup, this one made from dried hibiscus flowers. The rich scarlet color was eye catching, and the syrup was flavored with brown sugar, ginger, and cinnamon, giving it a unique taste that was almost autumnal, but the brightness of the floral still kept it summer appropriate.

I was obsessed with the hibiscus syrup. At home I liked to mix it with some club soda and enjoy it out on my deck. To the pitcher I also added a full container of fresh raspberries.

The last tea was the blue, which used a bergamot-forward black tea with lavender in it, accompanied by a lemon simple syrup. The final touch was fresh frozen blueberries in the jug. The end product would be a lemony delight with the sweetness from the berries keeping it from getting overly tart.

With my patriotic collection of teas ready to go, it was time to swap the baking out from the oven. The scent of fresh loaves of sourdough made my stomach rumble, even though I'd eaten a delicious breakfast with Rich. There was just something powerful about the alluring fragrance of fresh-baked bread. I knew if I was at home I would have ripped into the loaf with my bare hands before it even had the opportunity to cool.

Instead, I set the loaves aside to sit before lunch and put two trays of shortbread in. Even the uncooked dough smelled good—sugary, buttery, a little hint of sweetness from the dried strawberries.

Everything just smelled like *summer* in the kitchen, from the mason jar filled with fresh mint cuttings from pots on my front porch to the sunny rounds of lemon cut and waiting to go into drinks. It was nice to be so focused on the tasks in front of me. At no point did my anxiety creep in, and the only kitchen disasters were the ones my own clumsiness was responsible for.

I was just bringing the tea jugs out to the front counter when the back door of the shop opened and closed. I tensed for a moment, trying to recall if I had locked it and wondering if the person who was about to come down the hall would be friend or foe. In a sort of panic state, I held on to the heavy glass dispenser. I wasn't sure if my intent was to throw it at the person as a weapon, but the much more logical solution would have been to put it down so I could defend myself.

Daphne appeared, her blonde curls piled up on her head in a messy bun and a sequined Old Glory shirt paired with her denim cutoffs. "Oh gosh, Phoebe, do you need help with that?"

I realized, in my breath of relief to see her, I was still holding on to the heavy jug like an absolute moron. Daphne's offer of assistance only made me manage to feel like I was a borderline "golden girl" that my youthful employee thought needed to be saved.

"No," I replied stubbornly—even though the thing was legitimately very awkward to lift onto the counter. "I got it."

I quickly explained the day's drink blends to Daphne, and she went into artist mode, grabbing the little chalkboard we used to display our specials. She erased what she'd done up for the book signing, an evening I was sure now felt bittersweet to both of us, and set to work drawing up cutesy descriptions of each iced tea as well as the toasts we were doing for lunch.

While she worked on that, I finished hauling out the glass jugs and getting the bowls with featured loose-leaf teas set in front of their canisters.

A few minutes after Daphne's arrival, Imogen came through the front door. Her braids had been wrapped up into two space buns at the top of her head, and she sported a shirt with sparkly gold letters that simply read RESIST in all caps.

"I have a potentially controversial suggestion," Imogen announced.

I wiped condensation off the sides of the iced-tea containers and arranged our reusable tumblers so they were right out where everyone could see them. "I'm listening."

"I think we should put up a big display of Sebastian's books at the front table."

"Oh, Immie, that's terrible," Daphne said, holding a hand to her chest.

"No, no, wait. Let's hear her out." I had to admit Imogen usually had great marketing foresight, and whenever she wanted to do a specific table theme, it tended to boost our sales.

"Here's the truth, and I'm sorry, Daph, but I'm right. People are going to *want* those books. Especially the signed overstock. You put them out front because the gawkers are going to be here asking for them anyway, and then we don't have to point them out anywhere."

Imogen tossed a newspaper on the cash desk, and the first story on the front page was *Popular Nature Influencer Meets Foul Play*. I could tell someone at the paper was just dying to turn that *foul* into a *fowl*, but calmer editorial heads had prevailed.

I scanned the story quickly, but it was mostly things I already knew. It shared details of Sebastian's rise to fame online and his sudden death in town. One interesting tidbit was a quote from Melody: "Everyone who knew Sebastian loved him, and I knew him better than most. I think I can say on good authority that Sebastian wouldn't want us to dwell on this. He didn't believe in grudges; he said they were bad karma."

For that quote to have made it into the morning edition, she'd have had to be interviewed the same day as the murder. How had she gone from the bereft woman I'd left outside the B and B to telling people that the dead man would want to move on?

I didn't know Sebastian well, certainly not as well as she was claiming to, but if someone murdered *me* in cold blood, I'd want that person to be held accountable. Grudges might be bad karma, but killing someone was way worse.

I passed the paper over to Daphne, who had been pretending not to read it over my shoulder. She scooped it up and immediately started to flip through the pages to see if there was additional coverage. "Oh hey, they mention the Earl's Study in here. 'The victim had been planning to attend a highly anticipated nature hike presented by local bookstore The Earl's Study, following a successful book signing.'"

"Well, at least they didn't make us sound too bad," I said with a sigh of relief.

"And they mentioned us," Imogen continued. "So we should definitely put those books out front and center, because you know people will be asking."

Daphne made another face of displeasure, but she didn't argue this time, which made me feel like even she could admit it was a good idea. There was bad taste and then there was just smart business. I had noticed that after the passing of a celebrity, streaming services would suddenly have a bunch of older movies with that person front and center on the browsing page. This was no different.

Imogen was right, because I could already see a few people queued up outside waiting for us to open, and I suspected they weren't here for our delicious iced tea. I glanced at my watch.

"If you can get it done in ten minutes, I'm all for it. But we can't change tables around while people are in the store."

Imogen gave me a little mock salute and then set to work clearing off our front display table. She didn't leave any of the bird-related books we had put there, but she worked like a whirlwind, taking all our remaining Sebastian Marlow books out of the front window display in the stacks and leaving that space empty for the moment. I normally would have preferred something there, but I knew that on a short day, when everyone and their dog would be here to ask about the murder, a vacant window display wouldn't be on anyone's radar but mine.

With a minute to go before my deadline, Imogen plopped a framed photo of Sebastian that we'd had on his meet-and-greet table in the middle of her new display and raised her hands in the air like she'd just broken an Olympic record. "Done."

"Okay, Grimogen Reaper, maybe let's tone our enthusiasm down a bit; it's supposed to be a *memorial* table." But admittedly I still chuckled over how proud of herself she was. She was typically fairly stoic, so I liked the brief moment she was letting excitement shine through.

She opened the door right at ten, and our first wave of customers barely let her get out of the way before swooping in.

Imogen would definitely get to gloat with a big round of *I told you so* later, because nearly every single person through the door in the first hour made a beeline for our Sebastian table display.

The signed copies were gone in the first thirty minutes we were open. It was a little ghoulish how excited people were to get their hands on one. And, of course, the questions came in fast and furious. People wanted to know everything—if we had any idea who the killer was, if one of us was the killer, if Sebastian's ghost was haunting the store, if we thought someone else might be next on the killer's list.

This last point I hadn't considered much, but after overhearing the argument with Melody this morning and tying it to what Honey had said, I *was* a little uneasy. It seemed as if Melody—if she wasn't guilty of the murder herself—might know too much. And if that was the case, then she could be in some real danger.

I decided to head over to the B and B when my shift was done just to have a quick chat with her. I didn't need to mention what I'd heard at the river, but I could try to gauge where she was emotionally and maybe see if she'd let something slip that might help me determine if she was the villain or a possible victim.

A lot depended on what Rich and I learned from our little stakeout later, and I was sure he wouldn't approve of me nosing around and having face time with Melody beforehand, but I also figured if she was guilty of something, then our conversation might drive her into action, which Rich and I would spot later.

I should *not* be as excited for a stakeout as I was, but I knew the entire reason I got butterflies in my stomach thinking about it was because I was looking forward to that alone time with Rich.

As I got ready for our busy day, I noticed a familiar form pass by the front window. The short figure with distinctive glasses grabbed my attention right away.

"Hey, Daph." I turned my attention to my adorable nineteen-year-old employee, someone who would definitely be able to get Connor talking a lot more easily than I could. "I just spotted Connor Reeves go by. Why don't you catch up to him, see how he's holding up with all this Sebastian stuff? If he's feeling up to it, you could pick his brain a little about social media for the shop."

Daphne and Imogen both looked at me like I'd spoken in another language. I gave Imogen a quick warning glance, because I could tell she was about to say something. Daphne asked, "Are you sure? It's going to be so busy."

"I'm not suggesting you go for hours, just tell him we're thinking of him, okay?" I wanted to ask her to specifically grill him about Melody or Deacon, but that might be too obvious. "Come back in fifteen or so. Imogen and I can hold down the fort."

I took a twenty from the till and handed it to her, and she ran off to catch up with Sebastian's social media manager.

"What was that all about?" Imogen asked as we watched the sprightly blonde head out. "Since when are we a counseling service?"

"I have some . . . reservations about the people in Sebastian's inner circle. I think Connor might be a weak link to spill. Detective Martin *did* ask me to keep my ears open."

"I don't think she meant you should enlist your employees in subterfuge, but I like where your head is at." Imogen gave an approving nod, and we got to work.

\* \* \*

The shortened morning flew by. Daphne had returned from her coffee meeting with Connor—and I hadn't failed to notice how smitten he looked when they walked back—but I hadn't been able to grill her about what had gone down. We were simply too busy. While people might have been coming in to grab copies of Sebastian's book, they were leaving with bags full of books, loose-leaf tea, and cup after cup of iced tea. We were sold out of bread before twelve thirty, and it was all I could do to make the small fridge meet the demands of our thirsty customers.

I hammered out a quick text to Amy, seeing if she might have space in her walk-in cooler. I had the *supplies* to make more tea, I just didn't have the space. She wrote back in minutes saying she did and it was all mine if I needed it. The moment we had a lull between customers, I shoved a fistful of cash into Daphne's hands and sent her to the grocery store.

"I need whatever berries they have, I don't care." I could make adjustments on the fly as needed; I was just grateful I'd made enough of my various simple syrups for a week, because a week was turning into a day.

All the chairs in the reading area of the bookstore were occupied, even Bob's usual haunt. My heartbeat skipped a step, and I worried he might have gotten out in all the hubbub, which was precisely why I'd been nervous to bring him today.

I left Imogen in charge of the cash register and headed into the reading room, my stomach in my shoes and knotted with worry.

Evidently my worries were unfounded, because I found Bob curled up on the back of a chair occupied by a little girl, her sleek black hair in pigtails and a picture book open on her lap. I scanned the store for her parents and spotted a smartly dressed Korean couple standing by the pastry display who seemed to be likely candidates.

Bob had an eye on her in the meantime.

I gave him a quick pat on the head and then returned to the front counter to help Imogen.

The rest of the day passed in a blur of red, white, and blue.

As we got toward closing, I finally had a free moment to pester Daphne about her meeting with Connor. I had to be careful about my questions, though, or risk her realizing I'd sent her out on something of a spy mission.

"So, how'd your coffee with Connor go? How was he feeling?"

Daphne took a stack of books I'd offered her and started filling the new release section with them. "It went by in such a blur. We went into Amy's place, and it was so busy we were practically shouting at each other. He's *so* smart, Phoebe. He started from nothing, but he was intuitive, and he taught himself everything he knows. That's so hard to do in the industry. I think he's part of the reason Sebastian got so famous, you know."

I thought Sebastian being very hot and charming probably had a lot more to do with it than algorithms, but I kept that to myself.

"Did he talk about Sebastian?"

"Not really. He said they weren't friends, exactly. He's really worried about his job now that Sebastian is gone, and I can't blame him. It's a tough industry. He told me that Travis from the publishing house already left town, so he doesn't know what that means for the book and his job now."

It *was* interesting that Connor seemed more interested in his job prospects than his dead boss. The news about Travis being gone also struck me as suspect—hadn't Patsy told everyone to stay put?—but I focused on information Connor might have spilled to Daphne.

"Did he mention Melody at all?"

Daphne took another stack of books. If she realized I was giving her the third degree for clues, it didn't show. "Nah, I think he might have said something like it being hard to work with her, especially now, but nothing else."

*Especially now.*

Interesting.

I left Daphne to finish putting the books away, wishing I'd gotten more from her conversation but definitely more curious about Connor's part in all this, and especially his relationship with Melody. They'd been thick as thieves at the signing, but suddenly *now* she was hard to work for.

I wanted to know what that meant.

# Chapter Seventeen

I was the last to leave the Earl's Study, and it was a bit of an effort to chase out the final stragglers politely before locking the door up for the evening. Since the streets were still bustling with people, I had a couple of last-minute customers sneak their way in before I could get the ones who were already there rung up.

It was close to six thirty by the time I shut everything down and after seven before I had the bread dough for tomorrow mixed and set to rise and the cookies prepped in their happy little dough logs in the fridge.

I was incredibly grateful for the successful day we'd had, but I was exhausted. The demand for Sebastian's books had far outstripped the remaining stock we had, and I had needed to place an order to satisfy local customers who wouldn't mind waiting a couple of weeks to pick their copies up. I'd directed the tourists—who'd made up the bulk of our customers today—to check out our other offerings despite their disappointment.

Imogen had been right: the birder's popularity and untimely demise had created a feverish demand for his books and anything remotely connected to him. Someone had bought a used copy of Henry David Thoreau's *Walden* simply because she remembered Sebastian mentioning it as a favorite during a live stream once.

We'd needed to refill the iced tea six times, which was a new record and a sign that I was going to need to invest in a serious upgrade to keep up with demand going forward in the summer.

I'd barely had a chance to look at my phone while I was working, so I was surprised to see a text from my brother, Sam, waiting for me.

I can check their bar and license status, case history. That's about it.

I quickly grabbed the business card I'd gotten from Amy and gave Sam Andrew's full name. I didn't figure he'd reply right away, especially given the holidays.

While I had my phone out, I shot Detective Martin a quick text asking her if she knew Travis had left town. Him leaving when I knew Sebastian's entourage had been told to stay in town was suspicious to say the least.

Surprisingly, Patsy replied almost immediately.

We checked his alibi, he was on a video conference call for hours, multiple witnesses. We let him go.

Oh. Well that took Travis off the list of potential candidates, then. I slipped my phone into my pocket and focused on finishing my closing tasks.

As I checked the tins of loose-leaf tea to see what I would need to bring refills for in the morning, someone tapped on the glass of the front door.

"We're clo—" I started to say, but when I looked up, I saw Honey standing outside waving at me.

It was a rare treat to see her in my store, since I usually visited her shop or we would hang out at my house after hours. Since she worked most of the same hours I did and didn't have additional staff, it wasn't easy for her to get here when I was open.

There was a woman I'd never seen before standing next to her, but based solely on their striking resemblance, I had a suspicion they were related.

I skirted around the counter and opened the front door with a jingle of greeting, ushering them inside before any of the curious tourists still thick on the streets thought we might be open. Amy was still open next door, and the smell of sugar and butter wafting through her door into the evening air seemed to be distracting most passersby. She'd been going over twelve hours on her own; I wasn't sure how she was still alive over there.

Honey and her visitor followed me into the store, where I led them into the tea shop side, indicating one of the small empty tables near the counter.

"Phoebe, I want to introduce you to my mother."

The woman's resemblance made perfect sense now. Honey was the spitting image of her; she just had a few more lines around her eyes and a bit more pleasant roundness to her face and body. Unlike Honey, she didn't wear her hair cut short; hers was in long dread-locks pulled back with a striking silk scarf. But like Honey, she seemed to have an affinity for adding a little blonde to her hair, based on a few of the locs I could see peeking out.

"Phoebe Winchester." I offered her my hand to shake, and she took it, giving it one firm pump, then pulled me in for a tight hug.

"I'm Karma Westcott. It is such a pleasure to meet you. My baby has done nothing but talk about you since the minute you moved into town. Been a real long time since we heard of anyone learning about their gift so late in life." She released me from the tight embrace and held me out at arm's length as if to get a good look at me. "Mmm, pretty girl. That husband of yours must have been a damn fool."

"Oh, well, I like you already." Honey had told me on numerous occasions that her parents were slightly hippie-ish in their lifestyle, hence her full name being Honey Moonbeam, so it seemed *possible* that Karma was an assumed moniker, but it suited her.

"Come on, baby, sit here for a minute and let me get a look at you." She guided us over to a table, where the three of us clustered together. The tables weren't really meant for this many people, but we made it work.

Karma took my hand in hers, flipping it over so my palm faced up. She started to trace the lines in my skin, mumbling mostly to herself about a *split love line* and a *mound of Venus*, things that I really didn't know the meaning of, but she understood as easily as reading a book.

I darted a quick glance to Honey, wondering if this was normal, but she was fully absorbed in watching her mother work and nodding along to the things Karma was saying. Obviously, they were speaking a language that wasn't yet mine to understand.

Karma gently set my hand down on the table and patted it. "I see plenty about you here, but not what I need to know."

Again I tried to gauge from Honey what she meant, but Honey seemed a little disappointed.

"Um, please don't interpret this as me not being so thrilled to meet you and appreciating the unexpected palm reading, but what exactly is going on here?"

Karma shot her daughter a look that I had seen innumerable times on my own mother's face. It was so unexpectedly familiar I automatically shrank back as if I had done something wrong myself. "Honey, you didn't tell her I was coming?" Karma asked.

"Mama, I didn't have a chance. I needed you to see what was going on, and I couldn't figure it out on my own."

Karma clucked her tongue at her daughter, then turned her attention to me. "I'm sorry, I thought you knew I was coming."

"Honey told me that she might mention my, uh . . . issues to you, but no, you being here in person is a bit of a surprise to me, I'll admit."

"Well, I suppose it's a surprise that can't be undone. I want to see if I can help you sort out your messy-magic situation. Swear I haven't heard of anything like that happening to an adult witch in decades. Do you have any ideas what might have started it?"

I gave a helpless shrug. "I don't know of any one thing that might have initiated it, but I do know it seems to be triggered by stress."

Karma mulled this over for a moment. "Honey tells me that your main gift is probability magic, is that right?"

I nodded. "I can do other things, but from what I've been told, that one is pretty rare."

"Very. You're one lucky witch." Karma smiled at me as if I'd just been told I was a lottery winner. While the magical gift had saved my life—more than once—I wasn't sure if I was always all that grateful to have it. Being a witch was a blessing and a curse all rolled into one. I regretted that I was coming into it so late and wished I'd had twenty extra years to hone my skills. As it was, I often felt as if I were sitting in on an exam for a class I'd never been able to attend and the questions I got right were just good guesses.

I suspected that my skills and control would grow over time, but I still felt like I was miles behind on being a witch and that having such a rare and powerful gift like probability was something that should have been granted to someone who knew how to *use* it.

I explained to Karma what I'd learned about stress triggering the new incidents and what I'd been doing each time. By the time I was done, she was nodding along, and for the first time since things had begun to go wrong, I wondered if there might actually be some hope of stopping it.

"Seems to me like a pretty similar situation to what happens with teenage witches when they're having some big feelings and it interferes with their abilities. Since you never got a chance to get used to it while you were younger, it's popping up now because you've got some stressors in your life—naturally, we all do—but you never got a chance to manage both magic and stress before. Baby, don't you worry, you're not broken, you just need some coping skills."

"I'm sure my old therapist would agree with you." I was making jokes, but inside, the wash of relief I felt was akin to what I remembered feeling after paying off a giant chunk of debt. Even if just for a moment, my soul felt lighter and a burden had been lifted from my shoulders.

*You're not broken.*

I hadn't even realized this was something I'd been thinking about until the moment she said it wasn't the case. The way I needed to hear those words was unlike anything I'd ever felt before. I was divorced, living alone with a cat, starting my life all over again with new friends, new gifts, and new opportunities, but sometimes I still felt like something must be wrong with me. I was the problem; the fault was mine.

But it wasn't.

I was okay.

I could fix this.

I didn't even realize I'd started to cry until Karma reached across the table to wipe a tear from my cheek. "It's okay, baby. You're going to be just fine."

# Chapter Eighteen

Karma and Honey left about thirty minutes later after I insisted on making tea for both of them. I wanted to ask Karma a million questions about her own gifts, but she was too busy asking me about myself for me to turn the tables.

It was nice to just talk about silly, unimportant-seeming things rather than the dark, heavy topics of misfit magic and recent murder. It wasn't until they'd left and I'd locked up behind them that I realized I'd completely forgotten to ask Honey about her eerie words regarding Sebastian's death.

Had she had any more dreams or done another reading? I wondered if the runes might be clearer now. Maybe the notion of the wrong person dying was more conceptual, implying his death was wrong because he was young and had his whole life ahead of him. Or did the runes mean what I *thought* they meant, that Sebastian had not been the intended target of the murder? If it was the latter, were we barking up the wrong tree by focusing our attention on Melody and Deacon?

Maybe the killer had had someone else in mind entirely and Sebastian's room swap had proven deadly for him.

I mulled this over on my bike ride home, with the familiar, comfortable weight of Bob in his backpack along for the ride. It was still bright out when I pulled the bike alongside my house and leaned it up against the patio railing. Rich would be by after dark to pick me up for our stakeout, so I had time to kill.

While Rich and I were planning to keep an eye on Melody tonight, something was still bugging me about the little room shuffle that had meant Sebastian wasn't sleeping where he'd originally intended to.

I decided that since I still had a few hours before Rich came by, I would head over to the B and B and talk to the owner.

Leaving Bob at the house, I made the short walk back to the B and B. The streets were bustling with activity, and when I entered the little mansion, I was happy to see that the owner—whose name I thought might be Andie or Audrey—had her hands full talking to a small group of guests. None of the guests gathered around her check-in desk were a part of Sebastian's original party. She was so occupied, she didn't see me come in, so I figured there was no harm in just ducking upstairs to see Sebastian's room for myself. The police were done with their investigations of the space, so it wasn't like I'd be interfering with an active crime scene.

I tiptoed up the big stairs, waiting for someone to call up to me and stop me, but when no one did, I took it as a sign from the universe that this was meant to be and moved to the upper floor. I knew which rooms I had rented and who they'd originally been assigned to, so I headed to the one I was certain Sebastian must have swapped for.

There was no crime-scene tape on the door—or any of the doors—but I quickly realized my error. I had no key.

My magic might have been wonky lately, but this did seem like a good opportunity to try a simple spell I shouldn't be able to screw up. I held my palm up to the lock, under the DO NOT DISTURB sign, and whispered, "Open."

Every lock on every door clicked open with an audible *chunk* sound.

*Oops.*

I'd have to remember to relock them all when I left, and perhaps not try any other spells until I had a better handle on what was happening with my magic.

I opened the now-unlocked door and ducked inside, shutting it softly behind me. The room was messy, clothing tossed about, take-out containers on one counter, a stack of Sebastian's previously published books piled up on the dresser next to some loose paperwork.

But I quickly realized this couldn't be Sebastian's room.

For one thing, the bed—while unmade—was still covered in linens, and since Sebastian had been killed in his bed, the linens and mattress would have been removed. The DO NOT DISTURB sign on the door had kept anyone from tidying up in here, but there was no mistaking that the contents of this room belonged to a woman.

A lacy bra dangled over the back of a chair, and while Sebastian had his share of ladies cooing over him, the bra coupled with high heels, several dresses, and some makeup on the nightstand told me I had just come into a room that definitely didn't belong to Sebastian.

Which meant this must be Melody's room.

Not *exactly* the person I'd wanted to investigate, but now that I was in here, I wasn't going to throw away the opportunity. I kept my ear tuned for noises in the hall, then slowly moved around the space trying to see if she had helpfully left out any notes that said *I killed Sebastian, and here's why.*

I wasn't quite *that* lucky, but what I did zero in on were the papers littering the top of the dresser. I flipped through them, finding printed itineraries for the trip and a list of room assignments I'd sent Deacon before the group arrived. As I skimmed over it, my brows drew together in confusion.

Sure enough, Sebastian had been booked for this room, number 203, and Melody must have taken the room across the hall that was originally intended for Deacon, number 204. So when she'd said she never should have let him swap rooms, she'd meant swap with *her*?

Maybe their rooms had just been shuffled around after booking; certainly the inn manager could have addressed requests as people arrived. There were plenty of logical reasons for people to end up in different places, especially given Sebastian's insistence on a good view. But if Sebastian had *died* because he was in the wrong room, was *Melody* the intended victim?

Or had Sebastian been moved intentionally to make it easier for the killer to get to him, since Melody's original room was right next to the fire escape?

I set the itinerary down and picked up another document, this one a bank statement. Melody's name was on top—confirming my suspicion that this was her room—but there was also a note saying that the account was managed on behalf of Backyard Birdman LLC.

I was a bit perplexed. Hadn't Melody *just* taken over as Sebastian's manager after Deacon got fired? This statement was over a month old and showed a robust savings of thousands of dollars.

But why would Melody have been handling that kind of money on Sebastian's behalf if she hadn't been his manager at the time?

Floorboards creaked in the hallway, and I panicked. The room was large, but there weren't a ton of options for hiding, and if those steps were coming this way, I wouldn't be able to get out of the room without being seen.

I dropped to the floor and squirmed under the bed, hoping the draping bed skirt would hide me from observant eyes. It also meant I could barely see what was going on in the room.

The door to the bedroom opened and I sucked in a breath, trying to keep myself calm and hoping that all my various parts were safely tucked under the bed. This would be the worst possible time for my mischievous magic to act up, so I tried to focus on deep, soothing breaths rather than the idea of getting caught.

Decidedly masculine shoes entered, with a thick sole, military-style boots. The boots moved in much the same path I had originally taken, obviously scouring the room for something.

A hand rifled through a suitcase on the floor, and I held my breath. The person moved away from the suitcase empty-handed and then stood in front of the dresser for quite some time.

After what felt like an eternity, the boots moved back in the direction of the suite's door and vanished back into the hallway. I waited for a full minute before wriggling back out from under the bed, and my gaze immediately landed on the dresser.

The bank statement was gone.

It had been right on top when I'd gone into hiding, and now it was gone.

I didn't have much time to reflect on The Case of the Missing Bank Statement, because footfalls came back in the direction of the room.

"*Seriously?*" I hissed under my breath. "Remind me never to do this again," I added to no one in particular.

Back under the bed—and just in the nick of time, as the door quietly whispered open and a *different* pair of male feet entered, these ones wearing what looked like beat-up sneakers. I'd been so sure it would be the same person that now I had even more questions than before.

This person made a beeline for the suitcase on the floor, and once again I held my breath, just begging my magic to behave itself a few more minutes.

Whoever was visiting this time was not on a mission of finding something, however. He buried something *under* Melody's clothing and then wasted no time at all ducking back out of the room.

I waited one minute. Two. Surely the moment I got out from under the bed, this time Melody herself would come waltzing into the room. Instead, everything was quiet, and I finally got out from my hiding spot. I knew I had to get out of here or risk getting caught. Luck and magic wouldn't make me invisible forever, but I needed to know what had been buried in the suitcase.

Lifting one of Melody's dresses up, I spotted a pair of black leather gloves.

Black leather gloves that appeared to be stained with blood.

# Chapter Nineteen

I raced home, my thoughts a blur. I tried to make sense of what I'd learned as I fed Bob his dinner and scarfed down a quick bite of some leftover pasta I had in the fridge.

I needed a distraction to let my thoughts run wild, and the best way I knew how to do that was to make some tea. I headed downstairs to my tea storage and pulled out the list of teas we had nearly emptied at the shop that day. I was stunned by the sheer volume of tea sales we had made. I'd been confident that the iced tea would sell well on a hot, sunny day, but what I hadn't been prepared for was the number of people who had wanted to buy the loose teas to take home with them.

I'd also nearly sold out of my reusable travel cups and ceramic mugs. I was going to need to place a new order tomorrow, which I had been sure I wouldn't need to do for months.

Today had been a *very* good day for business, which made my heart happy. One of my main worries after moving here had been that I wouldn't be able to keep Eudora's legacy with the store alive, and it was becoming obvious day after day that I was not only succeeding but perhaps even exceeding all the great work she had done for the store. Modernizing it for the new generation, allowing for online sales, and establishing a social media presence had taken us further than I ever could have imagined the little shop going, and I hadn't even been in charge for a full year.

Yes, there were going to be lulls, and yes, it was far too soon for me to start congratulating myself. I did, however, feel a spark of inspiration while thinking about all the positives. I wanted to make a tea specifically to thank our customers and to embrace my aunt's memory of giving.

I filled up some jumbo freezer bags of the teas I needed to restock—there were simply too many for me to use jars—and set those bags on the stairs leading back up to the main floor so I could grab them later. Then, rather than going to Eudora's big book of recipes or checking one of the recipes on a card inside the premade mixed teas, I grabbed the big glass mixing bowl I used to make tea and took it over to the ingredient shelf with me.

I decided that whatever spoke to me from the big glass jars and metal tins was what I would use to make this new tea.

Since I was a big fan of black tea, I started there for my base, filling the bowl with some big scoops of the rich-smelling leaves. There was just something about black tea that *smelled* like tea to me—not quite as earthy-grassy as green tea, not as light as white tea. I knew most of my friends had grown up trying a basic black tea as their very first (an orange pekoe was a classic first tea), and I always gravitated toward it as my favorite.

Of course, growing up around Eudora meant I'd learned quickly about different tea bases and all the most common blends. Not a lot of preteens grew up on rooibos mixes or jasmine handpicked by their adventurous aunt on a different continent.

Black teas were better paired with sweet or citrus mixes instead of fruitier offerings, which usually went well with green or white. I was going to buck that trend, though, because I adored the way freeze-dried strawberry tasted with the black tea.

I grabbed the strawberries, some vanilla sugar, some lemon rind, and elderflower. The white elderflower petals and the subdued pink hue of the strawberry would make the loose tea look beautiful and eye-catching, while the strawberry would help infuse the liquid with a rosy shade.

I brought all my ingredients back to the table and started to mix them together. I roughly chopped the strawberries to make the pieces smaller so each scoop was sure to get some. Even though the berries were no longer fresh, the freeze-drying process had locked that summery sweetness in, so as I chopped, the air was filled with the tart and candy-like fragrance of fresh berries.

The lemon peel had been dehydrated so it would stay preserved longer, and as I dropped the long, bright-yellow strands into the mixture, my fingertips came away smelling of sunlight and lemonade.

The sugary vanilla made me think of fresh sugar cookies, and the elderflower had a unique, bittersweet and almost spicy scent, with a hint of honey as the fragrance lingered in the air. I mixed all the ingredients together until the bowl resembled beautiful confetti. I smiled at my work, proud that I had created something new and wholly original to honor my aunt's legacy and to thank the people who had helped me keep it alive.

Grabbing an empty storage tin from the bottom shelf, I filled it up and put a fresh label on the outside—the first one on the shelf with my writing on it—that said *Gra-tea-tude*.

The remaining mixture in the bowl went to a big bag for me to take to the store tomorrow and give away to anyone who made a purchase. I'd fill up some twenty-five-gram bags when I got to work in the morning.

Making the tea was the most relaxed I'd felt in days. The stresses that had been weighing me down had vanished, if only for a little bit, and when I stepped away from my worktable, there was nothing floating in the air around my head.

Bob was watching me from the top step of the staircase, his striped orange tail flicking. He didn't particularly enjoy the basement and rarely came down even if I was there, but he did like to keep an eye on me while I worked.

I didn't blame him; my general opinion of basements was that they were dark, spooky, and full of spiders. Being a town in the middle of the woods in the Pacific Northwest meant that there was no escaping the spiders. I couldn't do much about that, but I'd established a rule with them: if I don't see you, you can keep eating any critters you find inside.

The agreement seemed to work for the most part, though admittedly there had been one time when I pulled a canister of tea off the shelf and a big brown spider and I shared a mutual moment of abject horror before we both ran off. I never saw her again, but I assumed she was still somewhere in the house, avoiding me just as carefully as I avoided her.

I put all my bags of tea into a basket and carried them upstairs, putting them by the front door to take with me tomorrow. Bob trailed after me, sniffing my legs and the hem of my dress with intense interest, since I'd brought up foreign basement smells with me.

It was a good reminder that I was still wearing my little sundress, and while it had been a sweet and charming choice for my morning meeting with Rich, it didn't feel like an appropriate choice for a stakeout. It certainly hadn't been great for scurrying under a bed several times. But standing in front of my closet, I had to ask an even bigger question: what *was* an appropriate outfit for a stakeout?

My immediate thought was all black, perhaps some kind of turtleneck, but then I wondered if that might be more avant-garde beat poet or cat burglar rather than the ideal for sitting in a car for hours.

Plus a turtleneck would be much too hot, given the sticky humidity still clinging in the air. We were going to be punished for these nice sunny days with one heck of a storm in the next twenty-four hours, I could feel it in my bones.

I grabbed a pair of black capris that I would normally wear for yoga but would be comfortable if we did have to sit for hours. I topped them with a cute, lightweight sweater in a baby-blue shade. It was made of super-fine yarn, so while it had long sleeves and an off-the-shoulder neckline, it wouldn't be overly hot to wear. I had no idea if it was the right choice, but it looked cute and casual, which was the right vibe for this not-a-date event.

Heading back downstairs with my orange shadow in tow, I brewed up a fresh pot of coffee and was just filling a thermos with it when a knock sounded at my door. For a moment I paused, recalling Deacon's sudden appearance the day before. I was expecting Rich, but that didn't necessarily mean I should assume it *was* Rich.

When I opened the door a crack and saw the familiar tangle of Rich's unruly curls and his whiskey-colored eyes, I couldn't help but break out in a smile as I opened the door the rest of the way. "Good, it is you."

"Do you want me to come up with a secret knock or something so you don't need to check next time? A password, maybe?"

I held open the door, and he came in. "You're kidding, but these days that doesn't seem like such a bad idea."

"Okay, I propose *Bubbles*."

"Bubbles?" I gave him an incredulous look, not sure I dared ask why he had selected this particular passcode, but the curiosity was too much. "*Why?*"

"She was my favorite Powerpuff Girl."

"Oh my god." I rolled my eyes.

"Would you prefer *Buttercup?*"

I thrust the thermos into his hand. "You are still twelve years old, I swear."

Bob agreed, announcing, "Brow. *Mrreoow*."

"I think he wants to come with us," Rich said.

"Of course he wants to come with us. Bob always wants to come. But we're not bringing a cat on a stakeout. I can't believe I, the woman with a space-age cat backpack, have to be the one to set that boundary."

"It wouldn't be his first time investigating a murder," Rich reminded me.

I gave a little shudder, recalling the time Bob had inadvertently helped me find a body. I hoped to never relive that particular adventure.

"I think he's going to have to sit this one out."

Rich leaned over and scratched Bob behind his ears. "Sorry, pal, I did my best."

Bob gave a happy little *brr* sound and then wandered off into the living room, where he settled onto the couch, obviously none too upset over being left out of our plans.

I locked up the house and followed Rich to his car, which was the definition of nondescript. It was navy blue but might have been black or gray or dark green, depending on the light and how hard you looked at it. I couldn't even have made a guess of the brand; it was just a standard sedan that could have belonged to any cop or soccer mom or first-time car owner. It had been parked behind my store for months on and off, and yet it still felt like the first time I was seeing it.

As if reading my puzzled expression, Rich chuckled. "Eudora."

"Hmm?"

"Eudora put a spell on the car. It helps keep it from being too recognizable, so the longer you look at it, the harder it is to describe. It's pretty handy when you don't want anyone to notice you."

"Well, *that* is a cool use of magic. I wonder how she did that."

Rich shrugged. "Beats me; I'm just glad it still works even though she's gone. It's actually very advantageous in my line of work that no one knows they're being watched or followed because they can't quite remember if they've seen the car before or not."

"I could see that being very beneficial."

He opened the car door for me and waited until I was sitting before handing me the thermos I'd completely forgotten I'd given to him. While he was circling the car, I glanced around the interior. I'd been expecting it to be messy. His apartment was clean, but I knew how much time he spent in the car, so I'd imagined it being full of fast-food wrappers and discarded drink containers. Instead, it was neat as a pin and smelled like the vanilla car deodorizer shaped like a pine tree hanging from his rearview mirror.

Had Rich cleaned his car out just for tonight's stakeout? I couldn't be sure, but the dust-free interior and suspiciously spotless fabric on the seats and floorboards made me think he'd taken it to a carwash at some point between our meeting this morning and him picking me up tonight.

Really, it was the completely clean floor mats that convinced me I was right, because considering how much it had rained the last few weeks, there was simply no way the mats were that clean unless he'd just done them.

I decided not to tease him about it, but I did smile to myself as I leaned across the front seat to lift his door handle and push the door open as he arrived at it. From that angle I spotted a small cooler sitting in the back, behind my seat.

"Did you bring snacks?" I asked, craning my neck to get a better look at the cooler.

"Can't have a stakeout without snacks, Winchester. That's amateur hour."

"And here I thought I was being so clever bringing us coffee."

"Hey, I never look a caffeinated gift horse in the mouth."

Dusk was barely falling as Rich turned around at the top of the street—since Lane End House was very literally named, there was nothing past it—and headed back into town. It was a short drive to the B and B on Apple Lane, but it took longer than expected with how crowded the streets were even now. Tourists and locals alike had turned Main Street into a party, with blockades set up to cordon off about six solid blocks from the grocery store all the way down to the gas station.

While most of the stores were closed, a few had opted to have evening hours or to set up booths outside and sell wares in a market-style environment. Seeing how busy it was, I knew next year I'd have to devise a plan to take advantage of all this foot traffic, but for today I wasn't upset about my plan to close early. Most shops had done the same to allow their staff time to go out and enjoy the holiday festivities.

People up and down the block had glow-stick necklaces and bracelets or combinations of the two they'd turned into crowns. Kids ran amok with sparklers waving in the air, and people sang along to pop hits being played by a cover band at the far end of the street. I couldn't see the band, but the acoustics of Main Street formed a kind of tunnel that brought sound downhill toward the grocery store, so as Rich navigated us away from the street festival, I could still perfectly hear a decent rendition of "Jack and Diane."

I wondered if Daphne and Imogen were out enjoying themselves, or if Honey was taking her mother around to show her just how much the town loved celebrating holidays. While I was missing my first Independence Day party, I had already experienced a good number of holiday events in Raven Creek. Halloween and Christmas were huge ones, but the town had even gone out of its way to plan activities for

Arbor Day and put on a celebration in November for the anniversary of Washington's statehood. That was when I'd learned that my house was actually older than the state, which made me extra impressed that it still existed.

Of course, Lane End House had gone through a lot of different phases, so only a small portion of the current house was what had originally been constructed, but it still gave me immense pride to be living in something that had evolved alongside my family tree.

The further away we got from Main, the quieter it got, and once we pulled onto Apple Street, all we could hear of the festivities was the faint thump of the band's bass and the occasional loud peal of laughter or cheering.

Rich parked a few houses down from the B and B and rolled the windows down just slightly before he turned the key off. Now that the sun was down, the humidity had dissipated, but there was still a thick, warm scent lingering in the air.

I pulled my hair away from my face, tying it into a messy bun on the top of my head so I could comfortably lean back and my neck wouldn't get sticky from the heat left in the evening. It seemed there wasn't going to be any air conditioning.

I caught Rich glancing over at me while I did my hair, but he looked away immediately when I turned my head in his direction.

The sky was the same deep purple-blue as a bruise, with fading hints of pink and lilac to the west. A few clouds had cropped up since I'd left work, but it still looked clear and promised to be a perfect night for fireworks. And since I had a pretty good idea how much the town spent on fireworks—after all, I technically paid for them—I anticipated it was going to be a good show.

Rich leaned his seat back slightly, and I did the same.

"Okay, what now?" I asked.

"We watch and we wait."

While I'd fundamentally understood that a stakeout was just sitting in a car and waiting, very little could have prepared me for just how astonishingly boring an actual stakeout was.

Rich and I sat in the car for close to two hours, watching the B and B. I took that time to fill him in on what I'd learned during my time at the inn earlier, and while he grumbled loudly about me doing *something so stupid*, he certainly seemed interested in what fragments I had picked up.

"Sounds like Melody might be in a little trouble with money, based on what you heard at the river and this thing with the missing bank statement. Embezzlement, maybe? Seems to me like she was up to no good."

"Embezzlement, you think?" Hadn't Deacon implied that Melody had only been interested in Sebastian's money? Not that I was necessarily taking his word for any of this. If the room swap had happened and Melody had been the intended victim, then Deacon was *still* a logical suspect.

"It would explain why her name was on an LLC fund. You said before she wasn't in charge until this week, so that does seem a little suspect."

"I'm more interested in the *gloves*. Were they the ones used in Sebastian's murder, or were they just meant to *look* like that?"

"I think we're going to need to let the police figure that particular plot out; that's above our pay grade. I'm curious to see what she gets up to tonight, though."

There was plenty of activity—the inn was fully booked with tourists; the murder hadn't changed that—so guests were coming and going all night, most heading in the direction of Main Street and others returning from that same direction. People carried ice cream cones or bags of popcorn or twisted potatoes on a stick. The smell of cinnamon-sugar mini doughnuts wafting through the partially open window nearly did me in.

My stomach growled loudly.

Rich chuckled. "Guess it's snack time."

He leaned behind me, his shoulder grazing mine as he rummaged around in the little cooler. He handed me a cold can of soda and a miniature bag of pretzels. While it wasn't street fair food, I was grateful for the bubbles in the soda and the salty goodness of the pretzels.

"Do you really do this every night?" I asked, munching happily on one of the pretzels.

"Every night? No. It's not always necessary for every case, but at least once or twice a week I have to sit in front of a seedy motel somewhere, or follow someone's husband or wife to see what they're up to. I think people hear *private investigator* and assume it's cool or glamorous, but it's really just a lot of waiting around for people to do something stupid. And if someone is hiding something, they're going to do something stupid eventually. It's just a matter of patience to be there to catch it."

"Sounds exhausting."

"When I'm by myself, I usually have headphones in and listen to a podcast or audiobook. Helps pass the time. Not sure there's any other way I would have read all the Wheel of Time books; those things are *dense*."

Being a bookstore owner, I was familiar with the epic fantasy series. "That is certainly a commitment."

"I've been listening to Stephen King's Dark Tower books recently. I like to pick a lengthy series; gives me something to look forward to if the stakeouts take a few days or more. But I'd say ninety-nine percent of my business is either catching cheating spouses or busting employees who are trying to take advantage of insurance policies. I do missing-persons cases privately now and then, and I sometimes help the police department in a consulting role. It pays the bills, keeps me busy."

"You don't really talk about your time with the police department very much," I said. Since he'd brought the police up, it seemed like a fair time to broach the topic.

"I guess there's not that much to say. I was with the Barneswood PD as a detective for twelve years, which is a limited field in a small town, but Barneswood has a little bit of drug-related trouble, so that kept my attention most of the time. The problem was I could only show up to so many scenes that involved an overdose or a kid taking drugs and crashing their tree into a car, and it just caught up to me. I showed up one day to a tough scene, and that was it for me. Put in my notice as soon as that case was closed and never looked back. Maybe it's me being naïve or small town—I don't know. I just don't think I can wrap my head around how city cops get used to it. It made me too sad. Ruined my marriage in a way too. I kept bringing those big feelings home with me until there wasn't room for her."

I hadn't expected him to open up quite so much. It was a fascinating insight into the man Rich had been before he'd come back into my life.

"And it's easier? Following around cheating husbands?"

"Heck yeah. That doesn't really do much to shake my faith in people. As long as there have been marriages, there have been cheating husbands."

I sipped my drink. "Tell me about it."

"Oh, man. Phoebe, I'm so sorry, that was completely thoughtless of me."

I laughed. "I'm pretty sure it was more thoughtless of him. I think you're safe."

"Still. Foot-in-mouth disease is a real problem for me. I'm sorry."

"Eh, don't be. You're right, there are always going to be husbands who cheat; it's sort of an unfortunate but reality-based statistic. I was just unlucky enough to be married to one. And now I'm not."

He tipped his can toward me and I raised mine, clinking it with a tinny *chunk* sound. "Cheers to failed first marriages," he said. "Better luck next time."

I flushed, and I was glad we were in a dark car so he couldn't see how red my face was. Before I was forced to think of anything clever to say, Rich said, "Uh-oh, heads-up. Here's our girl."

I put my can in the drink holder of the car and sat up straighter in my seat. Sure enough, there was Melody, jogging down the front steps of the B and B. Her walk had a determined speed to it, and she was wearing a dark-colored hoodie. She pulled the hood up as she headed in the direction of Main Street.

Rich leaned over and undid my seat belt, a move that caught my breath in my throat. I stared at him; he was so close I could smell the fresh soap on his skin.

"Wh-what now?" I asked.

"Now we follow her."

# Chapter Twenty

A ny sense of boredom I'd felt in the car was completely gone the moment Rich and I started to trail Melody from a safe distance. My heart was beating a mile a minute, and my thoughts were going even faster. I had anticipated we would keep an eye on her from the car; I hadn't thought this would become an on-foot mission.

Maybe I *should* have worn my black turtleneck.

Though that might have made me stand out even more, considering just how nice out it was. The oppressive humidity of the morning was gone and had been replaced by a pleasant warmth that made it the perfect evening to be outside and enjoying the weather and festive gaiety.

That seemed to be precisely what Melody had in mind. Despite the hood covering her head and the fast-paced walk that implied she was in a hurry, we discovered very quickly as we trailed behind her that she was on her way to Main Street.

She made a brief stop at Lansing Grocery, but Rich and I held back at the edge of the parking lot. Just when I began to get antsy with worry that she might have snuck out a back door or slipped away when other customers were leaving, she reemerged. Whatever she'd purchased—if anything—was small enough she didn't have it in a bag.

Continuing down Main Street, she slipped in and out of the crowd. Her dark hoodie made her hard to see, but Rich was locked onto her like a homing missile. I, on the other hand, was not accustomed to trailing people and kept getting distracted by the sights and sounds around me.

The band was back at it again, singing Stevie Nicks's "Edge of Seventeen." They had brought up a female singer to do the song. The voice had a familiar quality to it, and when I squinted up toward the stage, still several blocks away, I realized why.

Daphne. My sweet little Daphne was up on the stage with the band. She had tossed on a flowy, sheer robe over her Americana ensemble and had let her blonde curls hang loose around her shoulders. I couldn't believe the maturity in her voice as she sang the classic rock tune. She had the same raspy siren sound to her singing that Stevie did, just a little younger and a little less world-weary.

I'd had no idea Daphne even sang.

A hand clamped around mine, and I almost jerked it away out of habit until I realized it was Rich. "Come on, gumshoe, she's getting away."

We weaved through the crowd, and while I was no longer dawdling behind, Rich still kept my hand in his. It was nice, and familiar, even if I'd never held *his* hand before. This was the kind of human connection I'd been without since leaving Blaine, and it surprised me sometimes how much the simplest touch could scratch an itch for intimacy I hadn't known I'd missed so badly.

There must have been hundreds of people on Main Street. Some I recognized and waved to out of habit. I was sure Rich would have told me not to draw attention to us, but I thought it would have been weirder if I'd pretended *not* to see Charlie Bravebird from the pet store or the Tanakas who owned the plant shop next to mine.

I spotted Dierdre Miller's bright-red hair at one point but did not make an effort to get her attention or wave to her.

The air was filled with aromas that reminded me of a carnival. One booth was making kettle corn, which smelled sweet and salty and buttery all at once and made my mouth water. People passed by with cut-open bags of tortilla chips bedecked with a variety of nacho toppings like sour cream, salsa, jalapeño, and ground beef.

In the parking lot, where the summer garden center had stationed itself, a few games had been set up, including a dunk tank, where the town mayor—already sopping wet—was shouting fake insults at kids waiting in line with balls to throw at the target.

Melody didn't stop for any of this. She dipped past a tween girl waving a sparkler and skirted around a man wearing a flag-printed cowboy hat. When she was almost to the stage, I assumed she would have to stop, but she didn't. She took a hard left into a narrow alley between two stores, and for the first time, Rich paused.

"Son of a . . . ," he grumbled. He gave my hand a squeeze and then led us up to the alley entrance. There was no sign of her. We started to follow anyway but had made it only a few steps into the alley entrance when the sound of sneakers on pavement announced someone coming back our direction.

I panicked, thinking we should run, but Rich held my hand firmly, and instead of running, he pulled me up close to him. One moment we were trailing a potential murderer; the next, my back was up against a brick wall, our clasped hands still crushed between our bodies, and before I could get out the *what* that was on my lips, Rich kissed me.

Rich Lofting was kissing me.

My ears were suddenly on fire, and my head felt as light as if it were a whole bushel of helium balloons. A tingling sensation spread from my fingers and toes all the way to the roots of my hair.

The kiss was chaste on the kiss-o-meter scale, but try to tell that to my pounding heart and Jell-O knees. The moment someone brushed past us going back in the direction of the street party, Rich backed away.

He looked as flustered as I felt.

"Sorry about that."

Raising my hand to my mouth, I gently touched my lips as if trying to determine if I had imagined the whole thing. I would be lying if I said I hadn't thought about what my first kiss with Rich would be like, and in absolutely no version of those daydreams had it been like this.

Yet somehow this was better.

"Don't you dare be sorry about that, or I'm going to be furious," I said. "Now let's go after her."

Rich stared at me in dumbfounded silence for a moment before seeming to regain his composure. "Y-yeah. Yes. The person we were following, right."

I was more than a little pleased that even a spur-of-the-moment, pretend-we're-not-tailing-you kiss could melt my bones and turn Rich's brain to mush. It indicated that when we did it again under different circumstances, the chemistry would probably be off the charts.

We headed to the end of the alley opposite where Melody had gone. Whoever had come back through, Rich was pretty certain it hadn't been her, so we continued on our way. We were now slightly behind, but that didn't seem to matter; she was clearly heading west, which was the way she'd been going down Main, so unless that was just to throw us off her scent and she was doubling back, she was still going west. At no point had Melody turned around while we'd been on her tail, and I was pretty sure we were either far enough behind or well concealed by simply being locals at a street fair. She had no reason to believe she was being followed and didn't know who Rich was. We had plenty going in our favor on that front.

As we continued west down Beech Street, the din of the crowd diminished, even though we were only a block from Main and the party. The band was still playing, and though it felt like we had been at this for hours, Daphne was just finishing the final bars of her song. They kept her up for one more, and once the Stevie Nicks cover ended, she started to sing Pat Benatar's "Hit Me With Your Best Shot." It did not escape my awareness that Daphne hadn't even been alive when these songs were released, but she sang them as if they were radio standards.

Not only was it quieter on Beech, it was also darker. As we continued westward away from the party, we entered a more residential area. Here the smell of barbecue wafted toward us from back patios, and despite the lateness of the hour, kids ran around on the street, glow sticks waving. The fireworks were slated to start around eleven, and folks were already sitting on lawn chairs in their front yards, ready for a convenient and comfortable view of the light show that would be launched from the safety of the city hall parking lot a few blocks away from Main.

Rich lightly touched my arm and pointed up ahead, where a figure was moving at a steady pace down the sidewalk. The way she walked and the black blob of her hooded head told me that we'd caught up to Melody again, but Rich slowed his step, and I instinctively understood why. There was no easy way to blend in here, no crowd to hide within. If Melody looked back, we needed to look like we were just out for a casual evening stroll.

I was grateful there were so many people still outside bustling around, because it lent some credence to our projected cover story. *Lots* of people were out for walks or going back and forth across the street to check in with neighbors. We didn't look out of place.

We trailed behind Melody for another three blocks. The residential lots steadily got wider, and finally it was pretty clear we were almost on the edge of town. The street ended, turning back toward Main, and Melody kept going, even where the sidewalk became a sandy dirt trail headed into the woods.

Here we drew to a stop, because there was simply no way we could keep going after her into the trees and not make it very obvious we were following her.

"Where the heck is she even going?" I asked, almost as much to myself as to Rich.

He glanced around the area as if asking himself the same question, then his gaze locked on something just off the road, and he nudged me in that direction.

The sign had seen better days, with peeling paint around the letters and an overall sun-bleached fade that forced me to squint at it. It didn't help that it was surrounded by a thick swath of vines. But once I made out the words, one mystery was solved, only to be replaced by a brand-new one.

Melody had gone into the Bullock Memorial Bird and Wildlife Conservation Area.

The new mystery was—why?

# Chapter
# Twenty-One

Sweet Peach's was still open when we wandered back into town, with a special outdoor seating area set up where people could watch the fireworks. It looked like they had pulled some old booths out of storage, because the leatherette seating was cracked and discolored, but no one seemed to mind.

Rich and I grabbed one of the empty outdoor seats, but the way they were set up meant we had to sit side by side facing out to the street rather than across from each other.

I was hyperaware of his very existence as we pretended to read the menus we already knew so well. Jaspreet, a newer waitress, came out to take our order, and before she left to get our food, she set an unlit sprinkler for each of us on the table.

The band was winding down, playing a Boyz II Men cover, and while I couldn't see Main from where we were sitting, I had no doubt people were giddily slow dancing in the street. It was a truly delightful evening and a good reminder of why this town was so magical to live in, but I couldn't quite get out of my head the bizarre events that had led us here tonight.

"Do all your stakeouts end like that?" I asked, drumming my fingernails on the laminate cover of the tabletop.

"I have it on pretty good authority that *none* of my previous stakeouts ended in an on-foot pursuit that took me to a bird sanctuary."

I nodded.

The bird sanctuary was actually an old run-down estate that had belonged to George Bullock, the same precocious millionaire who had sold my aunt Eudora all the land and buildings he owned on Main Street. He had been famously reclusive, and after losing his wife and having a falling-out with his only son, he had decided the best thing to do would be to keep the properties with someone who would love Raven Creek as much as he had.

Evidently, he'd also been an avid nature enthusiast, because when he died, one of the conditions of his will was that rather than selling his property, the town was to turn it into a bird and nature conservancy area.

For a while the old mansion had been used to do lectures, demonstrations, and classes on conservancy and local birds and wildlife as well as basic tutorial sessions on how to care for injured animals. I remember doing at least one or two summer day camp sessions there in my youth and being totally in awe of the rehabbed owl and falcon ambassadors.

But in spite of the money George had left to keep the place running and the money Eudora had regularly siphoned into maintenance, there simply hadn't been enough interest to keep the institute part of the conservancy open. They couldn't exactly justify paying a full staff to stay on board when they couldn't fill classrooms, and Raven Creek was a bit out of the way for school tour groups.

It had been about fifteen years since the actual education center had closed, though I understood there was a local caretaker who tended to the maintenance of the house and grounds. Since the property was closed to the public and accessible only to visiting naturalists with a special pass, I had never seen the place as an adult. I'd heard people around town talking about how it was such a waste of a great location and how the mansion should have been torn down to make way for something else.

I disagreed. It had been George's goal to keep that place for the birds, and so it was kept. Was it a bit weird to have a gated-off mansion tucked back out of sight from the town? Sure. But what the heck else would that land be good for? It was remote, practically outside town limits, and while Raven Creek had a decent-sized population, it wasn't as if there were such a dire need for housing that anything new needed to be created.

Plus it was conservancy land, so it was a moot point. It was, quite literally, for the birds.

The real question was, what did Melody want or need on that property?

"What's funny to me is that with Sebastian's fame and popularity, I'm sure he and his crew would have been given a special pass to the park if they'd just asked for it." I was surprised I hadn't thought to suggest it to them, given his area of focus. Honestly, I usually forgot the conservancy was even there.

"Do you think there's an innocent explanation for it?" Rich asked.

"Like what? I mean, I'd love to give her the benefit of the doubt, but she's sneaking onto private property in the middle of the night, bundled up like she's off to steal cars, and all this while she's supposedly grieving the death of her boss and friend?" An idea occurred to me. "Maybe she *did* kill Sebastian and went to the conservancy to hide the weapon. Or maybe she found those gloves in her suitcase and decided she needed to get rid of them."

Rich mulled this over. "That's certainly a possibility, and something we'll need to present to Detective Martin so she and Detective

Kim can go check it out." That part I was on board with. It was one thing to trail someone we suspected of being involved in the murder, quite another to get ourselves tangled up in anything involving possible physical evidence. Plus I still needed to tell the detectives what I'd found at the inn earlier this evening.

I really wasn't sure what I'd thought we'd discover by following Melody, but things weren't looking great for her at the moment.

And yet there was something that perplexed me more. She had been *so* distraught when she learned about Sebastian's death, and it hadn't felt like acting or a fake-out. I had genuinely believed her tears. There was also still the matter of Deacon to consider. He, more than Melody, had had the motive to kill his former business partner and love interest. And he just kept disappearing on me, which felt highly suspicious.

If someone had put those gloves in Melody's room to frame her, maybe that someone was Deacon.

The first whistling firework spiraled up into the sky as Jaspreet brought out our food. For a moment, Rich and I just sat together, shoulders leaning in against each other and delicious diner food in front of us. It still wasn't our first official date, and yet it somehow felt like our thousandth. Being next to him was so comfortable that it was difficult to imagine being anywhere else *with* anyone else.

We might be on the trail of a killer, but it was also a wonderful moment to pause and be completely aware of the present. I had never felt so at home before. Not when I was with Blaine and not in Chicago with my family. This just felt so unbelievably *right*. I had come to Raven Creek because of two deep losses—my marriage and my aunt—but in coming here I had gained something beautiful and life-changing that I didn't regret for a second.

I reached over and took Rich's hand in mine, giving it a squeeze.

He glanced over at me and I rested my chin on his shoulder, marveling at the way the technicolor fireworks reflected in his eyes. His eyelashes were so long they made me jealous.

"Hey, you," he said, so quietly I could barely hear him over the crackle of explosives and the distant siren of an ambulance.

"Thank you."

"Thank me, for what?"

Wait. Fireworks. Distant and the growing sound of an ambulance.

I sat upright. "Do you hear that?"

"Talk about a subject change," he said, shaking off the romantic daze that had been washing over him. "Is that—"

"Sirens."

We listened a moment, wondering if there had been an accident at the party—perhaps someone had passed out or there had been a fight. Or a more horrible option to imagine was something going wrong with the fireworks. But they continued to bloom in the sky, sparkling night flowers in shades of red, blue, green, and a gold. The oohs and aahs of the Main Street crowd were audible even here, a block away.

The siren advanced, and then a different kind of red-and-blue flash zipped past the end of the block.

There were plenty of things in that direction, lots of homes and small businesses where an ambulance could be headed. But Rich and I shared a quick and immediate glance of concern.

"The B and B," he said first.

"The B and B," I answered back.

# Chapter Twenty-Two

S ince we were on foot, even at a jog we arrived at the Primrose Inn well after the ambulance had already gotten there. A small crowd of locals and a few guests of the hotel were milling around on the sidewalk, but Rich and I had no problem getting to the front.

Overhead, fireworks continued to whistle and boom, dulling much of the chatter around us. Someone was on their phone trying to find a new room to book, and I heard them grumble, ". . . can't be expected to stay somewhere after *two* murders."

A chill crept up my spine, and all I could think of were Honey's haunting words.

*The wrong person died.*

Rich had his hand on my back, angling me toward the front of the B and B. We had beat the police here, and we didn't even need to come up with an excuse to get inside; no one stopped us.

Unlike the morning of Sebastian's murder or even my visit earlier today, it felt like a funeral home inside. There were no clusters of guests arranged in different areas of the lobby; in fact, it seemed like most of the folks staying here tonight were only just beginning to realize something was wrong, as a few bleary-eyed patrons peeked down from upstairs mumbling about the lights.

I suspected, given the festivities, most people who were staying at the inn were out at the street party still. The owner of the B and B hovered nervously in the hallway outside one of the main floor bedrooms, still clutching the phone she must have used to make the call. Her face looked ashen, and she was muttering something to herself about not believing this could happen.

Rich approached her, putting a gentle hand on her shoulder. She almost jumped out of her skin, letting out a surprised yelp. "Oh, good heavens, Rich, you scared me half to death. I'm so sorry." Her hand, still with the cordless phone in it, went to her chest as if to check that her heart was still beating. She glanced past Rich to me, but she didn't seem to recognize me. Raven Creek was a small town, but not so small that I'd met every single person who lived here.

"Are you here with the police?" she asked me, and looked at Rich to see if he might confirm.

Rich shook his head. "Phoebe had some professional guests staying here, and we were just in the area and wanted to see what was going on."

This, as vague as it was, seemed to satisfy the woman, who gave a nod and gestured toward the back bedroom. "One of the guests had received a call." She held up the phone like perhaps she wanted to prove this point. "I went and knocked, but he didn't answer. I tried again, and normally I'd just leave it, but the caller did say it was quite urgent, so I tried the door, and it wasn't locked. I called his name, and when he didn't answer, I looked into the room, and . . ." Her voice drifted off and was replaced by an unexpectedly loud sob.

"Hey now, Audrey, it's okay." Rich took her gently by the arm and guided her toward the library area, helping to settle her onto one of the overstuffed couches and taking the phone from her hand.

"I just can't believe this has happened twice. I'm going to be ruined."

I wanted to allay her concerns, but I'd heard what people outside were whispering, and it was hard to blame them for not wanting to continue to stay at the inn. I probably wouldn't want to spend the night somewhere that two people had been recently murdered either. Not when the police hadn't tracked down who had done the first killing.

Were the two deaths connected?

"Can you tell me what you saw?" Rich asked Audrey in a calm, steady tone.

"Someone had . . . someone had st-st-sta . . ." Her voice drifted into a fit of hiccups and incomprehensible crying sounds. I had heard enough to gather that the victim, like Sebastian, had been stabbed.

Not a natural death, then.

If the murders were similar, there was a very real chance they were connected. What else could explain two men being killed in the same inn within forty-eight hours of each other? Unless the killer had a vendetta against Audrey or the B and B, the target was the guests involved and not the inn itself.

"Who was staying in the room?" I asked. I had been certain when I saw the ambulance that something had happened to Melody. She was the one who'd been skulking around all night. Perhaps trouble had followed her home. But Audrey kept saying *him*, which meant Melody wasn't the one lying dead in the main floor bedroom.

"Andrew Bachman. The lawyer. The one who was here asking everyone about their property."

A hundred thoughts went through my head at once, but the one that was blaring in my mind's eye in bright-red neon was a single name: *LEO*.

At least twenty people had been in Lansing Grocery to witness the fight between Leo and the lawyer, and I hadn't been the only one to hear the threats he had made. That was going to stand out to people, especially because of how out of character it was for my friend.

He'd been *so mad* on Amy's behalf at the shop earlier today. I didn't think he would actually have done anything, but his name was going to be connected to this, I felt certain. I also couldn't see how his death was connected to Sebastian's, unless Andrew had been the target all along.

Sebastian had swapped rooms, and even though his room had been assigned to Melody in my notes, maybe it had originally been meant for Andrew? I was beginning to believe that Sebastian hadn't been the killer's intended victim at all.

"Rich," I whispered. "We should go."

"When you just got here?" came a voice from behind us. "Why would you want to leave so soon?"

I turned to see that the voice did indeed belong to Detective Patsy Martin, who was wearing an expression somewhere between annoyed and amused, which she was trying her darndest to show as nothing at all.

I gave her a guilty smile and half wave. "Evening, Detective Martin."

"Mm-hmm," was all she said.

"Patsy," Rich added by way of greeting, going to give his former colleague a quick handshake. She allowed it, so I didn't think we were in *too* much trouble.

"Dare I ask what brings you two to the scene of a murder before even the police could get here?" She looked directly at me rather than Rich, and I knew she was going to think this had all been my idea no matter what Rich said.

"Let's have a quick chat," Rich offered. "Somewhere private."

Detective Martin sighed, then led us to the same small dining room where I had so recently seen the lawyer—Andrew—alive.

When we were all seated around the table, Rich and I gave her the breakdown, from the argument I'd overheard to my discoveries from earlier that afternoon about the gloves to following Melody to the sanctuary, right up to the moment we'd seen the ambulance come to the inn.

Martin listened, her expression shifting between interested, surprised, and frequently very, very annoyed, especially after I detailed going through Melody's room. "You should have come to me immediately after hearing that initial argument so we could have had Melody on our radar," she said, sighing. "I appreciate that you are so keen to help find out what happened to Sebastian, and I know I asked you to keep an eye open to things going on, but I *also* specifically told you not to get yourself into any trouble."

"In fairness, I didn't actually get *in*to any trouble," I said.

She cleared her throat. "Semantics aren't going to be your friend here, Ms. Winchester. And you." She pointed dramatically at Rich. "Of anyone, you should have known better."

"Well, now, we didn't actually know if Melody had any involvement. We followed her just to gauge if she *might* be involved."

"The two of you deserve each other. Wait here and don't touch anything." She got up and went into the hall, where I heard her giving someone directions to go to the sanctuary.

"Do you think Melody is involved in this murder too?" I asked Rich.

He craned his neck to see if Martin was coming back in. "I don't know. Did you get the sense that she had any connection to this lawyer guy?"

I shook my head. "Aside from them staying at the same place, there's nothing. As far as I can tell, I don't think they ever spoke to each other." Melody hadn't been in the room when I'd spoken to Connor and Travis after Sebastian's death; she had been outside.

"Do you know what Audrey was talking about, about him asking people about their properties?"

"Yeah, that's the other thing you should know about. He's apparently representing some big megacorporation who wants to buy up property in town to milk the tourist industry by making everything cookie-cutter. I guess he went to Lansing's to talk to Leo about selling the store, and things got . . . heated."

"Things with *Leo* got heated." Rich clearly didn't believe me.

"If I hadn't seen it with my own two eyes, I'd call me a liar too. But I swear to you, Leo was on the verge of knocking this guy's head off. I've never seen him so mad."

"Why didn't you say anything to Patsy?" he asked.

"Well, she didn't ask me if I knew anyone who had been in an argument with the lawyer, did she? And I'm not about to throw Leo under a bus. You and I both know there's no way he did this."

Rich thought about this briefly, for a moment longer than I would have liked him to.

"Rich. Leo didn't kill anyone."

Rich shook off whatever had stretched out his contemplation. "No, of course. There's no way. But you have to tell Patsy. She's going to find out about this one way or another, and it's better to come from you, who can vouch for his character, than some random person who might blow the whole thing out of proportion."

I groaned. "Yes, you're right. I know you're right."

With timing so perfect she might have a magical gift of her own, Detective Martin returned to the room and stood in the doorway with one hand propped on her hip. "I've got a team going out to scour the sanctuary, see if there's anything there. It would have been helpful for us to know everything earlier; we might have been able to get her in the act of doing something. As it is, we have an APB out for her, and one way or another we'll have ourselves a little chat with

Melody Fairbanks soon enough. Now I heard my name, so I suspect you might have a little more to tell me?" She raised a brow in my direction.

"You might want to talk to Leo Lansing about the lawyer. He didn't do anything, I guarantee you that, but you're going to hear about a bit of a scuffle at the grocery store the other day between Leo and the dead man."

"A scuffle? Like a physical fight?"

I shook my head. "No, though I think Leo probably felt like fighting him. It was a pretty loud disagreement, and I broke it up. The lawyer, Andrew, left, but it was a scene, and I wasn't the only one there. So best you know about it now."

"And do you happen to know if Leo Lansing has an alibi for this evening?" Detective Martin asked.

"I know the store was open later than usual; there's a chance he was still there tonight," I offered.

"Mm-hmm."

I'd been around the detective enough to know she made that particular noise when someone was trying to sell her something she didn't want to buy.

I hoped for Leo's sake he'd been on the sales floor all night with plenty of people to see him, because otherwise I might have just gotten my dear friend into a heaping pile of trouble.

# Chapter Twenty-Three

The dust from the street party had barely settled when news of the second murder began its rapid-fire spread through town. By the time I arrived at Sugarplum Fairy the next morning, Amy was stooped over a newspaper at the front counter.

"Can you believe this?" She shook her head to indicate that she did not believe it, whatever *this* was.

"Hmm?" I hadn't had enough caffeine to participate in guessing games this morning. It had been a long night and I had barely managed to get four hours of sleep. I was going to be a very grump bear today.

Holding up the paper, I saw the headline *Murder Times Two* with a lede that read *Sleepy Raven Creek struck by second homicide in a week. Is anywhere safe?*

While the conjecture was a bit over-the-top for me, they had a point. If two murders could happen in less than five days in *our* little town, then it might be time to see if the sky was falling, because things were looking pretty grim.

"I mean, I didn't like the guy, but I wanted him to leave town. I didn't want him to *die*," Amy said, largely to herself.

I was especially unsettled by the death of Andrew, because I still couldn't come up with a single way he was connected to Sebastian.

Two connected murders in a small town was bad but explainable. Two *unconnected* murders in a small town was going to have people locking their doors at night.

"Oh yeah, I heard about that." I was impressed the newspaper had managed to get an early edition out with the news. We had left the inn at around midnight, and the paper hit porches sometime between four and five.

Someone was burning the midnight oil at the local press office.

Since nothing usually happened in Raven Creek at night, I suspected the more likely case was that the editor of the paper had someone on the inside at the police department. Unless their lead reporter was the killer, which was unlikely but a more fun theory for me to latch on to than worrying about Leo being the new prime suspect.

I scanned the newspaper article upside down as best I could, not wanting Amy to feel I was overly interested. If she asked me questions, I knew I'd be unable to resist telling her the whole truth, and I didn't need anyone other than Rich and Detective Martin knowing I'd been around the inn for both murders. I might start getting a reputation.

Well, I already *had* a reputation, but I didn't need one as a weirdo who stalked crime scenes. Better to be thought of as that eccentric lady with the cat who might be a witch.

If it was good enough for Eudora, it was good enough for me.

I grabbed my boxes of pastries, leaving Amy to read up on all the latest information on the crimes. Thankfully, Andrew Bachman hadn't been internet famous, so I didn't think we'd have a big wave of customers in this morning looking for obscure law books. There was likely still going to be some trickle-down interest in Sebastian, but I also knew that word of a second slaying was going to scare quite a few visitors into leaving town earlier than they'd planned.

Sebastian had wanted to put Raven Creek on the map as the home ground of a rare bird species, and the lawyer had wanted to take advantage of our popularity to turn us into a booming tourist mecca for his clients. So far the only thing they had in common was that their deaths had managed to completely undermine what their goals in life had been for my sleepy little mountain town.

A cleaning crew was out in the streets with massive brooms, sweeping up confetti, discarded glow sticks, and more red plastic cups than I could count. The party had been a huge success, but it had certainly left behind one of the biggest messes I could ever recall seeing. Funny how people could come here and enjoy everything we had to offer but not care if they were leaving things behind worse than when they arrived.

I was glad my property money was going to help keep our streets clean.

I waved to the cleaners, only one of whom noticed—he doffed an imaginary cap in my direction. Back inside the store, I took a moment to appreciate past me and my staff for taking care to keep everything tidy even after the melee it had felt like in here yesterday.

There *were* plenty of empty spaces on the shelves, though, so I needed to focus on getting those taken care of. And since it was Tuesday, I also needed to get the new releases out on the shelves. I'd come in extra early to get as much of this done as I could before the store opened.

First things first. I put Amy's pastries on display in the cooled pastry cabinet, then got my own baked goods in the oven. I started with the Earl Grey shortbread, knowing it was going to be in demand as soon as we opened. I also double-checked to make sure we had plenty of iced tea on hand and made a quick list of things I'd need to order to start keeping extra stock at Amy's place.

Then I headed into the shop's basement. While on paper, it was nice to have the extra storage, the basement under the Earl's Study was not what I would call inviting. A narrow passage led to the extra-large storage room that had once been two separate storage spaces, as our shop had once been two individual buildings that were later merged into one. This was also where the shop's bathroom was, and I had gone more than one day simply not using the bathroom and rushing home after just to avoid coming down here.

It was tidy enough, with aging yellow laminate flooring, some peeling back from floods in the past, and the walls were lined with unfortunate wood paneling that had probably been here since the seventies. It too showed signs of water damage at the bottom, but nothing was moldy or needed to be immediately replaced, so any kind of basement upgrades had been put on the way, way back burner.

A couple of months earlier I had been able to get an enormous collection of books from an estate sale, and we were still slowly adding them to the upstairs collection as needed. All the boxes were piled up on wooden pallets just in case the copious amounts of Washington rain caused anything to back up. The lot of books had cost me thousands of dollars, and while I had already recouped those costs in resale, I wasn't about to risk losing the remaining stock to an act of God. No thank you.

Since the books were all a random mix—intentionally—I just grabbed the first box I could see and brought it to the bottom of the stairs. We'd gone through quite a bit of stock the last few days, and I expected we'd need about three boxes just to fill the holes in the used-books section. The only problem with our basement stock system was that none of the books down here were entered in our online database. This was by design, because we didn't want any online orders to come in for a book that we had no idea how to find. But it also meant that every time we opened a new box of stock, we needed to catalog it all from scratch. That was going to take time. I was grateful that I had entered all our new-release stock into the system ahead of time.

After dragging the three hefty boxes upstairs, I piled them up next to the cash desk so I could work on them while we were open if need be. I swapped out one tray off cookies for another, then dragged the new-release stock out of the office and up to the new-release wall.

I left a few hot-selling titles where they were and moved anything that was a couple of weeks old to the front table—which had been completely picked over by rabid Sebastian Marlow fans. I made them look as neat as possible and added one of our frequently used signs that read *New and Noteworthy*.

For the new-release wall, we had thankfully cultivated an air of chaos that people were accustomed to. Alphabet? We didn't need no stinking alphabet. At least not on this wall.

I unloaded the seven boxes of new-release stock in record time, thanks to my ability to take a slapdash approach. The wall could use a little tweaking later to make the style a bit more cohesive, but for now it was full, and anyone looking for a new book that had come out today wasn't going to leave disappointed.

A few of the new releases were special orders, and I put those aside on the cash desk to have Imogen do the calls and emails later letting people know their books had arrived. I had just enough time to haul the cardboard boxes out to recycling before the store opened to customers.

With a big stack of cardboard in front of my face, I almost didn't notice the thick manila envelope sitting on the back step of the shop. I'd driven in today—rain was in the forecast—so I knew it hadn't been there when I came, and there were only a few darkened raindrops on it from a new wave of bad weather that was just starting.

Someone must have just put it there.

I glanced around me to see if there was anyone around, but there was no sign of whoever had delivered this. Cautiously I tossed the boxes in the recycle bin and collected the envelope before retreating into the store. My curiosity would need to wait, however, because I was two minutes late to open the front door and there was already someone outside, huddling in on themselves against the weather.

I dropped the envelope on the counter in the kitchen so it was out of the way and unlocked the door to let my poor, damp customer in.

To my immediate horror, I realized it was Dierdre.

For a moment I was so gobsmacked to see her darkening my doorway that my manners escaped me. It was only when she cleared her throat and peered around me into the store that I realized I was blocking her entrance and forcing her to stand outside in the rain.

I became suspicious that perhaps she had been the one to dump the envelope on my steps, but that didn't make any sense; why would she come around the front right after sneaking something onto my path like that?

"Dierdre, this is a . . . surprise."

Given what had happened during our last meeting, I was stunned she would want to be within a ten-block radius of me.

"Good morning. Nice to see to you as well, Phoebe." She pushed down her hood and unwrapped a muted pastel scarf she had wrapped around her hair. It was pouring in earnest now, and the street cleaners had vanished. At least it looked like they'd gotten most of their work done before the weather chased them into hiding.

Dierdre took a few steps into the room and nodded toward the tea counter. "I don't suppose it would be too much trouble for you to make me a cup of something?" As soon as the words were out of her mouth, she looked as if she might reconsider them. I was shocked she was willing to take a drink from me, considering that the last time she'd sampled our wares she'd ended up under an honesty spell for several hours.

But she didn't take the request back, and there was none of the usual vicious undercurrent to her words. It didn't feel like she was here to pick a fight with me. I didn't know what had changed in the last couple of days, but I certainly didn't trust it.

"Yes, of course. What would you like?"

"Oh, I trust they're all good. Surprise me." She gave me an unusual look, as if the statement might be a dare, and I suspected she might be trying to catch me giving her magical tea again. While such an open invitation might have led me to pick something adventurous for anyone else, with Dierdre I decided to play it safe and picked a nice jasmine-peppermint blend. "Do you want milk? Sugar."

For a moment her expression became pained, and it occurred to me that perhaps this being-nice-to-me thing was a bit of a struggle for her. Her smile came across tight and forced. "However you think it would taste best."

"Honey, then," I said.

"Sure." She wandered over to one of the tables and pulled out a chair, the metal legs screaming against the tile floor. I winced. I poured the nearly boiling water over Dierdre's tea and checked the time on my watch to let it steep only so long. I added the honey now so the heat would help it melt and evenly distribute the flavor.

"So, um . . . what brings you here?"

"Well, I had originally planned to come by to talk to you about the space for my nephew."

"Oh?"

"Yes. After a bit of discussion about the housing opportunities locally, he has decided that he'd like to rent the apartment over the store."

"Ah." This wasn't at all what I'd expected her to say. "You know you don't need to ask me permission directly for that. I appreciate that you have, but the agency will take care of everything."

"Of course, but I just thought, given some of our . . . history, it might be best to ask you in person first. Out of politeness."

I almost snorted at that but managed to keep a straight face. If she was going to put in the effort to play nice, then so would I. And after what had happened during our last meeting, I still felt a bit guilty for what I'd accidentally done to her, so I swore to myself I'd be as civil as possible to her this morning.

"I don't have any issues with your nephew renting the space above the shop. It's actually a lot easier when you can rent the living space to someone operating the retail shop; it creates less friction between the store owner and the tenant. When I get the approval request from Mountain View, I'll sign off on it, don't worry."

She nodded gratefully. "He's a good boy, Dylan. I think you'll like him. I hope *everyone* will like him."

"Hmm," was all I could manage to say. I thought a lot of that was going to depend on how much like his aunt he was.

"Anyway, that's why I *originally* planned to come."

A little spasm of pure panic hit me like a bullet, and I was glad she wasn't looking right at me, because the moment she triggered my fight-or-flight, a whole stack of paper takeout cups started to float into the air. I grabbed them and put them back down on the counter.

"I'm sure anything else could wait until later, Dierdre. We just opened, and I do have an awful lot to do this morning." Where was the beeping alarm from the oven or the tinkling bell of another customer arriving? Who was going to save me from this horrible train wreck that was about to happen?

*Please stop, please stop, please stop.*

I took a deep breath in through my nose and out through my mouth, hoping it would be enough to steady me. I just needed to keep myself in check long enough to get her out the door.

"I heard the *terrible* news about what happened to Mr. Bachman last night. Imagine it—what an absolute tragedy. Man was only here to help the town, and then that big brute at the grocery store would go and do something like that to him."

I wheeled around, still holding the tower of paper cups in my hand. A few of them dropped from the bottom of the stack onto the floor with hollow *tok, tok, tok* noises.

"What did you say?"

"It's all over town. Betty Overland said she was at the store last week and saw Leo Lansing pick the poor man up by his collar and toss him right out of the store."

"That didn't happen," I said, almost breathless. Was that really what people were saying about Leo? And locals, no less. People like Betty Overland, whoever she was, should know better. They should know *him* better.

"Perhaps she exaggerated, but she's not the only one who saw it. Plenty of people are talking, and they're all saying that if someone in town killed Andrew Bachman, then the police should be looking at Leo." She shrugged as if this implication was completely obvious.

I set the cups down on the counter and barely had a chance to catch a full canister of loose tea that had begun to float up into the air. The contents of a basket by the till that contained pins and stickers was empty, and I looked up in horror to see that the knickknacks and my entire mug of pens were all hovering halfway up to the ceiling.

This was *terrible*.

"Dierdre, you have known Leo Lansing his entire life. You of all people should be the one telling these busybodies to turn their attention elsewhere." To distract her from looking into the foyer, I removed the tea bag from her cup and set the piping-hot tea down in front of her. She flinched, reminding me again what had happened the last time there was a hot drink between us, not to mention the last time she'd consumed something in my store.

I wondered if she was also focused on the word *busybodies*, something she had surely been called a time or two in the past. She took the drink and held it, for which I was grateful. I didn't think my glitching magic could snatch items right out of someone's hand.

Though I really didn't want her to hang around long enough for me to find out.

"Just because I *know* Leo doesn't mean people aren't capable of hiding who they really are. If you think it's so impossible for him to have killed someone, you tell me, Phoebe, did you think he was capable of threatening someone?"

I remained silent, because no response I gave was going to be a winner. I couldn't deny that what I'd seen from Leo that day at the store had been shocking, but there was nothing on this planet that would convince me my sweet, caring friend was the kind of man who could kill someone. And certainly not over real estate.

Dierdre took my silence as an admission of some kind and lifted her chin triumphantly into the air. I wanted to remind her that once upon a time she had been under scrutiny for someone's death and she hadn't liked that feeling very much, but I opted to keep my mouth shut.

She tied her scarf around her head and took a lid for her tea from the counter, slapping a five-dollar bill on the table before she left. I wasn't sure if she was so focused on her perceived win or if it was just that she was totally oblivious, but she batted a hanging pen and sticker out of her way as if they were annoying insects as she opened the front door.

Just when I thought she'd already had enough of the last word, she turned around and looked back at me.

"I don't think you can assume that *your* friendship is enough to make someone innocent. You don't have that kind of power."

She slammed the door behind her, and once she was gone, every tiny floating piece of bric-a-brac immediately fell to the floor.

# Chapter
# Twenty-Four

I had cleaned up most of the fallen items by the time Imogen arrived a little over an hour later, yet she still managed to kick a button under the cash desk the minute she stepped through the door.

She watched it shoot across the store with a baffled expression. "Did some kid knock over the pin container again?" She shook off her umbrella outside the door before slipping it into the umbrella stand we had next to the door. Her hair was in a bun, tucked under a hood. When she got into the dry safety of the store, she pulled out the tie that was keeping her hair up and let her braids fall around her shoulders.

"I accidentally knocked over the basket," I lied.

She crouched down and collected the pin from the ground, checking to make sure it was undamaged before replacing it in the basket.

"Pretty quiet in here today?" She peered around the store. One of our regular Friday night Knit and Sip ladies was browsing the used books with the slow patience of someone who had nothing else to do with her day, but I wasn't complaining; she had already stacked about ten books on the counter.

Imogen deposited her coat in the office before relieving me at the front so I could get the last of the bread loaves finished off before lunch. Given how quiet it had been all morning, I wasn't expecting much of a rush, but even on our most ghost-town days, we usually went through at least a full loaf of each.

I had made two easy, popular classics today. One was our cheddar jalapeño loaf, which I'd serve with either tuna salad or egg salad, depending on whether or not the person was a vegetarian. The sweet loaf was just cinnamon raisin, simple but delicious, and as I pulled a loaf of it from the oven, my nostrils were filled with the heady aroma of cinnamon, which always made me feel like it was almost Christmas. I'd serve that with a whipped honey cream cheese topped with some chopped hazelnuts. If any of the roasted hazelnuts survived, that is, because I kept snacking on them whenever I went into the kitchen.

With lunch prepped, I finally had time to face the manila envelope that had been taunting me on the kitchen counter while I waited for Imogen to arrive. I was nervous to open it, wondering if it was just a vendor leaving swag or an invoice or if it had something to do with all the deaths that had been happening in town. Everyone involved knew where to find me—Melody, Deacon, and yes, even Leo. If someone wanted to leave me a piece of evidence or something to point me in the direction of the killer, it would make some sense for them to leave it at the store.

I opened the envelope and nervously peeked inside. If there was a finger or an ear in there, I didn't want it to just slide out onto the counter and scare me out of my wits.

There were no body parts in the envelope but rather a slim stack of photos. I dumped them out onto the counter, and it took me a solid minute for my eyes to tell my brain what we were looking at. The photos were of the river near the footbridge, and for a second I was confused because I had seen this scene as it played out, but not from this angle.

There, unmistakably, was Melody and the man in the baseball cap who I'd seen her arguing with by the bridge. In fact, I could very easily picture my exact location in this scene, although the photographer hadn't captured it. I was just a hair out of frame, watching things unfold from the bushes.

I hadn't been the only one watching them, however.

Maybe *this* was why I'd felt certain I was being followed. Someone else *had* been there that day.

From this angle I could see very clearly who Melody was talking to, and it sucked every ounce of breath from my lungs. I dropped the photos back onto the counter once I realized.

Two formerly disconnected murders were not so disconnected after all.

The man that Melody had been arguing with that day was none other than Andrew Bachman, the dead lawyer.

Only the buzz from the oven telling me that a new batch of cookies were done was enough to pull me out of my horrified reverie.

I had a million questions to pile on the thousands I was already seeking answers for. How did Melody know the lawyer? Had they known each other before Sebastian's murder, or had they only met through that initial tragedy? There'd seemed to be a lot of pent-up familiarity between them by the river, leading me to believe they hadn't *only* met at the B and B. Something had driven them to meet in private, because otherwise any conversation between strangers could have taken place at the inn rather than in the woods.

I couldn't imagine why Melody would be in contact with a real estate lawyer. And had whatever they were talking about been enough to lead to not one but two murders?

The one thing I knew with absolute certainty as I looked at the photos was that they were my one golden opportunity to help clear

Leo's name. Because as far as I was concerned, Melody Fairbanks had just become the number-one suspect in both of these crimes.

She not only seemed to be secretly stashing some of Sebastian's funds, but she also had known Andrew. There was nothing coincidental about these murders.

I placed a quick call to Detective Martin, whose phone went right to voice mail, and then I put the photos in a freezer bag. They'd have my fingerprints on them now, but they might also have the photographer's, and I would dearly like to know who had taken them and brought them to me rather than to the police.

Someone knew I was poking around in this case—and in fairness, I hadn't really been subtle about it—but whoever had taken these pictures thought I could help. I was hoping I didn't prove them wrong.

I headed back out to the work floor, where it was as quiet as ever. The rain outside was pouring down in unrelenting sheets, and the sky had grown so dark it already looked like evening. Bob was sitting in the front window watching water drip down from the eaves, his tail flicking every now and then. Out of nowhere, as if possessed, he scrambled halfway up the window, paws and nails scraping glass, and when he landed, one of Daphne's little paper birds was hanging from his mouth.

"Oh, *Bob*, you little lunatic." I went to reclaim the bird from him, but he bolted off the window ledge and hid under one of the chairs, where reaching him was just going to be too annoying to make it worthwhile. He started to bat the paper bird around with his paws, making sure it was good and dead.

"That's his third one this morning," Imogen informed me. "He has been hiding them around the store. I think we might need to do a scavenger hunt at some point to reclaim the missing flock."

"I don't know what's gotten into him today. Those birds have been up for almost a week, and I don't think he even noticed them until now."

"Or did he just spend a week planning his attack?" Imogen tapped her temple. "Bob's no fool."

As if to agree with her, Bob let out a muffled yowling sound from under the chair. The bird was stuffed in his mouth. "Yeah, pal, you killed it. Good job."

This was why I didn't let him outside unless he was on the deck with me. I would like to keep my newfound bird friends in one piece.

I had far too much time that afternoon to think about the photographs. It was so miserable outside that even old Mr. Loughery didn't show up, and I could hardly blame him for wanting to stay comfortable at home with the company of Frodo the cat. If I didn't have a store, I'd be doing the same.

Thinking of Mr. Loughery and Frodo, I was slapped with a stark reminder. The cats! The cats from Barneswood were slated to be delivered tomorrow, and I'd been so preoccupied the last few days I had done almost nothing to prepare for their arrival.

The kennels were built, thank goodness, and we were only taking two cats to start—though we had enough room for four.

"I completely forgot about the new fosters that are coming tomorrow," I explained to Imogen, to give reason for my suddenly stricken expression.

"Oh shoot, that's *tomorrow?*" Evidently, I hadn't been the only one who had put the cats entirely out of my mind. We all must have collectively thought, *Oh, it's okay, I'll take care of that later.* Only later was now.

I went down to the basement, both to check for water, thanks to the deluge outside, and to grab all the supplies I'd put into storage for precisely this event. The basement remained dry, and also spooky, so I hauled the bags from Charlie Bravebird's pet shop upstairs, hoping I didn't need to make any more trips to the dungeon for the rest of the week.

"Charlie needs to give you a blue ribbon for being his best customer," Imogen said, rifling through the bags with the curiosity of someone filming a shopping haul montage.

Dragging everything over to the designated kitty corner, I spent the next hour making sure all four kennels were ready for feline guests. I filled up the litter boxes in only two, but when I was done, each suite had a small covered bed where the cat could relax and also hide if they were feeling shy, a litter box, food and water dishes, some cozy blankets donated by the Knit and Sip crew, and a slew of toys that might tickle the cat's fancy. Each kennel door also had a small chalkboard affixed to it where we could write the cat's shelter name and some basic information about their age and temperament.

When I was done, Imogen brought over something I hadn't seen her working on, and when she handed it to me, I could barely believe it was *her* doing it. Her cheeks reddened. "Don't you dare say anything."

She had made a little paper bunting that said *WELCOME* in multicolored flags. I bit my tongue at her request, but as soon as I'd hung it on the outside of the kennel, I turned around and forced her to submit to a tight hug.

Imogen wasn't big on displays of warmth or affection, but she did wrap her arms around me and give me a hug back. "You worked really hard on this. I know those cats are lucky."

My heart was full.

Bob pressed his face up against the metal cage doors, trying to get a good whiff of the new toys inside. He set down his paper bird, now thoroughly crinkled and damp, and reached a paw into the lowest kennel door, hoping to grab a spring toy I'd left in there.

"Bob, that's not for you," I scolded.

But a cat is going to do what a cat is going to do, and Bob eventually did succeed in getting the little spring toy out. It went skittering across the hardwood and so did he, a furry ballistic missile on a mission.

"Ah, let him have it. He could probably use the exercise," Imogen teased.

Bob *was* a little on the portly side, so I acquiesced. It wasn't as if he were disturbing anyone. The sole customer we'd had in the store was gone.

I was thrilled the cat condos were now ready for their guests and jotted down a note on the staff reminders pad for Daphne to get some social media posts up about the cats during her shift the next afternoon.

When an hour and then another passed without a single visitor, I decided it was time to throw in the towel. The storm showed no signs of relenting, and there was no sign of any foot traffic out on Main.

"I'm calling it. Let's close early."

Imogen, who had been reading at the counter, set her book down. "Are you sure? I don't mind staying if you want to head home. I really don't have anything better going on tonight anyway."

I hemmed and hawed about this and then finally agreed to let her stay. Sometimes it was nice to be out of the house, and it didn't seem like she was in a hurry to leave. I was planning to pay her either way, but at least this way we'd be open in case anyone wanted to stop by for a reprieve from the weather.

Bundling Bob up into his backpack, I grabbed the photos I'd left in the kitchen, double-checked that everything was ready for me in the morning, and bid Imogen farewell, making her promise to close up anytime she wanted if she decided she would rather leave early after all.

"Yes, because sitting here with a cup of tea and a book is such a terrible way to spend a rainy afternoon," she quipped after me.

Hard to argue with that.

I wanted to head to the police station to see if Detective Martin was in. She still hadn't returned my phone call from earlier, but I expected there was a lot on her plate, given that our sleepy little town had just had two back-to-back homicides. I decided I'd wait to hear from her. I wanted very badly to show her these photos, hoping they might help clear Leo of any suspicion, but if she was busy, I couldn't force her to be available.

Leo was probably lying low, and I considered stopping by his house to check on him, but I was honestly more worried about finding him *not* there. If the police had taken him in for questioning, I couldn't help him avoid that. The fight had happened, and it was inevitable that he was going to be asked about it eventually.

Instead, I bypassed all immediate responsibility and went home.

I released Bob, who headed directly into the living room and made himself comfortable on the back of the couch in a now-permanent Bob-shaped divot. He looked about as happy and cozy as only a napping cat can be. I'd have loved nothing more than to join him for a late-afternoon doze, but my brain wouldn't turn off.

This new information about Melody and Andrew was helpful, but it wasn't a smoking gun. I grabbed my laptop and an apple from the bowl on the kitchen counter and plopped down on the sofa. I did a quick search on both Andrew's and Melody's names and then their names together. Absolutely zero hits with their names combined; the only thing that seemed to connect them was that their names had both recently appeared in articles in the local paper.

Then I tried to search any connections between Sebastian and the lawyer.

Again, only the newspaper.

Since I couldn't exactly point to the paper's sole features writer as the killer, I was left at square one. Whatever the connection between Sebastian and Andrew had been, I couldn't find it, and I didn't understand how Melody was involved.

Whatever it was that had brought the three of them together, though, it had been worth killing over.

# Chapter
# Twenty-Five

It was another hour before I got a call back from Detective Martin, which was precisely the amount of time it took for me to come up with a compelling but utterly insane theory about Melody and Andrew belonging to a secret society and Sebastian being killed because he'd learned about their connection.

I should never be left to my own devices when there's an unsolved murder on the line.

Martin came directly over from the police station, and I was pacing the living room when she arrived.

"Let's have a look at these, then," she said, following me into the formal dining room. Since I never actually *ate* in the dining room, it had become sort of a catchall for things I was trying to purge from Eudora's house but hadn't found the right new home for yet.

There were stacks of books I knew I'd never read but suspected might have too much value to just donate. Boxes of clothes that weren't quite my style lined the wall, but again, these were so eclectic—and some of them quite high-end brands—that I thought I might be better doing online consignment than just taking them to goodwill. And then there were Eudora's papers. I had banker's boxes stacked three tall lining the whole dining table, and I was only about a quarter of the way through reviewing them.

Considering Eudora had once hidden millions of dollars' worth of land title deeds in a photo album, there was no way I was just going to shred everything in those boxes without going through it first. Who knew what other secrets she might be hiding?

"Moving in or moving out?" Detective Martin asked, eyeing the fortress of cardboard.

"Moving on," I replied. "It's all my aunt's stuff."

"Ah. Well, I imagine over her life and in a house this size, she probably amassed a pretty impressive collection."

"She amassed *collections* that would put the British Museum to shame."

"The British Museum doesn't know the meaning of the word." Her lip quirked up. She held out her hand for the photos, and I was happy to oblige, giving her the freezer bag I'd been carrying around with me. I'd been scared to let them out of my sight since getting home, as if they might grow legs and wander off of their own free will.

"Did you touch them?" she asked.

"I did. I wasn't sure what they were until I had them out of the envelope, and I also don't usually carry around gloves just in case I stumble across evidence."

"Given your proclivity for *stumbling* across crime scenes, you might want to start leaving some in your purse."

Her voice was so deadpan I wasn't sure if this was a joke or not, but the twinkle in her dark-brown eyes told me there was no malicious intent behind her words. She was teasing me.

At least I had moved beyond the *it's suspicious this woman keeps showing up at crime scenes* phase of my relationship with the detective. I'd found my way to her good side, and I hoped that by bringing her this evidence, I might stay there.

"Next time I won't open any surprise mail, I promise."

"You don't happen to have a camera installed behind the store, do you?"

While that would have been wise, considering there had been situations behind the store in the past, it was just another thing on a lengthy to-do list that I hadn't yet gotten around to.

"I don't, sorry."

She shook her head. "I'll check with your neighbors. If they have something, maybe our delivery person was caught making the drop. Not holding my breath, though." She had on gloves and was handling each photo individually, tipping it this way and that under the dim light of the overhead chandelier. "I'm also not holding my breath that our shutterbug left any prints on these. I see some, but I suspect those might be yours. We have your prints on file, though, so it'll be easy to eliminate you."

A small mercy that made up for how utterly humiliating it had been to get printed in the first place. It didn't matter that I was perfectly innocent of any crimes; the simple act of being fingerprinted had been enough to make me feel instantly guilty of something. I'd almost confessed to the one time in junior high when I'd stolen a bubblegum lip balm on a dare. I'd admitted it to my mother so quickly I hadn't even given her an opportunity to suspect something was wrong. I was *not* cut out for a life of crime.

"Thank you for sharing these with me, Phoebe. I hope this will help us, and it certainly sheds some interesting light on the case, I can't deny that."

"Did you find anything at the sanctuary?"

"You know I can't tell you that."

"Did you find Melody?"

"No, she never did come back to the inn last night; we had a cruiser out front and an officer inside. Her *things* are still there, however, and we think it'll only be a matter of time before she has no choice but to show her face. We didn't find any sign of those gloves you mentioned, though. Or any bank statements."

Well, that was interesting. Maybe Melody *had* tried to ditch the gloves.

"What about Deacon?"

She shook her head. "In the wind too, I'm afraid. You think he might be responsible for these?" She tapped the bag of photos.

That actually hadn't occurred to me, but it made sense. "It wouldn't be the first time he targeted me as a possible ally. Considering how he showed up here a couple days ago, there's a chance he might think of me as someone trustworthy."

"Well, if he should reach out to you again, be careful but keep him close. I'm not sure who is to blame for these murders, and this investigation keeps getting messier by the day, but I would very much like a chance to chat with both him and his friend Melody."

Part of me wondered, perhaps morbidly, if the reason we couldn't find both of the cases' best suspects was because one of them had taken the other out. I didn't say this out loud, but based on the grim expression Detective Martin was wearing, I wouldn't have been surprised if she was thinking the same thing.

Detective Martin donned a RCPD ballcap and tipped the brim in my direction before reminding me to be careful.

"Seriously, Phoebe, keep your eyes open, but keep your guard up. Someone, or more than one someone in this case, knows you're involved, and that could make you a target. The *second* you don't feel safe, I want you to call me, and if I don't answer, call the station directly, okay? Please take this seriously."

"Trust me, I am."

She disappeared into the rainy night, leaving me alone in my big house as dusk fell over the town. I *would* listen to her warning, but my curiosity about the case far outweighed any concerns I had over my personal safety. I didn't believe whoever had left me the photos had done so as a threatening gesture. I thought they'd done it because they believed I could help.

Which brought me back to Detective Martin's question about Deacon. Was it possible he had been out in the woods at the same time as me and captured the argument? And if that was the case, had he been out there following Melody, or had he been following me?

That last question gave me enough pause that I went to double-check my locks for the third or fourth time that evening. I might not be an obvious target for the killer, but that didn't mean I wanted to make myself an *easy* target if that changed.

Dinner would be leftover sourdough, since I had a fridge full of tuna and egg salad and two full loaves of bread. I'd made Imogen promise to take home the other two. I couldn't believe how quiet the day had been. It made me all the more grateful for our beautiful weather on Independence Day, which meant we'd made more than enough money to guarantee that a few slow days weren't going to hurt our bottom line.

The bad weather also hadn't done anything to dampen our online sales. I was going to need to set aside a good chunk of my day tomorrow to catch up on those, because there were too many to just leave them for another day.

Plus we were finally getting our first kitty guests from the Barneswood Humane Society, and despite all the other messy business in my life, I was super excited to see which cats would be coming to stay with us at the store.

I was just about to sit down to a tasty dinner sandwich when my phone pinged to alert me to a new text.

Honey's name was on the screen.

Can we come over? My mom might have an idea about your little . . . problem.

Recalling how lucky I'd been with Dierdre's lack of observation this morning, I knew this was an offer I couldn't turn down.

I'm home, come on by.

Honey replied immediately. Hope you're hungry because Mama has been in the kitchen all day.

Magic *and* a hot meal?

Maybe this day was turning around after all.

# Chapter
# Twenty-Six

Honey and Karma arrived about fifteen minutes later, both huddled under one umbrella. Honey was carrying an overstuffed tote bag that appeared to be filled with Tupperware containers. I ushered them in from the front porch and took them into the sitting room.

As nice as the living room was for watching TV, it wasn't the ideal location for an actual conversation. The couches were too soft, and the layout of the room made it difficult to talk to more than one other person.

I almost never used the sitting room, so it was still set up exactly the same as Eudora had left it. I had lit a fire in the massive fireplace that was connected to both the sitting room and kitchen, because the drafty old house was having temperature mood swings and even though it had been sticky hot the previous day, there was now a distinct chill in the air thanks to all the rain. The fire made the sitting room feel cozy, and I loved the smell of burning wood.

Through the two grates I could see Bob curled up in his bed on the hearth in the kitchen.

Honey handed me one Tupperware container after another, describing each dish as she went. "That's honey jalapeño corn bread.

That's shrimp with dirty rice. This one is akara." She shook a container that appeared to be filled with golden-brown coins. "They're deep-friend patties made of black-eyed peas. You'll love them. And *this*, this is chicken mafé. Phoebe, let me tell you . . ." She made a little chef's kiss gesture. "You haven't lived until you've had my mama's chicken mafé. You're not allergic to peanut butter, are you?"

While I didn't immediately know how peanut butter was involved, I assured her I was totally fine to eat it. The container with the chicken was still warm to the touch, and when I opened the lid, my mouth immediately began watering. The chicken was coated in a reddish-gold sauce, and there appeared to be a stew-like mixture of vegetables cut up with the meat: carrots, onion, potato. The scent was heavenly, a little sweet with hints of tomato, ginger, and something perhaps a little umami, maybe fish sauce?

Whatever it was, I couldn't resist the urge to snatch out a cube of potato and pop it into my mouth. If I'd thought the smell was good, the flavor was beyond comprehension. I'd been about to eat a tuna salad sandwich for dinner when food like this was an option? It was sweet, salty, rich, and creamy. The spices sang, and even the bed of rice the whole meal was settled on was the fluffiest I'd ever seen.

Heaven in a Tupperware container.

"This is incredible. I can't thank you enough." I closed the lid and set all the food on the coffee table, knowing full well that the instant I locked the door behind them I was going to turn into a pure glutton and just sit on the floor with a fork in one hand and a napkin in the other, devouring everything in sight.

Bob must have smelled the chicken, because he had snuck into the room at some point and was pointedly sniffing his way around the table.

"None for you, mister," I scolded. But everyone in this room knew he'd get to try some when I finally sat down to eat.

"You girls are too skinny. I don't know what this town is feeding you. I said to Honey, I said, 'Baby, you need to eat some proper home cooking, because you're wasting away to nothing.' And so I made something nice for her, and for you."

"Thank you, Karma. This all looks insanely good."

"You're welcome, baby. Now I'm sure what you really want isn't comfort food, so let's get down to business. I do my best thinking while I'm in the kitchen, so all day today I was thinking to myself, *Karma, how are you going to help that poor girl?* And somewhere between the dirty rice and the mafé, it came to me." She clapped her hands together loudly, spooking Bob, who had climbed up onto the table to investigate the shrimp. He darted out of the room.

"Mama, you're scaring the cat," Honey scolded.

"Oh, pshh, he's a big boy, he'll be okay."

Indeed, Bob poked his head back around the corner not even a minute later, the siren song of shrimp simply too powerful for him to stay away.

"How are you going to help me fix my problem?" I asked, steering us back toward the subject that had brought them here tonight. I didn't want to be rude, but the promise of no longer making random objects around me start floating was too enticing to ignore.

"Witches usually grow out of our magical hiccups pretty quickly as teens," Honey started.

"But because you started so late in the game, your magic is having a hard time adjusting," Karma explained.

"Yes, I think we got that part figured out already. But aside from going back in time and telling teenage Phoebe she's a witch, what else can we do to help me through this midlife magical puberty?"

Honey snorted, but Karma didn't seem to think my joke was very funny.

"I'd tell you to get a little therapy or go on some good antianxiety medication if I thought we had time for that." She clucked her tongue at me.

I might have found her suggestion offensive at a different point in my life, but I'd be lying if I said I hadn't considered medication a few times while dealing with this. A little Xanax every now and then would probably stop me from sending fruit levitating in my kitchen.

"What we need to do is tell your magic not to worry so much," Karma said.

Honey nodded along.

I was completely lost.

"I'm sorry, you want me to . . . have a heart-to-heart with my powers?"

"In a sense." Karma started to pull more things out of the tote bag that had been nestled under all the food. There was a huge chunk of smoky quartz, a mason jar filled with water, several freezer bags packed with dried herbs, a whole box of salt, at least a dozen candles, and a sharp-looking bronze blade that Honey had told me once was called an athame. They were ceremonial knives used by some witches, depending on their practice. "Honey, help me with the table."

Honey got up from her armchair, and the two women moved my hefty coffee table off to the side of the room.

"Okay, you can sit right here, sweetheart." Karma tapped her toe on the center of Eudora's huge Persian rug.

I did as I was told, even though I still had no idea what was happening. They wanted me to talk to my power? While I understood that magic was a strange thing to have control over, I had never thought it was a sentient thing that I could just hold a conversation with.

Surely there was more to this than what Karma was suggesting.

I just needed to trust the process.

Sitting cross-legged in the middle of the carpet, I immediately set my hands on my thighs like I was about to start meditating. I wasn't much for mindfulness, but I'd apparently watched enough YouTube videos that I thought this was the best way to sit. I was ready for yoga but not a tête-à-tête with my witchy powers.

"You got a good vacuum?" Karma asked, picking up the box of salt from the table.

"Uh, pretty good, I guess?"

"Okay, good." Then she set about pouring the salt directly onto the rug.

I almost made a noise of protest but bit down on my cheek before it emerged. I had to trust that Karma knew what she was doing. She'd been a witch for decades longer than I had and had raised one of the smartest women I knew. If anyone was going to have an idea of how to fix this, it would be her, so I let her continue with her efforts.

My Roomba was going to have a field day with this later.

Next to Karma, Honey was lighting the small white candles they had brought with them. She followed behind her mother, who was drawing a circle of salt around me, and Honey placed five candles at equal distances around the circle.

When the last candle was placed and the circle was closed, it was as if a window had been shut and blocked out all the sound and air from outside, except it was blocking out the sound of the room.

I felt a chill creep over my skin as the warmth from the fire disappeared.

I took a deep breath just to remind myself I could breathe.

While I'd never been inside a deprivation chamber, I had to believe this was exactly like what it felt like. My heart hammered, and sweat beaded my forehead.

On the coffee table, the individual food containers that the Westcott women had brought with them started to lift from the table, as did a collection of wooden coasters and several small framed photos on a nearby desk.

I shut my eyes tightly, trying to will it to stop, but the muffled voice of Karma broke through the invisible wall around me.

"It's okay, Phoebe. Let it happen."

I took a deep breath and opened my eyes, horrified to see that small objects all over the room were now halfway up to the ceiling. Whatever Karma and Honey were doing was making things worse, not helping.

"I can't do this," I said, barely able to catch my breath because my pulse was tripping all over itself.

"You're doing great, I promise you. This is okay."

I didn't see how it was possible that making everything that wasn't bolted to the walks in a whole room float eight feet in the air was okay, but Karma's voice was calm and reassuring. I *wanted* to believe her.

She glanced around me, taking in just how much of a midair disaster I'd created. Bob, meanwhile, was no longer put off by my glitchy abilities; he was balanced on the back of an armchair, reaching out to grab the Tupperware container with the shrimp and rice. His paw clipped the edge, but he only managed to send the plastic dish wobbling away from him.

He started to wiggle his haunches, but Honey plucked him up quickly, sensing as I had that he was about to make a jump for it.

"You'll get some later, Bob. Just be good for now," Honey scolded in soothing tones. She set him on the floor and he stayed by her feet, staring up at his forbidden snack, the tip of his tail twitching violently.

"Phoebe, do you grant me permission to cross your barrier?" Karma was crouched in front of me, pulling my attention back to her.

"Yes?" I really wasn't sure what any of this meant. Honey had grown up not just employing her natural hereditary witchy abilities but practicing a more traditional form of witchcraft as well. She made potions and poultices. She used candles and herbs and crystals. I didn't know what any of this meant beyond the few things she'd educated me on over our friendship.

"Thank you," she said, then picked the huge chunk of smoky quartz up from the ground. "Can you hold this?" She passed it to me, and the moment her hands crossed the line of salt on the floor, the suffocating sensation dimmed for a second. The warmth of the fire tickled my cheeks; the rain pattering heavily on the window became audible.

When she retracted her hands, leaving me holding the heavy crystal, everything dulled again.

How bizarre.

She took something from Honey and passed it across the barrier, again creating the strange opening between whatever space I was in and the reality of my living room, as if she were parting a curtain between rooms. Bob paced in front of me but seemed to be aware of the invisible wall between us; he didn't try to get any closer, which made me unspeakably sad. My inability to snuggle him in that moment meant I'd never wanted to do it more.

The item Karma passed me this time was the bronze-hued knife. I almost resisted taking it, but she placed it firmly in my palm before retracting her hand and sealing me inside my terrible little fortress. I stared at the knife in one hand and the heavy crystal in the other, then looked to the older woman for even the slightest idea of what I was supposed to do.

"Put the crystal in front of you." She tapped the rug, and I mimicked her, although it was like trying to listen to instructions that someone was yelling at me underwater. "Now take the knife and cut your palm."

I stared at her, holding the knife totally still against my knee. Surely I had heard her wrong.

There must have been something obviously mistrusting in my expression, because she gave me a soft smile, nodded, and then mimed drawing her thumb across her palm. "It doesn't have to be deep, but you gotta spark the magic, sweetie."

I gestured to a candelabra floating about three feet to her left. "I think it's pretty active already."

"You want help or you want to be sassy? I'm plenty used to sassy—I raised this one." She jerked a thumb in Honey's direction.

"Excuse me, don't go pointing any fingers at me right now, I'm just an innocent bystander." Honey was actually an innocent partici- pant, because she'd mixed together the herbs they'd brought into a metal bowl and set them alight and was now fanning the smoke around the room.

This was *nuts*.

I took the knife, whose blade now looked especially sharp, and drew it across my palm. While I barely even touched metal to skin, I still let out a surprised hiss of pain, and stared as blood bloomed across my skin. The cut wasn't deep and actually looked and felt less painful than the scrapes already on my palm and knees from my tumble down the hillside a couple of days earlier. In fact, I doubted anyone was even going to notice this new cut in a day or two.

I held my hand up so Karma could see, and she gave me an appreciative nod. "Good girl. Now put your hand on the crystal."

In for a penny, in for a pound, I guess.

This time I didn't hesitate or make faces. I just pressed my palm against the smoky quartz.

The second flesh met stone, the entire world disappeared.

# Chapter
# Twenty-Seven

Wherever I was, I didn't have a body anymore.

I was surrounded by white light and the faintest humming noise, as if I'd left the mortal world and been transported inside a fluorescent lightbulb. Except the light here was warm and inviting. It felt the way it did to close your eyes and turn your face toward the sun on a beautiful summer day.

It was just my mind and the light.

I would have liked to have my hands back, though.

Was I dead? Had Karma's spell gone all wrong and killed me? I found that rather than being scared of that prospect, I was remarkably calm. No body, no problem. There was also nothing to focus on here, making me wonder if I had eyes. There was just brightness, the humming, and a soothing calm unlike anything I had ever known before.

"Hello, my sweet girl," came a familiar voice.

Since I had no eyes and no body, I couldn't look around, but I instinctively understood there was nothing to see, and I didn't need sight to know who that voice belonged to. I'd recognize it anywhere.

"Auntie Eudora?"

I didn't have a mouth, yet I knew she could hear me just like I could hear her without ears. It was an understanding. A warm glowing sensation washed over me, making me feel peaceful. Loved.

"Oh, Phoebe, it's so good to see you."

I wasn't sure if she *could* see me, but I also didn't know how any of this worked.

"Am I dead?"

She laughed. Though I couldn't hear a laugh, I *felt* the lightness of the way Eudora's high, bright laugh filled a room.

"No, no. This is a temporary space. You're not really here. I'm not really here. I'm an imprint, just part of your memory to help make this easier for you."

That made me sad. I had wanted this to be a moment of connection, of being together with someone I'd lost, and despite what she was saying, something in my heart told me she was real.

"Are you going to help me?" I asked.

"Yes."

"How do I fix this?"

"Fixing implies something is broken. You aren't broken. You're not a thing that needs to be fixed."

"Tell that to the inanimate objects around me trying to make a bid to join the space program."

"I see your sense of humor remains unchanged." She sounded both amused and frustrated, which was a combination I was beginning to understand I made a lot of people around me experience.

"If you can't laugh at yourself . . ."

". . . someone else will do it for you," she finished, as it was one of her most beloved turns of phrase. She'd use it to remind me not to feel too sorry for myself, because in life there's only ever one person who is going to be by your side from start to finish, and that's you.

"I wish you were here," I told her.

"I wanted to tell you so many times, but we didn't know. I *thought* you might have the gift, but then you moved away so young and I just couldn't watch for the signs. I figured when nothing happened by the time you were an adult, it wasn't going to happen. But still, I tried. I sent special teas; I made you jewelry and sent things that might boost your power, hoping one day you would tell me things were happening to you, but that day never came. I'm sorry it came when I couldn't help you."

"Me too."

"I've left things behind. Things in the house that will help you."

"I found the deeds."

"Oh, those old things? Well, that's good, but that's not what I meant. You'll know what I mean when you find it."

Since I had no idea what she was talking about, I had to assume I hadn't found it yet.

"How do we fix . . . er . . . how can I stop the accidental glitches? Karma said it's something I would have figured out when I was young, so there has to be a solution."

"You have almost thirty years of pent-up magic swirling around inside of you, wanting to get out. That's why things keep going awry; that's why you keep letting your magic control *you* rather than you controlling your magic."

"Then what's the solution?"

"I think I just made that clear."

"I beg to differ."

"Tone, Phoebe."

"How can I have a tone if I don't even have a voice?"

I didn't need to see Eudora's face to know the *precise* expression she would be making if we were physically together.

"You're bottled up. Like a can of soda that's been shaken and left to sit."

It dawned on me then what she was suggesting. And while it was a logical solution, it also sounded like madness as I processed it.

"You have *decades* of pent-up magic inside you," she goaded.

"I need to let it all out."

"You need to let it all out."

\* \* \*

I was dragged back to the real world with a gasp and a popping sensation in my ears. I sat in the middle of the salt circle panting for breath, my hand still pressed to the crystal in front of me.

Karma and Honey were both staring at me with wide eyes. When I looked at the carpet, I realized all the salt had blown outward as if an explosion of air had sent it flying.

I blinked, shocked by how dim the light in here was compared to the liminal space I had just been in.

"What did you see?" Honey asked, unable to keep the curiosity out of her voice.

"I didn't see anything."

She exchanged a quick glance with her mother. "It didn't work?"

Karma put a hand on Honey's arm. "She didn't say that, did she? Did you, sweetie?"

I shook my head. "I went somewhere, but it was . . . it was nothing, it was just light. And Eudora was there. I think it was her, anyway. It was her voice, inside my mind."

Honey opened the mason jar of water and handed it to me. "Full-moon water. It's safe, it'll just recharge your energy."

I hadn't realized I was thirsty until she handed me the container, and once the sweet, clear water hit my tongue, I drank half the jar thirstily, only stopping to come up for air.

"What did your aunt say to you?" Karma asked.

"She told me how to get my power back under control."

Karma and Honey exchanged another excited look, something that demonstrated an entire unspoken language between mother and daughter. Then they waited expectantly for me to speak again.

"That's the thing . . . Apparently, I just need to find something that will let out about three decades of pent-up magical stress. No big deal, right?" I laughed, but it didn't feel particularly funny.

As I drank the rest of the water from the jar, Honey helped me to my feet. "We're on the right track, Phoebs, I promise. We'll find just the thing that will help. The most logical thing would be a spell. A big one."

"Do you have a spell in mind?"

"Well . . . no."

Karma also shook her head. "There isn't really a scale for which spells take more energy. I think we're going to need to do some digging to find something for your level that might do the trick. But Honey is right, we're getting somewhere. This is really positive." She came over and gave me a big squeeze. "You did great. Now why don't you go sit outside on that nice covered porch of yours and get some fresh air while Honey and I get things cleaned up in here."

I glanced up to see that all the floating objects were still stuck in midair.

"I appreciate the offer, but this is my mess. I couldn't ask you to clean it up."

"Nonsense—you didn't ask, I offered. And you weren't the one who poured salt all over the rug, now, were you?"

I was too exhausted to fight an unstoppable force like Karma, so I listened to her suggestion, grabbing a throw blanket from the living room and heading outside into the cool night air.

The humidity that had clung to Raven Creek for the last several days had broken, and while it was still pouring rain with the distant sound of thunder rumbling in the background, it no longer felt like being wrapped in a hot, wet towel when I stepped outside the door.

I slung the thin throw blanket over my shoulders and took a seat on my porch swing, which I had added cushions to for the summer with the goal of sitting here to read regularly. I didn't get much reading done, but I did like to sit out here and watch the birds at the feeders.

The door to the house hadn't closed all the way behind me, and Bob came marching out. Rather than making a dash for freedom, he sniffed the air for a moment, warily eyed the falling rain, and decided his best course of action was to join me on the swing.

He jumped up and crawled into my lap, kneading my thigh with his powerful little paws. His nails kept snagging on the blanket, reminding me I needed to cut them soon, but he just took it as a sign he should lie down.

Soon he was curled into a ball, his paws covering his face, and purring loudly.

I felt calmer than I had in weeks.

I might not know exactly what spell would stop my magic from going haywire, but I at least knew my problem could be fixed.

That was a start.

# Chapter
# Twenty-Eight

"It's cat day!" I announced to Amy as I flounced into Sugarplum Fairy. I was carrying a damp bouquet of flowers that I had cut from my garden that morning and arranged in a spare mason jar I'd found in the basement. I placed the jar on the counter and did an enthusiastic little dance-shuffle.

"Wow, I haven't seen you this excited about something since that time you found out there was a Christmas cat pageant and you got to make Bob wear one of those sweaters the knitting ladies made for him."

"What *isn't* exciting about a Christmas cat pageant?" I asked.

"I don't have an answer to that question."

Amy was not a cat person. It wasn't that she didn't like cats, she had assured me, but she didn't particularly trust any animals that were *that* self-sufficient. She had grown up in a family that owned dogs, and I knew that if it weren't for her grueling schedule at the bakery, she would probably own about ten Scotties.

She *did* appreciate that I had become a bit of a crazy cat person since adopting Bob. If someone had asked me five years ago if I'd ever be a cat person, I would have laughed them out of the room. Blaine and I hadn't owned any pets; we both worked long hours, and he was so rigidly opposed to being responsible for something that we couldn't even discuss a pet, let alone children.

I wasn't sorry, in retrospect, that we didn't have children. It wasn't that I didn't like kids, but as I'd gotten older, I'd realized that I liked my life without them, and I was also happy we hadn't had to force any young children to endure our less-than-amicable divorce.

Amy smelled the flowers I had brought her. "These are beautiful, thank you. Now, be honest, is it only the cats that have you in a good mood?"

"Isn't that enough?" I asked.

She raised a brow at me, her lips quirking into an all-too-knowing smile. "I saw you and Rich together at the street party."

While I assumed she meant she had just seen us in the same place at the same time, I was immediately brought back to our scintillating and unexpected kiss, and my entire face turned red. Not the smoothest way to deny things.

"I mean, we hung out."

"Oh my goodness, you two are exhausting. It has been *months*. Just admit you're crazy about each other and put the town out of its misery."

"The whole *town* knows about me and Rich?" I could have died and been buried under a rock and never shown my face again.

"Of course the whole town knows. How do you think we keep ourselves occupied? We certainly can't look inward at our own problems; we need to spend all our time talking about what everyone else is doing. And *everyone* has been waiting for you two to stop lollygagging and just get on with it." She grinned. "So get on with it."

I didn't ask what *it* entailed to our apparently townwide audience. But after the events of the Independence Day street party, it did feel like Rich and I had finally burst the will-they-or-won't-they bubble. Still, we hadn't talked about it since, and I hadn't even had much of a chance to think about my own feelings regarding how it had all gone down.

As first kisses go, it might not have been romantic, but it was memorable.

"Don't push me," I said, rubbing my cheeks to chase away some of the redness. I probably only made it worse. "I need to take it slow."

"If you take it much slower, you'll be going backwards, just keep that in mind." She handed me my usual boxes and an iced latte. "I think I've finally got the iced version nailed down, so tell me what you think."

I took a sip and, without even meaning to, let out a long *mmm-mmm* sound before I'd even swallowed it. I wasn't sure what she'd done, but this *was* different and better than her previous efforts, even though those had all been delicious as well.

"This is *incredible*."

Amy did a fist pump in the air. "Yes! I knew this one was the winner."

"What's different? I mean, don't get me wrong, I loved all the other ones, but this is just amazing." I took another sip, closing my eyes as the flavor washed over me. I was going to gain twenty pounds this summer drinking these.

"It still has the Nutella, of course, but I used a different kind of espresso, technically a ristretto. Then I used a hazelnut *creamer* instead of the hazelnut syrup I put in the other one, and that really seemed to do the trick in terms of the flavor. If your reaction is anything to go by." She laughed.

"Yeah, this is amazing."

"Thank you for being the guinea pig for it. I knew you'd be kind but honest."

"I'm happy to test anything you ever want to throw my way."

"Noted. And have a very happy cat day. I hope they don't last long because people are so excited to adopt."

I hoped the very same. We were a small town, and it was difficult to get to a shelter with any ease unless you wanted to drive over thirty minutes each direction to get to Barneswood, which was our next closest "big" town. My goal was that in bringing the cats *to* people and eliminating a lot of the distractions from the bigger shelter, these sweet kitties would more easily find new homes. Now we were going to see if my little gamble paid off.

I took my pastries and my already half-finished iced coffee and headed back to the store, where Bob had made himself comfortable in his usual spot and the empty cat condos looked ready for their new tenants. I'd rechecked the emails from the shelter about ten times already this morning, and the cats were scheduled to be delivered before noon, so it could really happen anytime this morning.

After unloading all of Amy's delicious-looking goodies and getting my own cookies baking, I did some nervous tidying, too excited for the arrival of the cats to really do much of anything else. When Imogen arrived a couple of hours later, she took a look around the store and then at the feather duster in my hand. "I see."

"Don't look at me like that."

"Uh-huh." She took her coat to the office and returned a moment later with more cookies to put on the empty tray in the display case. We'd had better luck with customers this morning than yesterday; either it wasn't raining as badly, or people had just accepted that the bad weather wasn't going away and decided it shouldn't hold them back. "Give me that," she said, snatching the dusting wand out of my hand. "The store is spotless. You're being a weirdo."

"Dusting never hurt anyone."

"Tell that to the poor disenfranchised dust bunnies you're making homeless. For shame."

I rolled my eyes and got off the little stepstool I was on, which Imogen folded up and put away.

"I tried to tell her she didn't need to do it," Mr. Loughery said with a chuckle from his usual chair.

"Don't you two start ganging up on me."

"It's not my fault he knows who's right." Imogen winked at the old man, who blushed furiously.

A car pulled up in front of the store as I was about to head into the kitchen, and all three of us peered through the window to watch a young woman in khaki pants get out, then open her umbrella in a precise routine. She must have seen us watching, because she waved.

"I think your new children are here," Imogen announced.

"Oh, how exciting," Mr. Loughery said. "I was hoping I'd be here to meet them."

"You thinking of getting another one already, Mr. L?" Imogen asked.

He chuckled again. "No, no, Frodo is definitely enough work for an old codger like me. But I am sure curious."

"Grab the door for me," I said to Imogen, running outside so I could help the woman with her umbrella as she struggled with something in the back seat of her car.

"You must be Phoebe Winchester?" she said. She was in her midtwenties with an explosion of freckles across her cheeks and muted red-brown hair that was curly and had probably doubled in volume thanks to all the humidity. "I'm Iris Keller from the Barneswood shelter. We've only met through email—it's nice to finally meet you face-to-face."

"Ditto. I'd shake your hand, but then we'd all get soaked."

Iris laughed. "Yeah, don't worry about it. You've got everything ready for these guys?"

She had sent me a very detailed list of their requirements ahead of time. "And then some," I confirmed.

"Awesome." She pulled two carriers out at the same time, and I followed after her with the umbrella. I definitely got wet, but she and the cats were covered as we all went into the open door where Imogen was waiting.

I shook off and closed the umbrella, then showed Iris over to the cat condos.

"Oh my goodness, you really went all out. This is so exciting." She looked up at the sign that said *Bob's Place*. "Family memorial, I assume?"

I coughed a little, my cheeks growing flushed. "Uh, no." I pointed to the orange lump, who was so tightly wrapped up in his chair it didn't even look like he had a head. "Bob."

"The name was my idea. He inspired me to get a cat myself," Mr. Loughery said proudly. "I'm the first one on the board." He pointed to the little bulletin board I'd put next to the kennels where I hoped to feature all our success stories. Sure enough, there was a photo of Mr. Loughery and Frodo right in the middle.

"I love it." She set the two carriers down on the floor and the reached into an interior pocket of her jacket, handing me two laminated pieces of paper. "Little fact sheets on your newest residents."

I didn't have time to look the sheets over before Iris opened up the first of the carriers. From inside she pulled a handsome tuxedo cat, more black than white, with a half-white and half-black face. The cat had striking green eyes that were already taking in the room.

"This is Indigo. He's seven and was an owner surrender. They unfortunately moved states and couldn't bring him with them. He's been with us almost a year."

"*Mowwwwww,*" said Indigo.

Bob immediately uncurled from his ball and stared wide-eyed in the direction of the new arrival. The second he laid eyes on Indigo, he pinned his ears back in a pose lovingly referred to by cat owners as "airplane ears."

I saw his move toward being a grouch and clucked my tongue at him. "Bobert, put those ears away. You have not been cleared for takeoff."

He blinked at me a few times and stared at Indigo with open uncertainty, but at least he stopped hissing. He was going to need to get used to having cats around here if he wanted to keep coming to the shop with me every day.

Iris helped Indigo into one of the top condos, where he started to sniff out his surroundings before hiding inside his covered cat bed.

"Don't worry about him. He'll come around in no time. He's a big lovebug. I think people are just put off because of his age, and also we have a lot of trouble rehoming black cats. Superstitions and whatnot." She shook her head sadly.

I caught a glimpse of Mr. Loughery adjusting in his chair, and I knew he was *dying* to tell Iris that Frodo was a tuxie, but he seemed to decide better of it and sat back in his chair.

"Mr. Loughery knows all about how great tuxedo cats are, isn't that right?" I offered for him.

"The best. They're just the best."

Iris smiled at him in agreement, then took the next new arrival from its carrier. This one was a striking-looking calico, much smaller than Indigo was. She blinked her almost-yellow eyes at me and wriggled in Iris's grasp. "And this is Coco. Coco came in to us with a litter of kittens, and she's basically just a baby herself, poor thing. The kittens all got adopted, and she just couldn't find a home. She gets a bit stressed out at the shelter, so we thought this might be a better environment for her to thrive in."

The small cat twisted like she might make a run for it at any moment, so Iris hustled to get her placed in one of the lower condos. Without even a pause to smell anything, she jumped into the litter box and cowered there.

"Oh, that poor baby," I said, crouching down to look at her.

"Yeah, she'll need to decompress a little. Don't be surprised if she never becomes really *warm*. I don't know what happened to her before she came to us, but she really doesn't trust people. Especially male people."

"That makes two of us," I heard Imogen say from behind a bookshelf. I think she was pretending not to be interested, but I kept seeing her peek around the corner to catch a look at the cats.

"And that's it. We'll have these guys with you for a month, depending on what happens. If they get adopted before then, awesome, and if not, we will look at rotating them to fosters or back into the shelter. You can remind people we're no-kill, so the cats will stay with us until they're adopted, no matter what. There's an online application form you can direct them to if they want to adopt, and we usually process those in twenty-four hours when we're able to. We will email you all the paperwork they need if they're approved. We also talked to Mr. Bravebird at the pet store—thanks for putting us in touch with him—and anyone who adopts from you will get a twenty-five-percent-off deal to get everything they need from him."

"Wow, that's so generous of him." Perhaps the hundreds of dollars I'd spent there since taking ownership of Bob had made him warm to me.

"Everyone just wants to see these cats find homes." She smiled at the two now-occupied condos. "Let's hope this plan works. It was a real pleasure to meet you, Phoebe. You have my email and my number if you have any questions or need anything at all. Keep me updated."

"Of course."

And like that, Iris was gone, toting two empty cat carriers and an umbrella back to her waiting car.

Mr. Loughery, Imogen, and I all gathered round the condos, peering into the suites Indigo and Coco would call home temporarily. Indigo's green eyes shone out from inside the cat house. Beneath him, at my feet, Bob had plopped himself in front of Coco's space. Unlike how he'd reacted to Indigo, he seemed curious about her as opposed to enraged. She was still hiding in her litter box, her little black ears sticking up over the lip.

"Let's give them a little breathing room to get settled," I suggested. While I could have stood there all day myself, just waiting to see if the cats would emerge, I knew it had to be scary for them to be in a foreign environment and they needed time to adjust.

The three human observers moved off, Mr. Loughery reclaiming his chair and picking up his current John Grisham. Imogen and I returned to work, but Bob staunchly refused to be moved and turned himself into a ginger loaf in front of Coco's cage.

I was going to shoo him away, but I noticed that once the humans were gone, she cautiously raised her head over the side of the litter box and sniffed the air in Bob's direction. There was no flattening of ears and no hissing from either of them. A good sign, perhaps. I decided to just leave him be for now, thinking maybe he could help coax the mistrusting calico out of her hiding spot. I'd love for her to at least start hiding in her cat bed instead of the litter box.

I watched Bob a little longer, transfixed by his steadfast devotion to Coco, like he was a guard ensuring no one bothered her. Was this a sign, perhaps, that he was a little smitten with the new arrival?

*You don't need another cat, Phoebe*, I told myself.

*But maybe* Bob *needs another cat.*

The lunch hour rush was soon upon us, though it wasn't as busy as it might be on a normal day. While more people were braving the bad weather today, it was still quieter than I'd like for midweek in the summer.

Imogen was drinking a cup of the new Gra-tea-tude tea blend I had made. I'd brought some samples for the staff, figuring they deserved some thanks as well. "Phoebe, this is *really* good. I think this needs to go into our regular rotation."

I had tried my hand at one or two other blends for seasonal offerings, but I had left them as one-offs, never remaking them once they were gone. Imogen's suggesting that Gra-tea-tude was good enough to stay around permanently made me flush with excitement. "You think so?"

"Definitely. You have the knack. Eudora would have loved this."

Her mention of my aunt brought me reeling back to the previous night in my living room. I wished I could understand what had happened to me during Karma and Honey's spell. I *wanted* to believe I'd spoken to my aunt, but Honey herself had assured me ghosts didn't exist. So if I hadn't been speaking to my aunt's spirit, was there another way it could have been her, or should I just listen to what the voice had told me and believe it was my own mind offering me comfort in the form of something familiar?

No, I couldn't just downplay it like that. I knew somewhere deep in the pit of my stomach and in my blood that I *had* been speaking to my aunt, my real aunt. Whether that meant she was a ghost, an angel—I had no idea, but I believed what she'd told me.

Maybe I should have been scared by the prospect of having spiritual conversations with a dead woman, but quite the opposite was true. I felt relieved, lighter, and more prepared to take on this weirdness that was happening to me and my magic.

It also made me believe that once I'd restored balance, I might be better able to control the powers that until this point had largely controlled me. And that wasn't just a relief, it was *exciting*.

On some level, I'd resisted the knowledge of my witchy skills. I had played with a spell here or there but never really dived deep to find out what I was capable of. It was time for that to change. Me being a witch wasn't going anywhere, and hiding from my powers had only given them an opportunity to take over. No, I wanted to see what could happen when I was in the driver's seat.

Imogen and I handed out packets of the tea to customers buying both tea and books, thanking them for making the trip in in such bad weather. The extra sample seemed to encourage and delight people, and at least one customer set their bags down to go buy more things.

Had I accidentally made the tea magical?

I shook my head, reminding myself that none of these people had actually drunk the tea yet and this was just the happy result of good customer service.

People who came in for lunch or to shop all gravitated toward the cat condos, and there were cooing sounds as people put their fingers through the bars. Indigo, as Iris had promised, warmed up quickly. He would butt his head into people's hands and rub against the bars when people went by. He was also a real ham. He would roll over on his back and show his white belly whenever anyone stayed near him for more than a minute, and he also liked to show off how his new toys worked if anyone was watching him.

Coco, on the other hand, was as shy as—if not shier than—advertised. Bob had stayed by her cage, however, and at some point when we weren't looking had managed to make her feel secure enough to move from the litter box into her actual bed area. Now we could see only an orange-and-black tail sticking out of the covered bed, but I would call it good progress for the first few hours.

When I looked up again after clearing away a few empty plates from the tearoom tables, I noticed someone near the cat cages who looked vaguely familiar. It took me a second, but once he pulled out his camera phone and bent himself backward at an awkward angle to get a better view of the cages with his lens, it dawned on me.

It was Connor. He appeared to be by himself and looked slightly less polished than he had the last few times I'd seen him.

I'd gotten a little information on him from Daphne after their coffee meeting, but there was something nagging me about Connor, and I didn't want to miss an opportunity to speak to him directly. Tucking the plates onto the kitchen counter, I casually walked over to where he was standing.

"Connor?" I asked.

He jumped, startled by the interruption.

"Sorry, sorry." I held my hands up in an *I mean you no harm* gesture. "It's just me, Phoebe. I own the store, remember?" Like he might have somehow forgotten in the few days since we'd last spoken.

"Oh, yeah. Hi."

Close up, he looked even more exhausted and disheveled than he had from a distance. It had obviously been several days since he'd last shaved, and there were deep-purple circles under his eyes. It reminded me of the way Deacon had looked the morning we'd learned about Sebastian's murder.

"How are you holding up?"

For a second, I thought he might cry. His face crumpled, his expression giving away just how *not* okay he was. He rallied himself quickly, though, schooling his expression and taking a long, quivering breath before he answered.

"Had better weeks, y'know?"

I nodded, patting him gently on the arm. "We were so sorry to hear about Sebastian. And then Andrew too. It was shocking. Did you know him?" I tried to keep my tone casual and friendly, like I

213

was only curious, but I was desperate to know if there was any connection between the two men.

"You mean the lawyer?" Connor asked.

"Yeah."

"No. I mean, I might have talked to him in the halls at the B and B or something, but I never met him before that."

"Had Sebastian?"

Connor gave me a weird look, and I knew immediately I'd taken my questioning a step too far. He slipped his phone into his jacket pocket and sidestepped me, an eye on the door. I thought he might have come hoping to bump into Daphne but hadn't counted on being pestered by the owner.

"How is Melody doing? She was so upset the day they found Sebastian. I haven't seen her around, and I wanted to check on her."

This question was going to go one of two ways. It would either push him over the line and he'd leave here and never come back—which I figured might happen anyway, given how touchy he already was—or it might swing him in the opposite direction. It all depended on what his feelings toward Melody were.

I waited one second, then two. Connor wheeled around, a finger in the air pointed in my direction, and my pulse skipped a beat as I prepared for him to yell at me for overstepping.

Instead, he said, "Melody, ha! Like she's even been here. She went out two nights ago, and I haven't heard a single damned word from her since. Some freaking business manager. She's supposed to be the one taking care of everything, answering all these questions, *helping*, but instead she just has one of her little drama-queen moments and can't be bothered to do her *job*. Just because Sebastian died doesn't mean the work stops."

I would have assumed that was exactly what it meant. It wasn't like they could make content anymore.

"I'm the one left dealing with the emails, the fans, all these horrible comments on social media. I'm the one texting Sebastian's *mom* because Laurel can't get ahold of Melody. Me. *Me*. I'm just the social media coordinator, Phoebe. I'm not a trauma counselor. What do you even *say* to someone in that situation?" He threw his hands up in the air. "I know things got a little weird with the whole Deacon situation, but this wouldn't have ever happened if Deacon was still in charge. Deacon wouldn't just *leave*. Deacon wouldn't do a lot of the things Melody has done."

I wasn't sure what to say to that, because in my very limited experience with Deacon, he had proven himself very good at leaving.

"Did you say Melody has done this kind of thing before?"

"Like, flaked?"

I nodded.

"Oh yeah, all the time. She would show up hours late for things. Leave work early constantly. To be honest, I think Sebastian was planning to fire her, but then all that stuff with Deacon went down and there was no one else who knew all of Sebastian's needs like Melody did. But he told her before we came on the trip that it was her last chance to prove herself."

"Melody knew Sebastian was planning to fire her?"

"He wasn't shy about telling us where we stood. If someone wasn't pulling their weight, he'd let them know. And he let. Her. Know."

Well, well, that *was* interesting.

"And between us, I think there was a lot more she was hiding."

Before I could ask him for clarity, he spotted Daphne, who gave him an enthusiastic wave and stole his attention completely.

I had thought Deacon had the most obvious motive to murder Sebastian, but if Melody had known her career was on the line, it explained a lot about her behavior at the signing—acting like a hypervigilant den mother—and also might have given her the best reason to kill him. Although killing him wouldn't exactly secure her job futures, I imagined it would help her explain why she'd been released from her last position and couldn't easily provide a reference.

Was self-preservation enough to kill for?

Backed into a corner, people could do incredible things. It didn't explain the lawyer, though.

Unless the lawyer had seen too much.

I wondered if Detective Martin knew about this possible motive. Certainly she had to have been looking for Melody regardless, because it sounded like no one had seen her since the street party.

If she'd skipped town, surely there would be a record of her using a credit card or her cell phone, wouldn't there? So maybe she was still in Raven Creek, just biding her time.

But was she hiding *from* a killer, or because she *was* the killer?

I was about to urge Connor to give me more details about Melody when Rich burst into the shop, his hair dripping wet, looking like he'd just run a marathon.

"Phoebe, we gotta go." He waved me toward the door.

"What's going on?" Everyone in the shop was staring at him, so there was absolutely no way for him to keep whatever he was going to say a secret. But based on his ashen skin and shell-shocked expression, I didn't think he was about to make a declaration of love.

"They just arrested Leo."

# Chapter
# Twenty-Nine

H aving someone with inside connections went a long way at a police station.

Rather than stopping us when we entered, the officer at the front desk gave Rich a quick glance and then nodded his head toward the door, ushering us inside without question.

There was no way I'd have gotten the same treatment by myself.

Rich and I headed into the main area of the Raven Creek Police Department, and I was struck by just how *small* it was. It made sense, considering the town had to share its major-crimes detectives with an entirely different station forty minutes away, but it was a stark reminder of just how little crime our community was accustomed to dealing with.

There were three glass-paneled offices lining one side of the building, a door marked STAFF, four desks in the middle of the room cluttered with various personal effects to indicate they belonged to specific officers, and two closed-off doors at the back. One said INTERROGATION, but the sign had been handwritten on packing tape and stuck over an original sign that was still visible as JANITORIAL. The other had an official sign that said HOLDING, which must be where they had holding cells.

How many holding cells could Raven Creek possibly have? One or two where someone could sleep off having too much to drink? We weren't really in the habit of playing host to violent criminals here.

Detective Martin was nowhere to be seen, and neither was Leo, but we spotted Detective Kwan Kim leaning against the wall outside the makeshift interrogation room.

Every fiber of my being demanded I go over and ask him what the heck they were thinking to arrest an innocent man. Rich must have sensed the intensity vibrating off me, because he placed a gentle but firm hand on my shoulder and gave his head one silent shake.

I understood his message completely: *Let me handle this.*

I also knew he had included me in this trip only as a courtesy. Leo, Rich, and I had been thick as thieves growing up, and we had begun to rebuild that core friendship now that I was back. Rich and Leo were still tight; I was just the outsider finding my way back in.

But Rich knew I'd want to be here to help defend my friend, even if it was just as a glaring bystander.

"Hey, Kwan." Rich crossed the room and gave the detective's hand a shake. Detective Kim was a handsome man, probably pushing fifty but with no wrinkles to show for it. The only thing that hinted at his age was a little graying around the temples.

"Hey, man." The pair shared a quick bro hug, patting each other's backs before separating. "Look, I know why you're here, and you know what I'm going to say."

"He didn't do it," Rich said, his tone flat and firm.

"And we also hope that's the case, but we can't ignore witness testimony, Rich. We have at least a dozen statements—including one from Ms. Winchester there—confirming that Mr. Lansing had an altercation with the deceased prior to his murder. We also have an

eyewitness that says Mr. Lansing was in the area of the Primrose Inn on the night of both murders."

"He *lives* in the area of the crime," I snapped, unable to keep my cool.

Rich gave me a quick look of censure but then picked up my evidence to present it more calmly. "Kwan, he lives a block away from the inn. Some nights he walks home from the grocery store. That isn't a smoking gun."

"We need to follow the evidence. You know that as well as I do."

"You didn't need to *arrest* him," Rich said.

"We've had two murders in seventy-two hours. I have to think about the safety of the town and make sure that if we have a suspect who has shown the potential for aggression, we make every effort to keep the population out of harm's way."

I snorted. The idea of Leo being a risk to anyone was absolutely ludicrous.

"And he hasn't been *arrested*. Man alive, this town loves gossip. He came with us willingly—no cuffs or anything—to submit to some questioning. We can hold him for forty-eight hours without an arrest to either clear him or book him as we deem necessary."

The nuances of arrest versus voluntary detainment were probably going to be lost on a lot of people in town, especially when people were already spreading the rumor that he had been thrown into the back of a cop car and hauled off. Leo's existing reputation was that of an aloof outsider. His sheer size didn't help anything. He was a mountain of a man, both tall and wide, and looked like he could crush someone with his bare hands. I imagined some folks were already a little nervous around him, and this wasn't going to help.

"He didn't do this. I don't know why you're not out looking for Melody Fairbanks," I grumbled.

Detective Kim shifted his focus from Rich over to me.

"Ms. Winchester, I understand that you are upset about your friend at the moment, but I want to assure you that we are still exploring all avenues of this case, and we are absolutely looking for both Melody Fairbanks and Deacon Hume as persons of interest in this case. It just so happened that Leo was readily available to us and willing to talk, which will go a long way for him, believe me. What *doesn't* help him is having his friends come in here like they're trying to be the cavalry in an old-timey Western movie thinking they're going to scoop him up and rescue him. You let us do our jobs, and we'll find out who did this, okay?"

His tone was polite but brooked no opposition. He wasn't going to accept anything other than an agreement, and he'd made that perfectly clear.

"Has he asked for a lawyer?" Rich asked.

Detective Kim shook his head. "He has not. He doesn't seem too overly concerned about his present situation, if I'm being honest. I shouldn't be saying anything about it, but between us, since we're friends and former partners, Rich, I think what we've got here is just a case of wrong place, wrong time. I know Leo too, don't forget that, and I know as well as you do the kind of man he is. But we'd be lousy cops if we let him go because he and I have had a beer a time or two. And *that* is why I'm out here and Martin is in there. Because if there's anyone who can separate personal from professional, it's her." He gave us a meaningful look as if to say we ought to try to do the same, but there was no way.

I couldn't *be* professional about Leo.

"Could you do me a favor and update me if anything changes?" Rich asked.

Detective Kim looked thoughtful for a moment, and I thought he might say no, but whatever had gone down with him and Rich in

their years together working out of the Barneswood PD, there was evidently a sense of respect and compassion that remained even years later.

"Yeah, man. I'll let you know, if you just promise to stand back and let us do our jobs here, okay?"

Rich nodded, but I said nothing.

If finding Deacon and Melody would help us get Leo out of here faster, than that was precisely what I aimed to do.

# Chapter Thirty

Detective Kim had been as kind as he could be given the situation, and I was grateful to learn that Leo hadn't officially been arrested . . . yet. Still, I left the police station a bundle of rage. As I stomped back to the car, Rich chased behind me, grabbing me by the arm and pulling me to a halt in the middle of the parking lot.

It was still raining, though not as hard as before, but neither of us had umbrellas, so in a matter of seconds I was soaked to the bone, water dripping down my chin and into my eyes. We probably could have picked somewhere a bit more comfortable to have a heart-to-heart.

"Phoebe, talk to me. You've got this look on your face like you're about to do something you might regret later, and I brought you here, so it's gotta be up to me to talk you *out* of doing whatever it is you have in mind."

I huffed a fake laugh. I was a little mad at him right now for knowing me so well. "He's our friend, Rich; we have to get him out of there. You know how this town is. Audrey at the B and B. Leo and his grocery store. How are they supposed to recover from this?"

He made a helpless gesture.

"We need to figure out who did this, and *why*."

"There's a chance that these crimes have nothing to do with each other. I think we need to take that into consideration," Rich reminded me.

"Two people were killed the same way, at the same place, in the same week." I ticked the items off on my fingers. "I thought you were a good cop once."

His brows furrowed together. "Hey. I know we're both upset right now, but we are on the same team." He gestured back and forth between us. "So don't start building these walls up like I'm the enemy and I'm trying to keep Leo in jail. That's not what's happening."

I was suddenly glad it was raining so he couldn't see my tears of frustration. Rich was right, as usual. I was stressed out and frustrated, and he was the closest thing I could take those feelings out on. It wasn't fair to him, and it wasn't helping Leo.

"I'm sorry. That was cruel, and I didn't mean it."

He nodded tightly. "I'm kind of a jerk sometimes too when I feel helpless."

I wanted to argue that that wasn't what was happening here, but the more I thought about it, that was exactly it. I wasn't mad because he wasn't helping, I was mad because there really wasn't much we could do *to* help.

I had only one idea, and it was something we could do that wouldn't put us at risk and wouldn't make anyone at the police department mad at us. At least not immediately.

"I want to go talk to Audrey again," I said.

"At the inn?"

I nodded. "I don't know if there's anything more she can tell us, but if she was working overnight during both killings, she might have something to share that the police missed or that we didn't hear about. When Deacon came to talk to me, he said he'd spoken to Sebastian the night of the murder. But maybe he also interacted with

223

Andrew. Audrey might know. We didn't know what was going to happen to Andrew when the police might have asked her about Deacon. It's worth a try." I shrugged.

He waited a long time to answer me, long enough that I felt certain he was going to say no, but instead he gave one short nod, then said, "But if we're going to do that, we need to go get changed."

*　*　*

Twenty minutes later we were both dry and parked in front of the B and B in Rich's car. It took me back to the night of the stakeout, as we'd sat in almost this exact same place, watching the same house, waiting to see if Melody would make a move.

Melody was missing now, and so was Deacon, leaving us two prime suspects short of a closed murder investigation. Since Detective Kim had made it very clear that we couldn't go looking for them, we were doing the next best thing—asking anyone who had been at the inn that night if there was perhaps some new information they remembered now that they hadn't before.

It was a long shot, but short of running out and adopting some bloodhounds to go on the hunt for our missing suspects, it was the best idea I could come up with.

If I went back to the store, I was just going to stew on my anger over what had happened to Leo, and that wasn't going to help anyone. It would just make me a miserable jerk to be around—not exactly ideal when working in retail—and nothing was going to get done.

I'd texted Imogen and Daphne to let them know I'd be back later to collect Bob and to call me if they needed anything. From the sound of Imogen's reply, they had everything under control, which I'd known before I even texted.

I had the best staff, and I promised myself I would do something soon to show them how much I appreciated them. Sure, I told them

so often, but they deserved a special treat to really *show* them how I felt. My love language was gift giving; it couldn't be helped.

Rich and I dashed across the street—this time we had brought umbrellas—and managed to get from the car to the inn with minimal soaking. We let ourselves in through the front door, and it was a stark shift in mood the second we got inside.

The B and B was quiet as a tomb. A grandfather clock in the hallway ticked the seconds by loudly, but it was so silent overall that the patter of rain could be heard in every room.

Audrey was seated behind the front check-in desk, not bothering to hide her dismayed expression even as she spotted us enter. "Afternoon, Rich. Phoebe." She nodded. I was impressed she'd remembered my name, since we'd only been introduced at a crime scene and needless to say she'd been under quite a bit of stress that day.

She looked to be under quite a bit of stress now as well.

"Hi, Audrey. How are you holding up?" The tone of Rich's words conveyed an entire world of sympathy without him having to say too much. Audrey appeared as if she might start to cry.

"Terrible, if I'm being honest. We've had *forty-seven* cancellations, Rich. *Forty-seven.*" She waved a hand at her laptop screen. "They tell me polite lies, you know? Forgotten wedding plans, someone in the family got sick, relative died, credit card was stolen. None of them can just up and admit it, but they're bailing because of the murders. And who can blame them? Would you want to stay in a murder house?" Tears started to stream down her cheeks, and I wasn't sure she was even aware she as crying. "Do you know what the kids are calling it? The *dead-and-breakfast.*" She hiccupped a little sob. "That's too catchy. That's going to stick."

Rich rounded the side of the counter and gave Audrey a tight hug. Her shoulders trembled, and her hand fisted in the material of his jacket. "This town has a very short memory about bad things,

Audrey, we both know that. You run a great inn, and if *our* memory is short, the outside world's is even shorter. As soon as they find who did all this, things will be back to normal. Don't forget, there's not a heck of a lot of other places for people to stay."

She sighed. "Maybe I should have sold to that lawyer when he suggested it. I laughed in his face, y'know. But if I'd said yes, I could have retired early, could have been sipping drinks on a beach chair in Bali right now. But I'm *ruined*."

My ears perked up. "The lawyer asked you to sell too?"

Audrey nodded, grabbing a tissue from a decorative box on the desk and dabbing her eyes with it. "He said he would pay me three times what the house was worth if I would leave it intact for a new owner to take over. I couldn't do that, though, you understand? This was my parents' place, and theirs before. Some of the furniture in here is from my great-great-grandparents. I wasn't just going to up and leave that. But now? Who knows if anyone is ever going to stay here again."

Rich rubbed her back gently. "You're going to be fine. This is going to be fine."

"I wish I could believe that." She gave a mighty sniff. "Anyway, you all didn't come here to listen to an old lady moan about her problems. I don't suppose you're looking to rent a room?" Despite how puffy her eyes were, she still managed to give us a cheeky wink, which made me think she was going to be fine—and that gossip about Rich and I really *was* all over town.

"Oh. No, no," I said quickly. "We were actually hoping you might be able to answer a few questions about what happened over the last couple of days, just to see if maybe you remembered something you didn't before."

Audrey came out from around the counter, and we followed her into the library sitting area. "I'm not sure how much help I can be.

The police already asked a million questions, but I'll tell you whatever you want to know."

We sat around the little coffee table, Rich and I squished in side by side on the love seat and Audrey in a huge overstuffed armchair that made her look almost childlike.

"On July fourth, did you see Melody Fairbanks leave the inn?"

"Oh sure, she headed out that evening, said she was going to check out the street party and wouldn't need any dinner."

"Did you see her again after that?"

Audrey shook her head. "No, I don't recall ever seeing her come back, but we did have such a hullaballoo that night with the second murder, there's a chance she could have come and I wouldn't have seen her."

"Are there any other entrances to the house?" Rich asked.

"Not for guests, but there's a storm door in the basement and an exterior staircase on the back of the house. It was an old servants' entrance; goes from the backyard up to the third floor. But I keep that door locked from the inside, and I'm the only one with a key."

"No other way she could have come in, then, without being seen?"

"Nope. Like I said, she may have come in when we were otherwise distracted. I mean, she must have come in at some point, because a bunch of stuff was taken out of the room."

This was news to me. "Wait, some of her stuff is missing? I thought all of her belongings were still here."

Audrey looked confused for a moment. "Oh, well . . . I mean, not everything was removed. To be honest, I thought perhaps the crew had started shuffling rooms around again. Her suitcase is still here, but I remember doing her turndown service that night and seeing a wallet sitting on the dresser, but it's gone now. I just assumed she had come back to grab it later."

"And the police didn't take it? Are you sure?" It seemed odd to me Melody would come back just to get her wallet but not any of her other belongings.

Audrey nodded. "Very sure. They were going to wait until the lawyer was taken out before they went through everyone's rooms and they asked me not to move anything, and I guess when they went back a few hours later, the wallet was gone. They didn't find it in anyone else's room either. They must have asked me a hundred times if I was sure I hadn't moved it or anyone on my staff, but no, we didn't touch *anything*."

So at some point between when the murder was discovered and when the police checked everyone's rooms, Melody—or someone with access to Melody's room—had been able to take her wallet. Which indicated she was either planning to split and needed funds, or else she had something in her wallet that she was so desperate to hide she would be willing to face a run-in with the police just to sneak it out of the inn. I wondered if it had something to do with the bank statement I'd found. Was there even more to incriminate her in potentially illegal activity? A suspicious debit card, maybe?

I thought about my earlier encounter with someone who might know a bit about what Melody was hiding. "Is Connor back yet?" I asked.

Rich gave me a quizzical look, and I realized that with the hasty departure surrounding Leo's not-arrest, I hadn't told him what I had learned just before he arrived. I'd need to fill him in after, because right now we had bigger fish to fry.

"No, he's been out now for a few hours. Seems like a nice boy— what a frightful week he's had. He might be the only one of my guests who hasn't asked about a refund or discount, as if their bank balances are the only thing that matters at a time like this." She made a little *harrumph* noise, and I decided not to remind her that mere moments ago *she* had been making the murders all about her bottom

line as well. I knew she was upset—and who wouldn't be in this scenario?—but her double standard was interesting.

"Did any of the other guests leave early?" I asked.

She shook her head. "No, thank goodness. The police have asked that everyone stay put for the time being, just in case any additional questioning is necessary. That nice man from the publishing house did leave, though. Some sort of emergency that needed to be handled back in New York. He cleared all that through the police, though, I think. At least that's what he told me when he checked out. He was very nice, paid full price for his room even though he was leaving early. Wish everyone was like that."

I mulled all this over, trying to decide which avenue to pursue next. If Connor wasn't here, I couldn't ask him about Melody's vanishing act—even if could have, I wasn't sure he'd be much help—and I already knew from Patsy that Travis wasn't a suspect anymore, so his exit wasn't news to me.

In retrospect, Travis was an illogical suspect anyway. Sebastian had been on the cusp of a very lucrative book tour, and with his stardom on the rise, there was surely going to be talk of a second book. And sure, book sales went through the roof after someone died, especially tragically, but a dead writer—especially one on the verge of possibly discovering a previously lost species of bird—wasn't going to be the same kind of cash cow as a live one.

Rich leaned forward in his chair. "Audrey, you said the two other entrances to the house are locked from the inside. Would you mind if we just went and had a look?"

I raised an eyebrow at him. The police would have checked those doors already, wouldn't they? What was he hoping to find?

"Oh sure. Follow me." She got up from the armchair with a little effort but refused Rich's offer of assistance. "I'm not that old yet, pal."

He grinned at her.

We headed upstairs to the third floor first. All the guest room doors were closed, and despite Audrey confirming that almost all the guests were still present, the silence was thick. I heard only one muted conversation behind one door; otherwise, everyone else was either out for the day or being quiet.

At the end of the third-floor hallway was a door with a frosted glass window in it, letting in quite a bit of light considering how rainy it was outside. It made the hallway feel bright and cheery.

"This was the room Mr. Marlow was staying in." I already knew that wasn't correct but couldn't admit I had snooped around here on my own. She waved her hand at the door to Melody's room. "And Miss Fairbanks was over here." The room right across the hall. "Oh, gosh no, what a silly mistake; it was the other way around. The crew changed rooms on me and I keep forgetting, what with all this excitement. Originally, we had booked Mr. Marlow in the room that overlooks the street—it's what you had requested, I remember; I picked it because it has such a nice view of Apple Street—but at the last minute, after check-in, as a matter of fact, I think they decided to change things. I believe Miss Fairbanks mentioned that Mr. Marlow wanted the room with the blackout shades even though it only looks into the backyard. At that point I was getting quite busy because we had a last-minute check-in with Mr. Bachman, and I wasn't paying too much attention to the room swapping. Plus when I was doing turndown, everyone's suitcases look so similar. Of course, now that we're talking about it, I remember seeing Melody's things, but at the time they could have belonged to anyone, you know? People could sleep where they wanted; the changes didn't matter—it was just hard to keep track. And the lawyer was so lovely and patient during the check-in. He came right after they'd all gone upstairs. He'd been staying at another place over on Hummingbird, but they had also

declined his offer to sell, so he was going to try out a few different spots. He was lucky we still had a room available, honestly."

So Andrew hadn't bumped into the bird crew at the hotel during check-in. It was interesting, however, that he had ended up murdered, considering he hadn't originally been planning to stay at the Primrose. Audrey's memory also left something to be desired, considering she had confidently mentioned seeing Melody's wallet but then forgotten which room had been hers. Perhaps the stress of the murders was a bit too much for her.

I was right back to square one with figuring out who the *real* main target of the murder had been.

We checked the exterior door at the end of the hallway. Situated right between Melody's and Sebastian's rooms, it would have been an ideal entry point to get access to Melody's room, and also to kill Sebastian.

The door, however, was locked from the inside. And not just a bolt that could be turned by one of the guests; it was locked with a padlock.

Probably not up to fire code, if I thought about it, but definitely not as easy or perfect an access point as it seemed at first glance.

"Let's go have a look at the basement. Audrey, maybe have a look at getting a fire lock for that door instead. If anything were to happen here, I think you'd be liable, because that's not an exit." Rich patted her on the shoulder as we followed her down the stairs.

The basement of the inn was a lot like the basement at the Earl's Study. It was dimly lit, and an underlying dampness hung in the air, making it smell musty and unwelcoming. Cobwebs clung to the corners of doorframes, and I gave silent thanks to the universe it was just cobwebs and not freshly built webs.

Audrey pulled a cord on an overhead bulb, just barely giving the space light. Shadows deepened at the edges of the main room, and

the darkness of the storm outside didn't do anything to help alleviate the creepy, claustrophobic feeling of being down here.

"The boiler room is under the stairs. I've got seasonal decor in here." She tapped on a closed door. "Laundry is over there, and the storm door is this way." Another dangling bulb awaited us about ten feet from the first, and Audrey showed us the heavy double storm door at the far side of a fairly empty room.

There were footprints in the dust all across the room, telling me plenty of people had come and gone down here before us. The police had obviously made a search of the space, so I wasn't sure what else we could be expected to find, but it never hurt to look. Perhaps something had been overlooked.

The inn's storm door looked exactly like the one in my own home's basement, a not-uncommon design for old Victorian mansions of a certain era. These doors looked a little newer than mine, likely a replacement for the originals, because wood doors certainly weren't an ideal solution as they aged. These looked to be made of a laminated material, and like upstairs, these were locked from inside. A chain had been wrapped around the interior handles and was fastened with a padlock.

Audrey's proclivity for locking up emergency exits and entrances did make me question for a moment whether *she* was involved in the killings. After all, it was a bit strange that the only way *into* her house if bad weather hit and the only way *out* upstairs in the event of a fire were both sealed off, but I also figured that was just one woman's way of protecting her home.

I hadn't been here long enough to know what kind of issues Audrey had previously had with break-ins or maybe with guests taking things from the upper floor where she wasn't able to watch them. I realized I was just looking for anyone convenient to point a finger at if I thought it might help Leo.

"Locked," Audrey announced, rattling the chain by giving the padlock a shake. "And I keep the keys on me at all times."

"There's no way someone might have taken them out of a drawer and returned them without you noticing?" I asked.

With a flourish, she withdrew a long chain that had been tucked down the front of her dress. "Master key and the padlock key." The two keys glinted in the low light from the overhead bulb. "I think I'd notice if someone took them."

Well, that certainly eliminated one avenue of entry.

A loud *ku-thwak* noise made all three of us spin around at once. My once-calm pulse was now going a mile a minute, and Rich's posture had stiffened. His hand had gone instinctively to his hip, I suspect where he had once worn his service weapon, but upon realizing he was unarmed, he moved instead to stand in front of Audrey and me.

*Ku-thwak.* The noise sounded again.

"Is that the boiler?" I asked hopefully.

"Definitely not," Audrey answered.

We collectively edged in the direction of the noise, although I would have vastly preferred to unlock the big storm doors and head out that way instead. I was on the cusp of asking Audrey if she was perhaps washing a load of bricks in the laundry when we heard the sound again for a third time.

*Ku-thwak.*

What *was* that? I couldn't contextualize the noise to give me the slightest idea of what we were hearing. It just sounded loud and heavy. I was grateful for what little light the overhead bulbs offered, but every shadow we threw against the wall as we walked made me want to jump out of my skin.

I was glad there was nothing in the room for my powers to pick up at the moment, but that just meant I was channeling all my

anxiety inward and my brain was cooking up a million different horrible possibilities of what was making the noise.

When we got to the door that Audrey had said was for seasonal storage, the noise sounded again, and it was obvious it was coming from behind that door.

"Stand back," Rich insisted, stepping aside from the door so he could open it without being right in front of it, just in case something came hurtling out at him or someone inside was waiting to attack.

With the door open, the sound was louder, but no one came charging out. Nothing immediately happened after the door was opened, so the three of us peered around the corner and into the narrow room.

As Audrey had said, the room was obviously intended for seasonal decor storage, something a lot of homes in town needed to find extra space for. She had deep wooden shelves built on either side of the room, and they were lined with clear plastic tote bins, all of them labeled with various holiday and season names to make it easier for her to see which was which.

The totes weren't what was interesting, though.

At the end of the room was a window at ground level, probably about six or seven feet off the floor. That window was currently open, and the thing making the noise we had heard was the chain from the overhead light being jangled by a strong breeze from the storm outside. As the wind lifted the chain, the chain would fall back and smack loudly into the side of one of the plastic totes.

*Ku-thwak.*

While that mystery was resolved, it wasn't the only interesting thing in the room.

Beneath the window, currently being doused with falling rain, were a navy-blue duffel bag and a crinkled-up paper bag from a

fast-food restaurant. As we scanned the interior of the room, I could also make out a sad-looking blanket tucked away under one of the shelves and a few empty plastic bottles of water.

I didn't need to ask.

"None of that was here when I checked a couple days ago," Audrey said, her voice shocked. "Has someone been staying here?"

I entered the room before Rich could stop me. Whoever had been here was gone for now; they'd probably taken off when they'd heard us come down the stairs. I approached the duffel bag, whose zipper was open, and to avoid the risk of touching it with my hands, I used the tip of my toe to push apart the sides.

I gasped.

On top of a pile of clothing was the bank statement for the LLC in Melody's name. The one that had been stolen from her room while I hid under the bed.

Beneath the sheaf of papers was an unmistakable orange-and-brown button-down.

This bag belonged to Deacon Hume.

# Chapter Thirty-One

We found ourselves face-to-face with Detective Kim for the second time in less than an hour, and he seemed even less thrilled about it than we were. We sat in the library where we had just recently grilled Audrey—who was being questioned in the office by Detective Martin—and there was a chilly silence in the room.

I didn't think I'd felt quite so small under someone's piercing stare since my father had caught me sneaking in two hours late after curfew when I was sixteen.

I half expected Detective Kim to say he wasn't mad, he was just disappointed, because that was precisely what his stare was saying to me.

"I just want to ask you what you two *heard* when you left the police station. Because I know what I *said*, and I feel like perhaps we have two different interpretations of what my words were."

"We didn't go looking for Melody or Deacon," I offered.

"I don't know if minor details are going to help much in this case, Ms. Winchester. I asked you guys—nay, I *told* you—to stay out of this investigation and let us do our jobs. I don't think revisiting the scene of the crimes to interrogate a witness is staying out of it."

He pivoted his attention to Rich. "You should know better than this, Rich."

"I didn't see the harm. And if we're being honest, it's unlikely you'd have found the items in the basement if we hadn't come back." He gave his old partner a pointed stare.

A long and painful silence drew out between them.

"Are you hoping I'm going to thank you?" Detective Kim asked.

"No. I'm just saying you guys can't be everywhere and see everything. We're not police, that's true, but we're also not the Scooby-Doo kids bumbling into answers. We found something useful."

I was glad he was the one saying it and not me, because I didn't think Kim would be as restrained with his responses if I were the one speaking. I could sometimes come across a little indignant.

"Well, I appreciate your . . . efforts," Kim said sullenly. "I know you're trying to help your friend. But from this point forward, I'm going to have to officially ask you to remove yourselves from investigating this case, or I will have both of you arrested for obstruction of justice. Am I clear?"

My mouth hung open.

"But Detective Martin *asked* me to—"

"I asked you to listen and observe, Phoebe." Detective Martin had entered the room with Audrey trailing behind her. "I think we both know that I didn't ask you to take on your own investigation." She raised a brow at me, showing me she wasn't impressed that I would use her name to defend myself.

She was right, I shouldn't have thrown her under the bus like that, and my cheeks flushed hotly. I *hated* feeling like this, knowing I had misbehaved and was being called out for it. But every step of the way, what we'd done had been from a place of wanting to help. I'd wanted to help find justice for Sebastian out of a sense of guilt,

and I'd wanted to find answers for Leo to keep him out of the cross hairs of the investigation.

This wasn't the first time I'd been asked to mind my business about a murder, but it was the first time they'd threatened to arrest me if I didn't. I had no defense for that, and obviously Rich didn't either, because he said nothing.

Rich also wasn't saying he *would* stay out of it.

"All right, you two can go now," Martin said, keeping her tone even and level.

We waited until we were back in the car before speaking again, the patter of rain on the windshield one of the only sounds in the late afternoon.

"Say something," Rich insisted, breaking the silence.

I considered my options. I thought about discussing what we'd just been told and asking him whether or not he planned to listen. But he had no personal stake in this investigation; he was just along for the ride to help me. If the police told him to stay out on threat of arrest, he would listen.

He'd been a cop once, after all.

"Do you think Deacon was there the whole time?"

Rich sighed, tapping his palms against the steering wheel and staring out at the rain. He wanted to give me a lecture, I could tell. But he was holding it back.

"It's hard to say. They obviously checked the entire house after both murders, and there was no sign of him then."

"If he was coming and going through that window, there's no reason to think he wasn't just grabbing his bag every time the police showed up and hightailing it out until the coast was clear. It's pretty apparent no one knew that window was an access point."

Rich nodded his agreement. "Point taken."

"If he was sleeping there, that would explain how no one was able to find him at any of the other area hotels or during general sweeps. He had a safe place to hunker down and plenty of access to kill both Sebastian and Andrew."

"I'll admit this doesn't look great for Deacon, but we also can't ignore Melody's connection to the lawyer. They were arguing not long before his death, and if an argument is reason enough for the police to look at Leo, it should be enough for them to think Melody might have something to do with the lawyer's death. I just can't figure out why she might want to kill Sebastian. Though the bank statement is compelling if it *does* prove she was stealing from him."

"Oh, I have something for that," I announced, and quickly told him about the news Connor had shared with me at the shop.

"Huh." Rich ran his hand through his damp hair, creating a defined wave of curls that distracted me from our discussion for a few seconds.

"What if Melody and Deacon were working together?" I asked.

Rich frowned. "I could consider it if they were a couple or if they even passably liked each other, but from everything you've told me, the two of them couldn't stand each other."

"Maybe that was all a show for Sebastian and for this exact situation. So no one would think they could work together and everyone would write off the possibility. They *both* had motive, they *both* had opportunity."

"For Sebastian. But not the lawyer."

I rested my head against the headrest, staring up at the boring beige roof of Rich's car.

"We shouldn't even be talking about this, Phoebe. You heard Kwan. We're out. We've told them everything we can, and they can

come to these conclusions just as easily as we can. We have to let this go. *You* have to let this go."

"I'm the reason Sebastian was here, Rich. If he hadn't come, maybe he would still be alive right now."

"You can't think like that. If you're right about Melody or Deacon, they both had reasons for wanting him dead. They might not be good reasons—there's few cases where there are—but if they wanted to kill Sebastian, they were going to do it. It doesn't matter where he was. You can't blame yourself for this."

Logically, I knew he was right, but logic and guilt were rarely friendly bedfellows.

"And you can't blame yourself for Leo either. You had to tell the police what you saw; without your perspective they would have *only* gotten gossip. If anything, you helped them see what really happened there."

"For whatever good it did."

"It did plenty of good, I promise. He'll be out of there in no time. Man, I don't want to speak ill of the dead, but I'd have loved to hear what Andrew said to Leo to push him over the edge like that. He can't have just offered to buy the place. Other people have offered; Leo just sort of laughs them out the door and goes on with his day. If he was as mad as you say he was, then that guy really pushed some buttons. Makes you wonder what other buttons he might have pushed."

Something popped into my head.

Something I hated and wanted to ignore.

I glanced over at Rich.

"Oh no. I know that look. We're off this case, Phoebe. This is just *discussion*."

"Rich, I want to go talk to Dierdre Miller."

Of all the things I could have said to him in that moment—or any moment—I don't think either of us ever expected those words to come willingly out of mouth.

"I'm sorry, you're going to need to repeat that."

"I'd like you to drop me off at Dierdre's office." I checked the clock on his car's dash, confirming she was still likely to be there. It was only three, so I was confident that unless she was showing a house somewhere, she'd be in.

"What are you up to?"

"Do you actually want an answer to that question?" I smiled innocently.

"No, not if I want plausible deniability, I guess."

"Smart man."

"Never been accused of that in my life."

He started the car, and we headed to Dierdre's office. It was a mostly residential block, but there were three little offices in a business plaza at the end of the street. Dierdre, an accountant, and a dentist all shared the space adjacent to a tidy parking lot. I recognized Dierdre's cute little red car, confirming she was in.

"You sure about this?" Rich asked, eyeing the office building through the rain.

"Dierdre's not going to hurt me," I scoffed.

"I'm not worried about that; I'm worried about you ending up in a cell right next to Leo."

I swatted his arm.

"See, violent outbursts!"

"You think you're funny and you're not."

"I'm hilarious. It's one of the many things you love about me."

We both paused at the drop of the l-word, and before the moment could stretch into something awkward, I leaned over and gave him a quick peck on the cheek.

"One of many."

I didn't give him a chance to say anything, instead grabbing my bag and umbrella and ducking out of the car. I did hazard a quick

look back as I got under the protective awning of the plaza, and even through the rain and across a parking lot I could see a goofy little grin on his face.

Oh, I was in so much trouble.

I went from smiley happy bliss to walking into Dierdre's real estate office and seeing the woman herself.

My smile collapsed just as hers rose.

"Why, if it isn't Phoebe Winchester. I never thought I'd see the day you might step foot in my office. What a treat. What brings you in?"

I was sure she was already calculating the windfall she could make in commission on selling my house.

"I was actually hoping I could have a quick chat with you."

Our last two chats had ended with things floating all around the room and a coffee in Dierdre's lap. I hoped that by coming to her of my own volition and being mentally prepared for it, I might be able to escape unscathed this time.

In truth, since my encounter with Eudora the previous night, I was still feeling at ease magically. I wasn't cured yet, but I had a solution at hand, and just knowing that seemed to help. Placebo effect, possibly, but I wasn't going to overthink it if it was working.

This would be a real test of that newfound peace. If anyone could trigger my fight-or-flight, it would be Dierdre.

"Sure thing, I'm free." Her voice was sickly sweet, and I wondered if she was being so nice to me because I still hadn't signed off on leasing the apartment to her nephew. I wasn't *really* a vindictive person, and I wasn't going to take out my dislike of Dierdre on her nephew, whom I hadn't ever met before. But if *she* thought I might do that, I wasn't going to tell her otherwise.

She invited me to a small sitting area at the front of the office.

"Dierdre, I had some questions about Andrew, the lawyer, and what his plans were here. You said he was working for a company, but what company? I don't think anyone who's mentioned him has said anything about that."

Her expression shifted, and she looked a little green around the gills momentarily. "Oh, him. He told me his client wanted to keep their identity private until all the documents were signed."

"Did anyone actually *sell* to him? Audrey at the inn said he came to her after leaving a different B and B when they declined to sell to him. We both know I wasn't going to sell him anything. So was anyone actually interested in his offer?"

"He was only in town about three days before he . . ." Her voice drifted, and then she dramatically mimed a stabbing. "So he didn't actually have an opportunity to close any deals."

"To your knowledge, was anyone interested?"

She was quiet, and I imagined she didn't want to admit that she didn't have any deals in the pipeline, but she finally said, "I can't speak to anything that was handled directly by him, but anyone I connected him to politely declined the offer." She shuffled in her chair, now evidently uncomfortable. "Actually . . . I was in touch with someone in a real estate office over in Leavenworth, and Andrew had been there before visiting us. It sounds as though he didn't leave many positive feelings in his wake. He agreed to terms with a B and B owner there, making them promises about how much money they'd make, and they signed a contract without having their own lawyer look it over. Apparently, the contract gave Andrew the right to sell their property to a large corporation at *perceived* value. They ended up getting pennies for their property, and because they'd signed a contract with Andrew to mediate the sale on their behalf, it was all legal. Scummy, but legal. It sounds like this is something he's been doing all over Washington and Oregon. Usually he targets older

folks, widows, people who just want to retire comfortably, and he basically steals their property out from under them. He seemed like such a nice man too. I'm ashamed to have believed him at face value."

I was horrified but also not surprised. I hadn't even heard what he was offering before declining outright, and part of that was because rents were more affordable in Raven Creek than they were anywhere else in the state. People could still manage to own their own businesses without losing their shirt. However, I found it interesting that there was so much secrecy involved with who he was working for. Leo had told me Andrew had implied that a major chain retailer would be involved in taking over the grocery store. And the gist of what I'd gathered from anyone who had interacted with Andrew was that he was making similar implications about turning their little B and Bs into name-brand spots. Now, based on what Dierdre had told me, it sounded like he *was* working for some corporation, because it was obvious that whoever had put him up to this had no scruples at all.

Nothing, and I mean *nothing*, will dissuade someone in a small town from accepting an offer like hearing their space will be turned into a chain.

"I guess no one here thought it was worth it, thank goodness," Dierdre said, seemingly aware of where my mind was going. "It's one thing to sell to someone who wants to keep things around here the way they are. It's something else entirely to try to turn it into Disneyland. No one here wants a Starbucks on every corner; I think you know that better than anyone. I'm relieved no one was taken advantage of before . . . well, before he died."

I nodded, though I found her stance funny when only days earlier she'd been urging me to buy in so I could pack my bags off the profits and move back to Seattle. "Don't you think someone coming into this environment would know what the atmosphere would be

like, though? Why would he lead with the idea that properties would be turned into cookie-cutter chains? It was like he *wanted* to fail. I don't know what he said to Leo, but I have to imagine it was intentionally inflammatory. Leo just doesn't get mad like that. The lawyer had to have goaded him into it by pushing all the right buttons."

At this Dierdre rolled her eyes, and I worried she was about to launch into another monologue about Leo being a murderer. At which point I might become a murderer. She had that effect on me some days.

Instead, she said, "I will say in my dealings with him, he was very flashy about discussing money. He talked about how wealthy his bosses were, how connected they were, how this entire thing would help revolutionize the town and bring us into a new era of prosperity. It was all very lovely to hear, you know, like being on a first date where they tell you how beautiful you are." She tossed her red hair over one shoulder, letting me know that she was very accustomed to being told how beautiful she was. "But there were some things I noticed on our subsequent meetings as he went through town."

"Oh?" I wasn't about to ignore this, because Dierdre was the kind of person who paid attention. She watched everyone and everything around her, and if something seemed a hair out of place, she was going to spot it.

"For one thing, his suit. He wore the same one each time we met."

"That can't be *that* unusual for someone who's traveling. Who wants to pack a half dozen suits for a trip to a little town in the mountains?"

At this, she scoffed. "Phoebe, while *you* may not want to impress anyone with your wardrobe, that doesn't mean everyone else is equally careless about their appearance."

For a moment I wondered if I was still wearing my soaked ensemble from earlier that afternoon, but when I looked down, I confirmed I had on a nice pair of cinnamon-colored corduroy pants and a black short-sleeved blouse with Victorian lace details on the sleeves and collar. If anything, I looked dressed up compared to my usual tee-and-jeans uniform.

I let the barb slide off me, trying not to take it too personally. When I didn't rise to her bait, Dierdre continued. "A man in that position should have at least two or three good suits with him at all times. He wore the same one to every meeting. I could tell because it kept getting more and more rumpled, like he wasn't even bothering to iron or steam it every day."

I was about to ask who traveled with their own steamer, but I was sure that would just make her call me a wrinkly disaster, so I let it go.

"And then there were his shoes."

"His . . . his shoes?"

"Yes. Loafers." Her nose wrinkled so fiercely that I wondered if she had smelled something bad, only to realize it was her opinion about loafers in general. I was happy in that moment to be wearing my Chelsea rain boots and not my usual loafers, because I wasn't sure I would have survived the withering judgment.

"I'm sorry, what's wrong with loafers?"

"Why nothing, if you're a seventy-eight-year-old man with a time slot booked at the shuffleboard court. Or if you run a bookstore, I suppose." There it was. "But a lawyer in the business of brokering multimillion-dollar details . . . loafers? Absolutely not. Shined oxfords. A classic brogue if you're an especially elegant gentleman. But certainly not a *loafer*."

I had absolutely no idea what any of the terms she had just used meant, but she said them with such conviction I had to believe her.

246

"So he had one suit and bad shoes. Maybe he wasn't fashion forward. If he was busy running around for his clients, maybe he didn't have time to shop."

"Phoebe, my dear. The man wore Drakkar Noir cologne." She raised a meaningful eyebrow at me, as if this final piece of her puzzle should explain beyond a shadow of a doubt what she was trying to convey, but I was at a loss. My snobbery didn't cut as deep as hers.

She sighed, obviously frustrated by my stupidity. "He was *poor*," she declared. "He was *not* the lawyer of a wealthy firm. If you represent billionaires, you have to put yourself forward at the value they expect. No one doing business deals for a Fortune 500 company wears Drakkar Noir and loafers. A real lawyer wouldn't need to trick people out of their money the way he was. And given how he was presenting himself, it sounds to me like he wasn't particularly good at scamming people either."

I suddenly understood what she was saying, and I was momentarily too shocked to give words to the thoughts.

She waited for me to speak, a smug little smirk at the corners of her lips.

"Dierdre, are you saying you think this guy was just a straight-up con artist?"

"I didn't see it at first either, I must admit. He had a silver tongue, that one. And on the surface he had the right look. The Rolex was a nice touch. Probably a knock-off, but a good one. And when he pitched *me* the idea of an investment property portfolio, I had to admit that at first I was really intrigued. He certainly did his homework."

"But he was a fake?"

"Well, he certainly wasn't a lawyer for a major grocery chain or real estate mogul. I don't know what he was actually here for, but I think it's probably a good thing no one jumped when he made those offers. Or gave him any money for his investment schemes."

Offers she herself had tried to convince me to take only days earlier. I bit my tongue hard to keep from mentioning that part.

Something else rang a bell in my mind.

Dierdre had said Andrew had been in Leavenworth before coming here.

Leavenworth had been the last stop on Sebastian's book tour before he came to Raven Creek.

I somehow didn't think that was a coincidence.

# Chapter
# Thirty-Two

Everywhere this case brought me was somewhere new I hadn't expected to find myself. Perhaps there was a reason I wasn't a professional investigator like Rich or a police officer like Detectives Martin and Kim, because it always shocked the heck out of me to learn that people were being dishonest.

And such a *big* lie too.

If Dierdre's assertions were correct and Andrew had been a con man, then what was he trying to achieve? He hadn't managed to convince anyone to sign his cruel sales deal. But if Dierdre was right and he was also asking them to put money back into the town through some sort of investment scheme in Raven Creek's future, then there might be something to what he was trying to do.

Based on Leo's reaction and what I'd heard from Amy and other business owners, Andrew had been more off-putting than he was convincing. He'd had Dierdre going for a bit, but he'd needed her help to try to convince other locals, so his approach hadn't been one of hostility with her.

And if he had managed to convince someone to make an invest-ment, they were going to realize quickly they were investing in

249

nothing. At least I hoped my friends and neighbors had been smart enough to see through a scam.

What his ploy *did* do, however, was create an entirely new web of suspects for who could have killed the fake lawyer. If one of the homeowners or tenants he approached on his quest had agreed to take the deal he offered, then realized it was all a fake-out . . . well, there was plenty of motive.

The amount of rage someone in that scenario might feel was astronomical.

I recalled the way Audrey had wistfully talked about retiring early to a beach in Bali with all her financial concerns gone, then imagined it all amplified by a hundred for someone who had towering debt and a family to take care of. The right person pushed the wrong way might have decided that the lawyer had to pay for his lies.

So now it wasn't just a question of where Melody and Deacon were but the additional quandary of whether or not the entire town might have a motive to kill the man. I wished I could ask Leo exactly what Andrew had said that had set him off so badly. It might give me an idea of who else's buttons he could have pushed.

The other big problem was that I needed to share this information with the detectives, but I wasn't sure how to do that without letting them know I was still poking around. I could say I'd just bumped into Dierdre and we were discussing her nephew's lease when the topic had come up, but even in my head that sounded like a lie.

I should have asked Dierdre to call the police and tell them herself, but there was no way she'd do that without mentioning me, so I'd be screwed no matter what.

I was just going to have to take the heat and hope that the intel provided was helpful enough that they'd overlook my transgression.

A voice in the back of my head told me that the police might not even *need* to hear it from me. Surely they had run a background check on Andrew that would show he didn't work for a massive corporation.

But if it showed he was a lawyer, they might just assume he was being honest. Files between lawyers and clients were confidential, and since he hadn't told anyone the name of his client, there was no way to disprove him on paper. The notion that he was scamming people was just Dierdre's hunch, but it rang too true for me to ignore it.

Thinking about Andrew, I realized I hadn't checked my phone today to see if Sam had gotten back to me, and in fact, he had. There was a surprisingly long text—atypical of Sam—that read, Dude is a real piece of work, notorious history of making terrible contracts that border on elder abuse. Multiple bar complaints, but he's still practicing. If you're thinking of doing business with him, DON'T.

So Andrew *was* a real lawyer but not a very highly regarded one.

I sighed as I jogged down Main Street, clinging to my umbrella. I'd text Patsy as soon as I got home. Of the two detectives, she would go easier on me, and this kind of information was what she'd hoped I might be able to help with in the first place. I wasn't at a crime scene and I wasn't following suspects; I was just talking to another person in town.

They couldn't get too mad at me for that, I hoped.

The street was vacant, but I still had the creeping sensation someone was watching me. I looked over my shoulder, expecting to see a shadowy figure, but there was nothing. Still, I picked up my pace.

The store was still open when I arrived, and I was surprised by how early it was, even though the cloud cover made it feel like it was almost time to go to bed. Imogen was making tea for someone when I walked in, shaking my umbrella outside the door, and Daphne was at the cash desk with a whole packet of chalk pens spilled out on the counter.

As the door chimed, the pair of them looked up and smiled, then, realizing it was me, made exclamations of surprise.

"We weren't expecting you back today," Daphne said.

"Is everything okay with Leo?" Imogen asked, in almost the same breath.

"Mreow?" inquired Bob.

"Hello, hi, nice to see everyone. I'm back for my cat and my car, and then I promise to stop cramping your style. Leo is *not* under arrest; he had voluntarily submitted to questioning." I said that loud enough for any gossipy ears in the building to hear. "And no, I didn't bring you any treats," I concluded to Bob.

He returned to his place by the kennels.

"How's it been?"

"Slow. That weird social media kid was here for ages after you left. He asked a ton of questions about Leo and what we thought about the murders." Imogen made a face. "Little freaky, if you ask me."

"Immie, you're so mean," Daphne scolded. "Connor worked so hard for that job with Sebastian, and he was really good at what he did. It sounds like he had a really hard life, and with no degree or previous experience, no one wanted to take a chance on him until Sebastian hired him. He gave me some great tips for our social feeds." She beamed excitedly. "I have so many ideas."

Leave it to Daphne to turn Connor into her new best friend. I smiled at her. "That's awesome. You know I have no clue what works on socials; I'm still posting pictures of my food on Instagram, so I trust you. What are you working on there?" I pointed to the pile of markers in front of her.

"Oh, you'll love this," Imogen said, handing the tea over to her customer and thanking them. I was surprised that her tone wasn't sarcastic.

Daphne held up one of the little chalkboards that we had for the kennels. She had drawn Indigo's name in fancy script and added an adorable cartoon portrait of him next to his name. Underneath, in a variety of hand-drawn fonts and colors, she had given key word descriptions of him and his behavior but had also added cute fake information like one might find on a dating profile. *Likes: Churu treats, lap cuddles, and the Sunday New York Times (to lay on). Dislikes: Being asked when the Indigo Girls are getting back together and going to the vet.*

The sign was unbelievably eye-catching and charming and way more detailed than anything I'd have expected.

"Daphne, that's incredible."

She blushed. "Oh, I was happy to do it. I have great ideas for Coco."

"Has she come out at all?"

Imogen joined Daphne at the counter. "She very briefly emerged from her Coco-cocoon to sniff Bob, which I think made his entire afternoon, and then she went back into hiding. But it was a positive sign. A couple people already asked to take Indigo out, and he seems to love the attention. At least for now we've told people that Coco is just to be observed until she warms up to her new temporary home."

Imogen's thoughtfulness about the cat's needs warmed my heart. I was delighted to see my stoic and usually grouchy friend was getting involved in this new venture.

Daphne went to affix the new sign to Indigo's cage door, taking down the leaflet from the shelter that was there as a placeholder. She stopped and spent a good minute cooing at him through the cage bars before crouching down to give Bob a scratch behind the ears so he wouldn't feel left out.

253

As promised, I collected my cat and car and left the ladies to finish their shift without the boss looming over their shoulders. I was a good boss, and at least from my side of things I considered both of them friends as well as employees, but I also knew perfectly well the euphoric release that occurred the moment your boss walked out the door at the end of your shift. I wasn't sure what their little no-Phoebe freedoms were—whether it was the freedom to use their phones (something I allowed anyway) or to read at the counter (something else I allowed)—but I knew they didn't bother me.

Bob protested loudly when I collected him to go home, and I had to assure him that Coco would be fine without him for one night.

The fact that he hadn't moved from her side all day did not escape my notice.

*Phoebe, no.*

The rain was easing up slightly when I parked my car in front of Lane End House, so I scooped up Bob's backpack without bothering to open my umbrella and made a run for the porch. The old boards on the steps creaked under my heavy footfalls, but the newly replaced boards in front of my door were as silent as a whisper. A good sign.

Once inside the house, I released the wild beast from his shackles, and he set about sniffing around the entire main floor like he'd lost something. Was he looking for Coco?

*Does Bob need a friend?*

It was an idea I wasn't *quite* ready to give voice to just yet, and it was far too soon in Coco's stay to even consider it. But still, the idea was there, and Bob was feeding it with each new room he entered looking for a cat who wasn't there. Once he even let out a sad, long meow, like he was calling for someone other than me, and it was a lot for my tender, stupid, cat-loving heart to deal with.

I ended up feeding him dinner two hours too early in hopes that it would distract him.

I was moving the sitting room furniture back into place from where it had been moved the previous night when something caught my eye over the fireplace. I didn't spend much time in this room and spent even less of it at this vantage point on the floor, so I'd never really noticed a particular piece of Eudora's art mounted above the fireplace mantel.

With the coffee table back where it belonged, I walked over to the hearth and stared up. The piece really blended in if you were looking at it from eye level, which might explain why I simply walked past it every time I entered the room, but if I tilted my head at a certain angle, the low light from the dim overhead bulbs caught it just right.

It was a long, bronzed branch, maybe three feet long and the thickness of my thumb. On the branch were about a dozen chubby birds, huddled together like it was winter and they were hoping to get warm. Perhaps that was why Eudora had placed it over the fire—so the little metal birds could absorb the warmth all winter long.

But something about the birds bothered me. They were adorable, and I enjoyed the piece now that I knew it was there—I might move it to the kitchen side of the two-sided fireplace so I could appreciate it more—but it also made me think of something I couldn't quite put my finger on.

Birds over a fire.

Why was I thinking of birds over a fire as meaning something important?

And then it hit me.

When Honey told me about her dream, she'd said she had dreamed of a cluster of birds over a house, and in the end, the birds all flew away as the house burned to the ground.

A chill swept through me.

She'd said it was how she'd known that the wrong person had died.

Looking up at that sculpture when I did might have been the very thing that saved my life when the fire poker sliced through the air over my right shoulder and smashed into the rocky edifice of the fireplace hearth.

The poker sticking in the grate on its way up was also a big help.

Later, I might wonder if my aunt's spirit had anything to do with my luck, but in the moment, I spun backward, tripping over the coffee table I had just moved back into the center of the room and smacking my head on the love seat behind me.

A figure wearing all black with a thick woolen ski mask over their face was struggling to regain their grasp on the heavy metal poker.

From my place awkwardly stuck between the coffee table and the love seat, I couldn't manage to right myself, and a horrible thought occurred to me.

*If they get that poker free, I'm going to die.*

In different circumstances, at other points in my life, my probability magic might have kicked in at that moment to freeze time, help me get untangled and out the door. But that didn't happen this time.

Instead, Bob came into the room, and my would-be killer and I noticed him at the exact same moment, when Bob pinned his ears back and hissed at the person in head-to-toe black.

Bob hadn't been looking for another cat earlier after all; he'd been trying to warn me that something wasn't right.

My attacker wrenched the poker free and took one step, then two steps, not toward me but toward my cat. The same horrific certainty I'd felt about my own imminent death shifted, and a ripple of the most blood-curdling, horrific fear I'd ever felt in my life ran through my body from the roots of my hair to the tips of my toes.

I wanted to throw up and scream in equal measure, because this person, this monster who had tried to kill me, was about to attack my cat, and I knew in that moment I loved that fluffy ball of fur more than I'd loved most of the people I'd known in my life.

I'm not sure when it happened or how, but the coffee table was suddenly on its side and the love seat was three feet away from me against the far wall of the room. The already dim overhead lights were flickering, and the once-cold fireplace was suddenly roaring to life with a fire that threatened to overtake its confinements.

The room felt small and everything in it more distant than it had only a minute earlier, but I didn't have time to think about why. I just saw someone standing over my cat, and my entire being became attuned to making sure that nothing happened to Bob.

The cat in question was too busy trying to intimidate my attacker to notice what I was up to. He was flashing a mouthful of fangs, generating the ferocity of an actual jungle cat and swiping his claws out at the intruder's black-and-white Converse sneakers.

A grunt of pain told me that Bob had struck flesh, but he'd also tangled his nail in the person's sock, making him a sitting duck for retribution. Rather than attacking with a weapon, the intruder pulled their leg back, and I knew—could envision entirely—that their next step would be a hard kick to my cat's side that would likely be enough to incapacitate or even kill him.

Bob didn't have this same gift of foresight; he was just furious about being stuck and was taking it out on the person's leg with more swats and an attempted bite.

The world around me did not come to a stop.

It didn't need to.

I was in control this time.

# Chapter
# Thirty-Three

As the intruder arced their foot to kick Bob, I held my hand out and squeezed it shut into a fist.

The attacker's leg froze in place.

For one brief, stupid moment I thought, *Those shoes look so familiar.*

And then it struck me. I'd seen those shoes when I was cowering under Melody's bed and the person wearing them was hiding bloody gloves in her suitcase.

I knew time was still moving, though, with the fireplace crackling loudly from the blaze I had raised up from nothing and Bob ferociously growling as he struggled to both defend me and get his stuck paw free from the person's sock.

The attacker made panicked grunting noises as they tried to move their body and realized in horror that they couldn't. After a mighty struggle, Bob got his paw free and skittered across the room, hiding himself under one of the armchairs but still making plenty of noise to show he wasn't afraid.

With my cat safe, I approached the person and stood in front of them. While I couldn't see their face behind the knit mask, I did see

a pair of frantic brown eyes through the eyeholes, positively bulging with terror.

*Good.*

I had never in my life wanted to hurt another person, not in any real capacity. Even when I'd learned my husband was cheating on me, I'd been more interested in finding a way to never see his face again than in doing anything to physically hurt him.

But this person had come into my home, a safe space for me, and they had not only tried to kill me—or at least severely incapacitate me—they had been on the cusp of hurting the one creature on the planet who loved me unconditionally.

I wasn't going to stand for that.

I raised my fist, and with it they lifted a good three feet off the floor, dangling a few inches from the overhead chandelier. They continued to make muffled grunting noises, and it took me a moment to understand why they weren't screaming or swearing at me.

They couldn't move their mouth.

I had managed to take the gift I'd been given, one that protected me by freezing the world around me, and I had *controlled* it. I had funneled that ability to freeze time into a single person and stopped them in their very tracks.

While I was a little too high-strung at the moment to enjoy my success, I did pause for a moment to take in the scene above me and realize just how impressive a feat it really was.

I had done that.

And now I'd need to explain it to the police somehow.

I pulled my phone out of my pocket with my spare hand, leaving the other fist lifted, not sure if I needed it in order to keep the spell active but unwilling to take any chances. I was no longer worried about the police being mad at me for talking to Dierdre about the

lawyer, because I was pretty certain whoever had killed him and Sebastian was floating up around my ceiling right now.

Detective Martin arrived within minutes. They'd still been doing another search of the inn when I'd called, which meant they hadn't had far to come. When she walked into the sitting room where I was still standing, she took one look up at the ceiling, then one at me, and let out a long, low whistle.

"I have no idea how I'm going to put *this* in my report," she said, her voice remarkably calm.

"*Suspect detained by homeowner*," remarked Detective Kim, who had come to stand on the other side of me.

Why were both of them so *chill* about this? The person was *floating*.

"Hey, Phoebe," Detective Martin said in a soothing tone. "You can let them down now." She placed her hand on my shoulder, and Detective Kim withdrew his service weapon, angling it at the floor but having it ready just in case the person decided to make any funny moves once they were on the ground.

I unclenched my fist, and the intruder dropped roughly to the floor, landing with a thud. I could, perhaps, have been a little gentler about how I had done this, eased them down before releasing my grasp, but I didn't feel particularly guilty about the loud groan they let out.

"Are you going to arrest her?" demanded the masked assailant. Since it was the first time I'd heard their voice, it came as a bit of a surprise to me that I recognized it.

I'd just been speaking to the person a few hours earlier.

With Kim behind her for cover, Detective Martin approached the figure, who was collapsed on the floor and ripped their mask off roughly. Staring back at me, startled and flushed, was Connor. I thought back to the shoes I'd seen when I was under Melody's bed

# The Grim Steeper

and realized his had looked so familiar because he was the one who had come in and hid the gloves in her suitcase.

"*You?*" I asked, though it was fairly obvious that yes, indeed, it was him. "It was *you?*"

He looked at me, wide-eyed with horror. "You weren't even supposed to *be* here. I just wanted those bank statements you took. I saw you snooping around the B and B. I know you took those statements from Melody's room."

*That* was why Connor had just tried to kill me and my cat? To get back evidence I didn't even have?

He turned to the police. "You gotta lock that woman up. Did you see what she did to me?" His voice was higher-pitched than usual, and if it hadn't been for Detective Martin dragging him to his feet, he probably would have crab-walked himself halfway across the room and out a window to get away from me.

"Us?" Detective Martin asked, after she finished reading him his rights. "We didn't see anything out of the ordinary here. Did you see anything, Detective Kim?"

"*Suspect detained by homeowner,*" repeated Detective Kim. "That's all I saw."

The raging fire in the hearth had died down to a dull crackle, and Bob had emerged from under the armchair. He gave Connor one last good growl-and-swipe before dashing off to the living room, where he buried himself under a throw blanket.

Tough guy.

I still couldn't process what I was seeing. Of all the possible killers, all the truly strong motives, why would the one person who Sebastian relied on to get all his content be the one to kill him? Connor had job security, he had a connection to fame, he had the ability to travel freely for work. If what Daphne had said was true, Sebastian had hired the kid when no one else would. It seemed like a plum gig.

261

I couldn't understand why he, out of everyone who had been involved in this, was the one who had done it.

"*Why* did you do it?" It was the only thing I could ask, and it was a question that encapsulated so many of the things I was dying to know. Why attack me when he had already put me onto Melody's scent? Why kill Sebastian in the first place, and why kill the lawyer after that?

There were a thousand other things I wanted to know, but Detective Martin was leading him out my front door in handcuffs.

"I'm not telling you anything, you psycho. You witch."

Detective Kim was straightening out the knocked-over coffee table and then donned a pair of gloves before picking up my fireplace poker. "You mind if I take this with me, for evidence?"

"Please. I'm not sure I'm ever going to be able to look at it the same."

"You might as well come along after us, Phoebe. We're going to need an official statement from you, and you probably want to be there when we release Leo Lansing."

"Not really sure how I'm going to explain any of *this* with an official statement." I waved my hand around the room.

"Don't worry. We learned how to handle *this* from your aunt."

# Chapter
# Thirty-Four

I was sipping a terrible cup of police station coffee when Rich came bursting through the door and made an immediate beeline in my direction, like a homing pigeon who had just found its destination.

Though I was physically unharmed—Connor's initial swing with the iron had missed me completely—I had still been checked over by an EMT on arrival at the station, and they had insisted on draping a drab gray blanket around me just to keep any late-onset shock at bay.

At the moment I was doing okay, but I would have killed for a nice cup of chamomile right about now instead of the burnt leavings of an early-evening cup of joe that had been in the pot for heaven only knew how long.

"Are you okay?" Rich asked breathlessly. He crouched down in front of me, his hands and eyes doing a thorough search of my visible person to make sure I wasn't missing any limbs.

"I don't know. That really depends on whether or not you brought a latte with you, because this is awful." I lifted my coffee mug to show him, and then despite my complaints, I took a big sip. My face contorted miserably.

"What happened?" He pulled up a chair from a nearby desk. Even though we were in the middle of a police station and the alleged

killer in a recent double homicide was a few feet away in the janitorial/interrogation room, the main floor of the station was quiet.

The rain had let up outside, and the muted shades of an attempted sunset were coming in through the window, painting the floor a pastel shade of orange. I went to take another sip of coffee, but Rich saved me from myself, taking the cup from my hands and putting it on a nearby desk, where I wouldn't try to habitually grab for it.

"Thank you," I said. Pulling my itchy blanket around me, I tried my best to explain what had happened after he'd left me at Dierdre's office. The fake lawyer, the attack at home, and even the full gory details of my magic use. Rich knew I was a witch, but he still seemed surprised as I walked him through lifting Connor up into the rafters.

"I didn't know you could do that," he said with a hushed tone.
"Neither did I."

I hadn't really had much of an opportunity to think about the incredible magic I had done tonight. I had completely reimagined the way I used one of my most powerful magical gifts, and in doing so, it seemed I had become a better witch, or at least a more controlled one.

And while I had nothing to prove it yet, I also felt absolutely certain that the spell I had pulled off tonight was more than enough magical energy to count as the spell Eudora had hinted at in my vision. There might be too much adrenaline in my system at the moment for me to know for sure, but once I slept for three straight days, I was sure my bouts of accidentally levitating objects were behind me.

I hoped.

When I was done explaining the bizarre happenings of my afternoon to Rich, he sat back in his chair and let out a low whistle. "I think it's official. I'm never letting you out of my sight again."

I smiled and was about to speak when Detective Martin pulled up a chair and invited herself to join us. "If you think that is going to somehow keep her out of getting into this much trouble, you have got another think coming, my friend."

"Is he talking?" I asked, looking over my shoulder to the closed room like I might suddenly have developed x-ray vision. Unfortunately—or probably fortunately—I had not.

"Zipped his lip and lawyered up *real* quick, unfortunately."

"Does he know where Melody and Deacon are?" Now that I knew they weren't our killers, it was bothering me that neither of them had shown their faces. Deacon, it seemed, had been just under our noses at the B and B, but no one had seen Melody in days, and I was starting to get the notion that Connor might have a third victim out there just waiting for us to find her.

"No, he hasn't said a single word beyond *lawyer*. Well, other than to insist we should be charging you for assault." A little grin ticked at the corner of her mouth.

"Okay, can we talk about that for a second?" I lowered my voice because of just how quiet the police station was.

"If you're worried about it, we're not planning to charge you with anything."

"That's not really what I meant."

"I know what you meant, Phoebe."

I waited for her to say more, but when she didn't, I looked between her and Rich and made a *wtf* gesture.

"We should probably just tell her," Rich said. "I think at this point it would be silly to keep it from her."

Detective Martin scratched her chin, thinking about this for a second before giving a nod, more to herself than to Rich. "It's obvious by now that you've realized the powers you have . . . you weren't the only person in your family to have them, right?"

I wasn't sure if I should avoid the w-word, but since they had walked in on me making someone float, I didn't think semantics were really my biggest concern here. "I know that Eudora was also a witch, yes." I wasn't going to mention anything about any *other* witches in town, because I wasn't about to out my friends if their secrets were still their own. Honey didn't need the police department in her business.

"So, the thing is . . . when I suggested you keep your ears open in relation to the case, I was trying to figure out if you and your aunt had more in common than just a cat and a tea store, if you get my drift."

"You were *hoping* I'd use my magic to help solve the case?"

Martin gave a half-shrug *Can you blame me?* gesture. "Eudora would sometimes come in and help us with difficult cases from time to time. She was uniquely gifted, especially with finding missing things. I can't say we had a lot of murders to investigate back in her day, but what I did learn was that Eudora could get people to admit to just about anything if she had fifteen minutes and a pot of tea."

I knew precisely which tea it was, too, as I had accidentally used it a little too well once. Martin might not be aware that it was the tea and not Eudora who had been working the magic, but I supposed that in a sense, it was Eudora's gift for infusing her tea blends that made the Truth Be Told tea work as well as it did.

"So you had a witch on retainer."

"In a manner of speaking, though of course Eudora's efforts were all volunteer based. Whenever we would run into a situation where the normal path of the law was hitting a wall, she could usually . . . help us around that wall, if you know what I mean. When I asked you after Sebastian's murder to let me know if you saw or heard anything, I was hoping that you might be doing what she did, just in

your own way. Well, I think we can agree that your way is a little riskier than hers. A lesson I've learned the hard way."

"If you had told me that's what you were doing . . ."

Her stern expression cut me off. "Be real with me, Phoebe. You aren't the type to just sit at home and look in a crystal ball or pull out tarot cards or, I don't know, read tea leaves. You say you'll stay out of trouble, but you can't seem to help yourself from becoming a magnet for it. I *wish* you would do what your aunt did, because I never had to warn her off from crime scenes or ask her not to interrogate witnesses on her own. You and your aunt have a lot in common, but this last week has confirmed for me that you are *very* different people."

Rich was smiling, but the smirk vanished when Martin looked at him. "And you knew this whole time what she could do and didn't bother to let us know. Don't think I'll forget that, Richard. You were on the force when we worked with Eudora Black. If you had known we had another witch around, especially one with powers like hers, you should have told us."

Rich shook his head firmly. "Eudora asked me not to."

That was a bomb-drop of epic proportions. "What?" I asked. "Eudora talked to you about this?"

"Of course. When she asked me to watch out for you, she explained that your powers were going to be new to you, if they emerged at all, and that you were going to need time to figure things out. If your powers *didn't* show up, then fine, you go on and live a normal magic-free life, no harm, no foul. But if they *did* come in, she wanted me to make sure you had the time and distance you needed to figure out you were a witch and how you could use your gifts. Telling the police department wasn't going to be helpful to you in that regard. How could you figure out what you were doing if you were being asked to use magic to solve every other crime in town?"

I'd known that Eudora had asked Rich and Leo to look out for me after she passed, but I hadn't realized the extent to which she had told Rich about my potential abilities before even letting *me* know about them. I was hurt that she'd trusted him more with the information than me, but I supposed it had been a way to protect both me and her in case I didn't have magic.

"Based on what I saw tonight, I'd say Phoebe has figured out her magic just fine. I had no idea that sort of thing was even possible." Detective Martin shook her head. "Where did you learn to do that?"

"I didn't. That was the first time I'd ever done something like that." I didn't explain all my accidental levitations, because I was being honest. This was the first time I had *intentionally* made something float.

"It's pretty darned impressive. Spooky, but impressive."

It wasn't the best compliment I'd ever received, but I chose to take it as one.

"Phoebe, I have an idea, and it's not really aboveboard by police standards, but if we wait for this guy's lawyer to show up, I have a feeling we're going to have at least one more body on our hands, if you know what I mean."

"Melody?"

"Melody. I think he's done something to her, and I want him to confess to it, but he's not talking and nothing we say to him has moved the needle. He just keeps asking for a lawyer. Now, I can't let you into that room, as much as I'd like to, but there is nothing we say that's scaring him, and the only thing I know of that would spook him into talking is you."

"Detective Martin, that's not exactly ethical, is it?" I was mostly just teasing her. Connor had killed two people already, possibly one more, and if I could do something to help save a life or solve this crime, then I was game. "Tell me what I need to do."

"I just want you to stand outside the door where he can see you so when I go back inside, he gets one really good look at you, that's all."

And so, when she opened the door, all Connor could see when he got a quick glimpse of the outside world was me, standing between the desks, staring at him with the intensity of a post-prom Carrie.

"I'll talk," he said as the door slowly closed. "But you keep her away from me."

# Chapter Thirty-Five

The ground was spongy under our feet as we moved through the wooded path and under the blockade that was intended to keep trespassers from entering the Bullock Memorial Bird Sanctuary, the old mansion at the heart of the conservancy.

I couldn't help but appreciate the cosmic balance that was seeing this mystery begin and end with birds. It had been birds that brought Sebastian to Raven Creek in the first place, and now, among the birds, we were hoping to find Melody.

Connor had told the detectives he hadn't killed her, he had just incapacitated her to make it seem like she had skipped town. He had been hoping the appearance of guilt would be enough to keep the investigation focused on her, and in a way, he'd been right to believe that. So many of the people involved in looking for the killer—me included—had locked in on Melody's disappearance as proof that she was guilty of something or lying low for a nefarious reason.

Connor had insisted over and over again that he had no idea what had happened to Deacon, though.

Considering everything he had confessed to, thanks to my lurking outside the interrogation room, I had to believe he really *didn't* know where Deacon was. I was beginning to think Sebastian's ex

being in town was entirely due to Deacon wanting to get back in his former boss and boyfriend's good graces.

Connor had admitted to so much that we were halfway up to the old Bullock mansion and Detective Martin was still helping fit together a lot of the pieces I'd found on my own, but the motivations were as tangled as a spider's web. It was such a mess I wondered how it would have been solved at all without Connor foolishly breaking into my house to target me. If he had just left well enough alone, he probably would have gotten away with it.

As it was, it was a plot so thick Agatha Christie would have needed a few whiteboards to unravel it all.

"So you're saying Sebastian was never the target at all?" I was glad to be a regular runner, because the uphill climb to the mansion had others in our party huffing and puffing and taking breaks every few yards. Rich and Detective Kim were right behind us, but a few of the officers who had come along were having a really hard time.

"Yeah, that shocked me too, because that's what got all this started. But apparently it was all just a case of wrong bedroom, wrong time. Sebastian switched with Melody because he needed the blackout blinds, and that switch ended up being what killed him. The killer snuck in and stabbed who he *thought* was his intended target. Sebastian was just in the wrong bed. Poor guy."

The cursed Musical Bedrooms struck again. "So Melody was the target all along, then?"

"Yup. Hold on, this gets crazier. *Andrew* was the one who killed Sebastian."

"*What?* That's insane. So who did Connor kill?"

"Connor killed Andrew. Self-preservation, he claims. Apparently, Andrew was a pretty well-known scammer and had ways of making dirty money clean again. He had helped Melody set up that LLC, but she'd tried to cut him out of the payout—I think you

271

figured some of that out when you saw the bank statement and heard them arguing by the creek. Melody wasn't the only one on Sebastian's staff stealing from him, though; so was Connor. But when Andrew killed Sebastian instead of Melody, he told Connor that with the cash cow dead, he had no reason to protect them anymore and he was going to share all the details of their scams with the police. I think Andrew was hoping we would think Melody and Connor had committed the crimes together. Connor admitted to us that he made a deal with Andrew to buy his silence, but when they met up, Connor killed him. With Andrew gone, he planned to pin both crimes on Melody, which is why he hid those gloves in her room. Melody had no idea about Andrew's murder, so when Connor asked her to meet him out here on the fourth of July, she went willingly, because she still trusted him."

"Well, that certainly explains the mysterious meeting at the creek. Did Connor say he was the one who sent me those pictures?"

"No. We asked, and he claims not to know anything about the photos."

"We already knew Melody was probably up to something, but you said Connor was stealing from Sebastian too?"

Martin shook her head in disbelief. "According to Connor, the lawyer told him that Melody was using his real estate accounts to skim funds off the top of Sebastian's books, making it look like she was renting a studio space for an office that didn't exist."

"That explains the statement I saw perfectly!" I said triumphantly, thrilled that my little clue was somehow useful.

"She'd been doing this for *ages*, and I guess Deacon found out what was going on. She convinced Sebastian that Deacon was the one taking the money, which was why he cut Deacon out of his life. But Sebastian was starting to get an idea that it *hadn't* been Deacon who was lying to him, and the lawyer knew he had to cut and run.

Because Connor hadn't realized what Melody was up to and was running his own scam to steal from Sebastian. He was redirecting funds from several online accounts where he was posting Sebastian content without Sebastian knowing about it and taking the revenue for himself."

"And then Connor decided to tie up loose ends and just make Melody the scapegoat?"

"Exactly. He figured that with Melody on ice—hopefully not literally—she would take the blame for everything, especially when a forensic accountant started looking at the company's accounts and it became obvious what was going on."

"That's the most insane thing I've ever heard. Jealousy and a broken heart made sense to me. Losing a job made sense to me. But if Sebastian's death was an accident and this was all just about money, it's bonkers." It did now make sense why Andrew had been trailing after Sebastian's book tour, though. He hadn't planned to kill Sebastian; he'd been planning to shake Melody down for money and then kill *her* if she didn't pay up.

We had arrived at the crumbling steps leading up to the old Bullock mansion. The trees around the old house had developed a thick canopy overhead thanks to years without any kind of maintenance. In the dying light of evening, it felt like it was already night in here.

Detective Martin turned on a flashlight, waiting until the rest of the group caught up.

As the officers huffed up behind us, Martin said, "We did some research on Andrew after the murder, and while he isn't working for any known corporation and certainly isn't making corporate money, he is a lawyer and has a degree in tax law. When we went through his documents, it looked like he had done *extensive* research on the value of properties not only in Raven Creek but in a half dozen other towns in Washington and Oregon. He had a half-finished presentation on

the possible value of crafting an 'Out of the Box Tourist Center.' Basically, he was trying to find a town where he could create a cookie-cutter environment to sell to any buyer with enough money. We think he was testing the water here to see how hard it would be to get locals to buy into the pitch and invest their own money in it. When he started to double and triple the value of properties and still wasn't getting bites, that seemed to push him over the edge a little.

"That's why he was so desperate to get the money Melody owed him, so he could back up his ruse with real cash. When we talked to Leo, he said Andrew had told him that if it didn't sell, he was going to tear down the trees on the other side of the street and build a grocery store twice as big to put him out of business anyway. That seems to be the point where your friend lost his cool."

With all the officers gathered and armed, Martin looked at me and Rich. "You two stay out here. I could get in enough trouble just letting you tag along, so stay out of the building and let us do this, okay?"

For once in my life, I wasn't planning to argue. The police went into the building, and we watched their flashlight beams split up and move from room to room. After a few minutes we couldn't hear them anymore.

"Did Detective Kim tell you the whole saga?"

"It was like having someone explain all three seasons of *Succession* to me. There were too many double-crosses to keep track of."

"I can't believe after all this that Sebastian wasn't actually the target after all."

A group of crows settled into the branches over the house and started chattering loudly with each other.

For the second time that night I was reminded of Honey's haunting prophecy.

*The wrong person died.*

I had no idea how she'd known, but I was never going to doubt something she told me ever again. I didn't really believe in psychics, or at least I hadn't until today, but her words had been spooky and foretelling, even if she hadn't been able to point me to a killer or save the lawyer from getting a taste of his own medicine.

"Do you think she's still alive in there?" I asked.

Rich waited too long to answer, so I knew what he was thinking even though he said, "I hope so."

I was pessimistic as well, until a sharp cry from inside the mansion sent the crows scattering into the night air and beams of flashlights racing through the house to converge in a room on the house's second floor.

"Send in the EMTs," came a voice through the window.

A pair of EMTs had been along for the hike and were nervously biding their time next to us, but the moment they were called for, their unease transformed into focus. They picked up their heavy bags and the wheeled stretcher they'd brought and ran into the house together.

Radio sounds crackled through the night, and excited shouts of directions were too muddled for Rich and me to clearly understand the words, but the tone seemed to indicate they weren't bringing out a corpse.

A few minutes later the EMTs reemerged, two uniformed officers at their heels. On the stretcher—which bounced precariously over the uneven sidewalk that had fallen into disrepair—was the supine figure of Melody Fairbanks. She was pale like a porcelain doll, but her eyes were open and scanning the area around her. She looked weak, but I couldn't see any obvious sign of injury on her except dark bruising around her wrists and some superficial scratches on her arms and face.

Whatever she'd been through, she hadn't had a good two days, but she was alive, and that was more than two others could say this week.

The quartet disappeared into the murky darkness down the path, and the detectives and two other officers emerged from the house, their flashlights still bobbing in the night.

The officers silently headed down the path in a hurry, and Detective Kim gave Rich a quick clap on the back before following behind them.

Detective Martin pointed her flashlight to the forest floor, dusting her hands free of some unseen dirt or cobwebs. "I don't know if that's the luckiest girl on the planet or not. She's probably going to end up serving a little time of her own for fraud, but she's alive."

"Is she going to be okay?" I asked.

Martin nodded without hesitation. "He had her tied up upstairs in an old hidden passage between rooms. We missed it when we did that initial search after you directed us here, but this time she was making a heck of a racket in there. If she'd been unconscious or hadn't heard us . . . well. I don't think any of us would have ever found that pass. Right behind two closets. Connor had no problem with her never being found, let me tell you that."

I tried to think about what might have happened to Melody if Connor hadn't tried to kill me as well tonight, and for once I wasn't at all sorry for being too nosy to stay out of things.

It might have almost gotten me killed, but it had also saved a woman's life.

That made it worth every risk.

# Chapter
# Thirty-Six

I thought for certain the longest night of my life had ended when Rich and I left the bird sanctuary. The crimes had been solved; one killer was dead and the other was behind bars. And while I couldn't pretend that anyone's plans made sense to me, I also wasn't the kind of person who could kill someone over money, or real estate, or really anything else.

The motivations and logic of killers were never going to make sense to me, even if the plot was revenge or jealousy.

But it was jealousy who I found on my front porch when I got back to my house.

With Rich trailing behind me to make sure I got home safely, I didn't feel any immediate danger when I saw Deacon sitting on the porch swing, rocking back and forth. If anything, he looked more like an invited guest than a potential threat.

That said, I hadn't looked at Connor's baby face and seen a killer either, so I might not be the best judge of character.

Rich closed the distance between us and put a protective hand on my shoulder. I wasn't sure if it was more for me—so I knew he was there—or for Deacon, so the other man wouldn't try anything funny.

"Don't worry, buddy. I'm not here to hurt her or anything. I just wanted to see if you got my pictures, that's all."

The pictures.

In all this mess of twisted plans and nefarious schemes, I hadn't spent much time dwelling on who had left the pictures at my back door. Deacon had crossed my mind as a possibility, but I'd just gotten so distracted by everything else that I hadn't come back to the question of who had left me evidence. Detective Martin had confirmed it hadn't been Connor, but I hadn't stopped to think it might be Deacon.

"So that *was* you." Rich and I came up on the porch, and Rich pulled up one of the deck chairs for me so I could sit. The excitement of the evening was wearing me down, and I had dozed off in the car on the way here. Rich knew I was running out of steam, and I appreciated the kindness of such a small gesture.

He remained standing behind me, making sure that Deacon never left his sight.

"Were you following me around too?" I asked, thinking about all the times I'd been so sure someone was just around the corner, tailing my footsteps.

He blushed. "I know it was a risk, and there was a chance you wouldn't do anything about it. But I needed someone to know that Melody was up to no good. I'm sure she had something to do with Sebastian's death, and that was all I had to show to prove it. I took some other stuff from her room, but I wasn't sure I could go to the police without them arresting me." He must have meant the bank statements.

I glanced down and looked at his oh-so-familiar black military-style boots.

I gave my head a gentle shake. "Deacon, buddy. You're a few chapters behind on the updates."

"What are you talking about?"

Before I explained everything to him, there was something from Detective Martin's story that was bothering me. "When you came here to talk to me because you thought I might be a sympathetic ear, you told me this huge sob story about Sebastian firing you over your relationship."

"And that's what happened."

"But you didn't feel the need to mention that the actual reason he fired you was for embezzlement. You told me you quit."

Deacon shot up out of his chair, and Rich was in front of me in a heartbeat. "That's not *fair*. That's not what happened, and if Melody told you so, you can't believe a single thing that pathological liar says."

I grabbed Rich's hand, giving it a squeeze to let him know I was okay, and though he hesitated, he did step back.

"Deacon, sit down," I said, my voice thick with exhaustion.

To my surprise, he did so without any argument, reclaiming his place on the porch swing. His stress still showed in other ways—in the sweat on his brow, the way he was wringing his hands together. "I would never steal from Sebastian, and I tried to tell him that. I came here to try to prove that to him. I don't know if I wanted him back or wanted my job back or if I just wanted him to know he couldn't trust the people around him, but it was too late. I should have done more; I should have found another way to make him listen."

Deacon dropped his face into his hands and started to cry.

There wasn't anything I could do or say that was going to alleviate his guilt or bring back the man he'd loved. But I could at least offer him the truth. So I explained to him, as best I could, the convoluted machinations that had led to Sebastian's accidental death, the arrest of Connor, and the likely later arrest of Melody for fraud once she got released from the hospital. He absorbed the story with wide eyes and a mouth hung open in shock. I couldn't blame him for his reaction; I had probably looked much the same when Martin walked me through it.

When I finished, he sat back in the swing and stared out at the dark street, saying nothing. There wasn't much to say. Rich and I gave him the grace of shared silence so he could process the information I'd just dumped in his lap.

After a long, long time, he looked back at us and said, "Connor? Seriously?"

I nodded. "I know. He was really the last person I expected too. It made me overlook him completely."

"I thought of that kid like a little brother. I showed him all the ropes, helped him with everything. I was teaching him how to do *my* job so maybe one day he might be able to branch out on his own. Maybe that was my mistake too. Maybe I never should have let him know just how much money we were making."

"I mean, Sebastian was famous on a video app," Rich said. "How much money could inspire the kid to make a move this drastic?"

Deacon let out a little humorless laugh. "Last month alone Sebastian made a hundred and fifty thousand dollars in sponsorships, another twenty-five thousand on Patreon, and the ad revenue on his videos from YouTube and TikTok was worth fifty-eight thousand dollars combined. He was also doing Cameos—you know, those little videos people can buy for their friends? He made ten thousand doing those. In one month. One month. I don't think you realize just how lucrative it can be to be *famous on a video app*. There's a reason Sebastian was able to afford a full staff. He paid us all really well for our work. But apparently, for some people, it wasn't enough. They wanted a bigger piece of the pie."

"And you, you never wanted a bigger piece of the pie?" I asked, genuinely curious, given numbers like that, how Sebastian's former business manager had avoided the desire to pocket a little extra that had ruined two others on the same staff.

"No, Ms. Winchester. The only thing I ever wanted more of was his heart."

# Chapter Thirty-Seven

*Five weeks later*

"Okay, now I want you to blend in the onion. Gently—you don't want to take out too much of the air in the batter." Honey hovered near me at the kitchen table, watching me try my hand at making Karma's akara recipe for the first time.

I thought I was a pretty decent cook, but with Honey watching me like a hawk, I had to admit the African fritter recipe had my nerves going in high gear. Another time, maybe a month earlier, I'd have diced onion and habanero floating over my head, but I hadn't had any magical accidents since the night we caught Connor.

I followed Honey's directions, gently mixing diced onion into the caramel-brown batter. Beside me a waiting pan of oil was coming to temperature. The batter I'd made was a blended mixture of beans, spicy chili pepper, regular peppers, bouillon, and ground crawfish, but after having devoured the entire container of Karma's akara in one sitting, I knew I needed to learn how to make it myself.

"All right," Honey declared. "That looks perfect—you're ready to spoon it into the oil. Just be careful not to add too many at one time; they need a little room to breathe when you flip them over."

I did as I was told, impressed that Honey had resisted nudging her way in to show me and then taking over the whole process. She was bouncing on the pads of her feet, obviously dying to get involved, but she had promised to let me make it all by myself and had been true to her word, as much as it pained her.

While the fritters turned a beautiful golden-brown color in the oil, Amy popped her head in from the kitchen entrance. "Room for one more? Oh gosh does it smell good in here." She made her way in, easing her curvy figure through the too-small, too-occupied kitchen, but I loved having too many people in a kitchen. It was the one room of a house where I truly believed more was merrier.

Honey moved out of the way as Amy withdrew a tray from the fridge, displaying a truly glorious pavlova. "Voilà!"

The meringue base was huge and perfectly white, and the custard she had mounded in the center was almost the same color as the meringue. The custard was topped with liberal piles of blueberries and peaches and decorated with several well-placed dollops of whipped cream garnished with mint leaves and fresh flower petals.

Honey gasped. "Amy, that should be in a magazine!"

"It was, once." Amy winked. "Now, don't you two take too long in here; everyone is outside, and we're getting hungry. You might need to bring more of that strawberry iced tea out when you come too. The first batch is almost gone."

I had pulled the first few akara out of the pan and placed them on a waiting paper towel, where I dabbed them free of excess oil. Soon the whole batch was cooked, and I loaded them onto a big serving tray with a little dipping bowl of a yogurt sauce Honey had brought along with her. She carried a big jug of iced tea behind me as well as a platter of fresh heirloom tomatoes from my garden, cut into slices and served with super-fresh burrata cheese, garden basil, and a healthy glug of balsamic vinegar.

We headed out into the backyard, where several huge picnic blankets had been tossed onto the lawn in no discernible pattern, some overlapping others, some on their own, with an array of mismatched lawn chairs surrounding them.

On the blankets was every conceivable food one might want at a picnic. Huge wedges of watermelon, homemade elote corncobs, warm potato salad that was so fresh I could smell the bacon from ten feet away. From the barbecue grill that we had unearthed in the shed—and that miraculously still worked—Rich brought over a platter of perfectly cooked steak served on a bed of rosemary right from the pot at my back door.

Imogen plopped down two ice-cold bottles of sparkling rosé as she settled into her chair, then opened a cooler she'd brought to unveil bowls of the most stunning ice I had ever seen. The cubes were perfect little spheres, and each one had a real flower frozen into it. There was also a bottle of a homemade simple syrup that was a stunning pink color, labeled *Pink Lemonade*. "I might not be a good cook, but I can make one heck of a good cocktail," she declared.

Daphne had been across the lawn playing a game of tag with the Tanakas' granddaughter Emiko—or Miko, as she'd introduced herself—and the pair of them were giggling like mad as they approached the blankets.

Leo took the tray of steak from Rich and went around the circle, making sure everyone who wanted some was able to get a serving before the group descended like hungry dogs on the spread of food in the middle of the circle.

Detective Martin, who had come without Detective Kim, gave Leo a smile as she took the food from him, and without words, that smile conveyed a thousand apologies. Leo had told her a dozen times already he didn't have any hard feelings about being questioned, and because he was Leo, I believed that was true.

Everyone loaded their plates, the smell of propane and grilled meat, sunscreen, and sweet watermelon filling the air alongside peals of laughter and boisterous stories that got louder the more of Imogen's drinks we had.

The August sun hung low in the sky, and we were waiting for night to fall to watch a forecasted meteor shower, since my yard was the highest point in town to watch from.

With bellies and hearts full, jokes and tall tales spread through the group, and I looked around, marveling at this little family I had built just when I thought I had lost mine.

From the window in the back mudroom, a big orange cat sat with his face pressed against the screen, sniffing the summer air and watching us jealously. Beside him, a timid calico wrapped her tail around his, but did not run away or hide when she saw us watching her. Instead, she gave one slow blink and her attention darted upward, away from me.

I followed her hyperfocused gaze just in time to see a brilliantly colored bird land on top of my shed, then flit off to a nearby tree.

I wasn't the only one who saw it.

"Well, I'll be a monkey's uncle," said Mr. Loughery, pointing at the bird so the others could see. "But I think that boy might have just been right about that bird after all."

And as it turned out, the Pacific tanager—later renamed the Marlow tanager—*was* everything Sebastian had hoped it would be.

Rich planted a soft kiss on my temple, his arm loose around my shoulder.

We watched the bird until light faded from the sky, and as the stars began to fall, we were all right where we were meant to be, if just for one perfect moment.

# Recipes

## Blueberry Lemon Sourdough Bread

*I will not be offering a sourdough starter recipe here, but there's one in the back of* Death by a Thousand Sips. *You can also check with your local bakery, as they may be willing to give or sell you a cup of their active discard.*

3 cups bread flour
1⅓ cups lukewarm water
¾ cup active, bubbly sourdough starter
3 tablespoons white sugar
1 teaspoon salt
1¼ cups fresh blueberries
1 tablespoon fresh lemon zest

Combine flour, water, starter, and sugar in a large bowl. Stir until all dry ingredients are incorporated. Cover with a slightly damp towel and rest at room temperature for about 30 minutes.

Add salt, blueberries, and lemon zest, then knead for a minute or two until everything is thoroughly combined (try not to smush the blueberries too much). Re-cover with the towel and let the dough rise for about three hours, reshaping the dough roughly once per hour.

Shape one last time, then leave covered overnight on the counter. (If your kitchen is quite drafty, you can let it rise overnight in your oven.)

Place oven rack in the center and place an empty Dutch oven on it. Preheat to 450 degrees.

Turn the dough out onto a sheet of parchment paper. Create a design of your choice in the top with a lame or sharp kitchen knife. Remove the hot Dutch oven and place the parchment and bread inside. Place the lid back on.

Bake 56 minutes: 28 minutes covered, 28 minutes uncovered. Remove bread from the Dutch oven, remove the parchment paper, then allow to cool completely before slicing.

# Rosemary and Olive Oil Sourdough Bread *or* Rosemary Black Pepper Sourdough Bread

*I know some of you are like me and Phoebe and hate olives, so I'm offering both an olive lover's and an olive hater's rosemary loaf.*

4 cups white all-purpose flour
2 teaspoons salt
⅓ cup active sourdough starter
1¾ cup lukewarm water
¾ cup Castelvetrano olives, pitted and chopped (substitute kalamata if not available) *or* 2 teaspoons fresh-cracked black pepper
2 tablespoons fresh rosemary, finely chopped

Combine flour, salt, starter, and water in a large bowl. Stir until all dry ingredients are incorporated. Cover with a slightly damp towel and rest at room temperature for about 30 minutes.

Add salt, olives or pepper, and rosemary, then knead for a minute or two until everything is thoroughly combined. Re-cover with the towel and let the dough rise for about three hours, reshaping the dough roughly once per hour.

Shape one last time, then leave covered overnight on the counter. (If your kitchen is quite drafty, you can let it rise overnight in your oven.)

Place oven rack in the center and place an empty Dutch oven on it. Turn dough out onto a sheet of parchment paper. Create a design of your choice in the top with a lame or sharp kitchen knife. Remove the hot Dutch oven and place the parchment and bread inside. Place the lid back on.

Bake 56 minutes: 28 minutes covered, 28 minutes uncovered. Remove bread from the Dutch oven, remove the parchment paper, then allow to cool completely before slicing.

# Hand Pies

*The base hand pie recipe here is the same as the one in* Death by a Thousand Sips, *but I thought you might want Amy's new fillings!*

## Hand Pie Base
2 sheets puff pastry (cold but not frozen)

## Goat Cheese, Chive, and Fig Filling
1 log herbed goat cheese (can substitute 1 cup crumbled goat cheese)
2 tablespoons finely chopped chives
2 tablespoons caramelized onion jam (optional)
3–4 dried figs, soaked in water overnight, then drained and finely
    chopped (can substitute unsoaked dried dates, chopped)
Salt and pepper to taste

## Sausage, Cheddar, and Banana Pepper Filling
1½ cups scrambled eggs at room temperature
½ pound cooked breakfast sausage
½ cup shredded sharp cheddar
¼ cup chopped pickled banana peppers
Salt and pepper to taste
Each recipe yields 6 hand pies.
Preheat oven to 400 degrees.

Lightly flour your work surface. Take cold puff pastry dough and unfold onto work surface, then cut both sheets into six equal rectangles. This should give you twelve total rectangles.

Place six of the puff pastry rectangles onto a parchment-lined baking sheet.

In a medium-sized bowl, combine all ingredients to the filling of your choice.

Leaving about a ½-inch border, put a sixth of your filling onto each rectangle. Then, using water, wet the edges and place the reserved rectangles on top. Use a fork to crimp the edges until the hand pies are sealed, then cut a ½-inch slit in the top of each pie.

Bake for 20 to 25 minutes depending on desired color. Let cool for about 10 minutes before serving.

# Gra-tea-tude Tea Blend

*The amount of add-ins here can be changed to your personal taste; store extras in glass or metal jars in a dry area out of direct sunlight. For the loose black tea, feel free to order plain black tea in bags and just cut the bags open.*

## Vanilla Sugar

1–2 vanilla bean pods
2 cups granulated sugar

Using a sharp kitchen knife, cut a long slit in the vanilla bean pod, open it, and lay it flat on a cutting board. Use the back of your knife to scrape out the beans from inside the pod. Add the beans to 2 cups granulated sugar in a food processor. Pulse the sugar several times until the beans are dispersed; pour contents into mason jar. Add the empty vanilla pods into the jar for extra flavor.

## Tea Blend

¼ cup black tea (I suggest trying to find bulk loose tea at an Asian food market or bulk food store; this is roughly 50 tea bags)
2 tablespoons elderflower blossoms
1 tablespoon dehydrated lemon rind
¼ cup freeze-dried strawberries, chopped into small pieces (I'd recommend using a food processor, as they can be tricky to chop with a knife; include all powder remaining after chopping)
2 tablespoons vanilla sugar

Combine all ingredients in a bowl and mix with a spoon until evenly distributed. Store in an airtight container out of direct sunlight.

To serve, spoon 1 tablespoon of loose tea into your preferred steeping vessel and pour just-below-boiling water over top. Steep for 4–5 minutes, then remove tea bag/steeper. Enjoy plain or with preferred add-ins!

# Hibiscus Iced Tea Spritzer

8 cups water
¼ cup dried hibiscus flowers
2 sticks cinnamon
1 inch ginger, peeled

Combine ingredients together in a pot and bring to a boil. Let rest until cool, then strain the liquid into a pitcher.

Add about ½ cup to a glass with ice, then top with your favorite lightly flavored fizzy drink. Good options are Fresca, ginger ale, or flavored fizzy water.

# Chicken Mafé

*I will not claim that this is a traditional West African mafé. This is just my variation, and I am absolutely certain you will get a better and more authentic version in a West African restaurant, but if you want to give it a whirl at home, here's an option for you!*

12 cloves garlic (yes, *twelve*)
1 large piece of ginger, peeled
Salt to taste, divided
Pepper to taste, divided
2 teaspoons crushed red pepper flakes
2 pounds bone-in chicken thighs, skin removed
6 tablespoons flavor-neutral oil (like vegetable or canola)
1 medium onion, diced
3 tablespoons fish sauce
6 ounces tomato paste
6 cups water
1 cup creamy unsweetened peanut butter
½ pound green cabbage, cut into wedges
3 medium carrots, peeled, cut in 2-inch lengths
1 medium sweet potato
12 ounces yellow potatoes
White rice, cooked, for serving

The day before you plan to serve the mafé, prepare the marinade. Mince six cloves garlic and the ginger with salt, black pepper, and

crushed red pepper flakes to taste. Season chicken all over with salt and rub with the garlic mixture. Marinate overnight in the fridge.

Mince remaining six cloves of garlic. In a large pot, heat the oil over medium-high heat. When it is hot, add the onion and garlic and season with salt, then cook, stirring regularly, until the onion starts to turn translucent. Stir in fish sauce and tomato paste and cook until combined and slightly darkened. Stir in 6 cups water, scraping up any browned bits. Add chicken, bring to a boil, and turn heat down to a moderate simmer.

In a mixing bowl, stir a cup of the cooking liquid into the peanut butter, a little at a time, to loosen it. Add the peanut butter mixture into the pot and simmer for about 20 minutes. Add cabbage and carrots first, simmering for 10 minutes. Peel and cut sweet potato and yellow potatoes into bite-sizes chunks; add and simmer another 30 minutes until the vegetables and chicken are tender and the sauce has thickened. Add salt and pepper to taste, then serve over white rice.

# Acknowledgments

This book was a real testament to some of my biggest passions in life: books, tea, bird watching, and cat rescue. They say write what you know, and *The Grim Steeper* was my way of putting so many of the things I care most about in one place.

I am grateful to my mom for sharing her passion for bird watching with me. It's because of her that I can sit alone and say out loud, "Is that a yellow-rumped warbler?" She's the reason I spent a chunk of a recent research trip to California trying to find birds I'd never seen before. If you liked the idea of the app Phoebe mentions Sebastian creating, you're in luck: download Merlin immediately. It's free, and you will spend *hours* trying to identify birdsong near you. As a quick note, the Pacific tanager is *not* a real bird, but tanagers in general are very, very cool, and if you live anywhere that you can see them, go do that.

On that note, thank you to my friend and podcast cohost Darby Robinson—an honest-to-goodness park ranger—who answers all my goofy questions about local junk food brands and what might happen if you found a body in a National Park.

I want to thank my small but dedicated Patreon crew: Jenny, Rachel, Tracey, Coral, Tanya, Siobhan, and Catriona. You guys come

to my signings, you read every book with enthusiastic delight, and I couldn't ask for better fans. Thank you so much.

As far as cat rescue, forgive me for taking a serious moment. I have seven cats, and most of them came into my life because they were abandoned or the result of stray parents who should have been spayed or neutered. I, as well as many others, joke about the cat distribution system, but overpopulation and lack of care are things we can all help with. Cat rescues and TNR (trap, neuter, return) organizations take on the exhausting, heartbreaking, and endless task of helping to protect the stray and feral cat population of the world, and they need our support. If you're feeling so inclined, please look into cat rescues near you (shout-out to Rescue Siamese, Grateful Friends, Craig Street Cats, and so many others working in my hometown of Winnipeg). These are not-for-profit groups who only want to help animals, and they can always use donations and volunteers. If you're looking for rescues online who offer great social media content to go alongside their mission, please look up Miss Dixie's Kitten Rescue (South Carolina), Wonky Hearts Rescue (aka Megan and the Rescues; California), Poet Square Cats (Arizona), Kitten Lady/Orphan Kitten Club (California), San Bernadino Kitten Rescue (California), and Tabby Tails Cat Rescue (Ohio). You can see the hard work they put in day after day, the emotional toll, and you can learn a *ton* about why cat rescues matter so much. Cats bring us so much joy, and we should do our part to make sure they're able to have lives free from pain and suffering whenever possible.

Of course, this book wouldn't have been possible without my incredible editorial team at Crooked Lane. My eternal thanks to Melissa Rechter for believing in these books, and to my eagle-eyed line editor and copy editor for finding things that always get missed no matter how many times you reread a book. I feel so blessed to work with such talented and wonderful people.

And to you, who read this far. Thank you, thank you, thank you.